Praise for Karis Walsh

Set the Stage

"Settings are an artwork for [Karis Walsh] as she creates these places that feel so real and vivid you wish you could hop in a car or plane to go walk where her characters are to experience what they get to on the pages of her book…Her character work is as good as the places she's created, so they feel like realistic people making the whole picture enjoyable."—*Artistic Bent*

"[A] fun romance. It made me want to go this festival, which I'd never had any interest in before. *Set the Stage* is worth a read for fans of romance or theater."—*The Lesbrary*

"I really adored this book. From the characters to the setting and the slow burn romance, I was in it for the long haul with this one. Karis Walsh…is an expert in creating interesting characters that often have to face some type of adversity…There something new, something fresh about this book from Walsh."—*The Romantic Reader Blog*

Lammy Finalist *You Make Me Tremble*

"Another quality read from Karis Walsh. She is definitely a go-to for a heartwarming read."—*The Romantic Reader Blog*

Blindsided

"A jaded television reporter and a guide dog trainer form an unlikely bond in Walsh's delightful contemporary romance. Their slow-burn romance is a nuanced exploration of trust, desire, and negotiating boundaries, without a hint of schmaltz or pity. The sex scenes are sizzling hot, but it's the slow burn that really allows Walsh to shine."—*Publishers Weekly*

"Karis Walsh always comes up ~~~~~~ ~~~~~~ ~~~~~~~ ~~~~~~~~ances with interesting characters ~~~~~~~~~~~~~~~~~~~~~~~~~ rks." —*Curve Magazine*

Wingspan

"As with all Karis Walsh's wonderful books, the characters are the story. Multifaceted, layered, and beautifully drawn, Ken and Bailey hold our attention from the start. Their clashes, their attraction, and the personal and shared development are what draw us in and hold us. The surrounding scenery, the wild rugged landscape, and the birds at the center of the story are exquisitely drawn."
—*The Lesbian Reading Room*

Amounting to Nothing

"Great characters, excellent narration, solid pacing, interesting mystery, lovely romance. Everything worked for me!"—*The Lesbian Review*

Mounting Evidence

"[A]nother awesome Karis Walsh novel, and I have eternal hope that at some point there will be another book in this series. I liked the characters, the plot, the mystery, and the romance so much."
—*Danielle Kimerer, Librarian, Reading Public Library (MA)*

"[A] well paced and thrilling mystery revolving around two enigmatic women."—*Rainbow Book Reviews*

"[G]reat characters and development, a wonderful story line, lots of suspense and mystery, and a truly sweet romance."—*Prism Book Alliance*

Mounting Danger

"Karis Walsh easily masters the most difficult pitfall of a traditional romance. Karis's love for horses and for the Pacific Northwest is palpable throughout and adds a wonderful flavor to the story: the beauty of the oceanside at Tacoma, the smell of horses, the dogs, the excitement of Polo, the horses themselves (I am secretly in love with Bandit), the sounds of the forest. A most enjoyable read for cold winter days and nights."—*Curve*

Improvisation

"Walsh tells this story in achingly beautiful words, phrases, and paragraphs, building a tension that is bittersweet. The main characters are skillfully drawn, as is Jan's dad, the distinctly loveable and wise Glen Carroll. As the two women interact, there is always an undercurrent of sensuality buzzing around the edges of the pages, even while they exchange sometimes snappy, sometimes comic dialogue. *Improvisation* is a true romantic tale, Walsh's fourth book, and she's evolving into a master romantic storyteller."—*Lambda Literary*

Sea Glass Inn

"Karis Walsh's third book, excellently written and paced as always, takes us on a gentle but determined journey through two women's awakening…The story is well paced, with just enough tension to keep you turning the pages but without an overdramatic melodrama."—*Lesbian Reading Room*

Love on Tap

"Karis Walsh writes excellent romances. They draw you in, engage your mind, and capture your heart…What really good romance writers do is make you dream of being that loved, that chosen. *Love on Tap* is exactly that novel—interesting characters, slightly different circumstances to anything you have read before, slightly different challenges. And although you KNOW the happy ending is coming, you still have that little bit of 'oooh—make it happen.' Loved it. Wish it was me. What more is there to say?"
—*The Lesbian Reading Room*

"Risk Factor" in *Sweet Hearts*

"Karis Walsh sensitively portrays the frustration of learning to live with a new disability through Ainslee, and the pain of living as a survivor of suicide loss through Myra."—*The Lesbian Review*

By the Author

Harmony

Worth the Risk

Sea Glass Inn

Improvisation

Mounting Danger

Wingspan

Blindsided

Mounting Evidence

Love on Tap

Tales from Sea Glass Inn

Amounting to Nothing

You Make Me Tremble

Set the Stage

Seascape

Visit us at www.boldstrokesbooks.com

SEASCAPE

by
Karis Walsh

2018

Credits
Editor: Ruth Sternglantz
Production Design: Stacia Seaman
Cover Design by Sheri (hindsightgraphics@gmail.com)

SEASCAPE

Chapter One

Tess Hansen was still wide awake when her cell phone started to vibrate on her bedside table. She had been lying there for over an hour, feeling the small movements Lydia made while she slept—rhythmic, deep breathing and occasional shifts that made her naked body move against Tess's. The friction of heated skin against her own was arousing, but not enough to make Tess want to do anything about it. She had been trying to figure out why she felt so empty inside, even though this was usually the point in any relationship at which she felt the most alive.

She had met Representative Lydia Beckett at the Washington State Capitol Building, during a fundraiser for Evergreen College, and the attraction between them had been noticeable enough. They had spent the next few weeks trying to coordinate their busy schedules—admittedly busier on the congressional side than on Tess's—to find more than an hour or two to spend together. The foreplay of missed opportunities had led to last night's climactic date, and Tess couldn't understand why she felt so deflated by the whole experience. She had spent most of the evening wishing she hadn't declined the invitation to have a quiet dinner instead with her friends Cara and Lenae and see their newest litter of puppies.

Everything about Lydia made her perfect for Tess. She had made it clear she was wrapped up in her career right now and not interested in anything more serious than what Tess was willing to offer. She was smart and easy to talk to, smoothly efficient at the type of small talk that never crossed the line between interesting and controversial or personal. She was sexy and confident, unafraid to ask for exactly what she wanted in bed, at restaurants, or in life. So Tess had no idea why last night had seemed so flat and meaningless.

She had spent a disturbing few minutes probing her feelings for Lydia. Was she serious about her? Wishing they could have more than one night? Or was she simply wishing she had spent the night with someone else—maybe the woman she'd met at a bar two nights ago, or the new associate professor in Evergreen's comparative literature department? The answer to both questions had been *no*. Tess just felt bored, something she rarely experienced, and she wasn't sure why.

Tess almost welcomed the call because it interrupted her unsettling thoughts, but no one ever called with good news like promotions or winning lottery numbers at two in the morning. She carefully slid her arm out from under Lydia and rolled toward her phone, pushing her dark hair out of her eyes and squinting at the caller ID. Ugh. The sister.

She swiped the screen to answer the call but didn't speak until she walked across the room and shut herself in the bathroom. She perched on the edge of the tub, her muscles clenching at the feel of uncomfortably cold tile under her naked thighs, and her stomach doing likewise in anticipation of talking to one of her family members. She lifted the phone to her ear.

"Tess? Tess, are you there?" Kelly sighed loudly into the phone, expressing her usual irritation with her younger sister.

"I'm here, Kelly. What's wrong?" Tess kept her voice pitched low, but she heard movement in the other room that sounded like Lydia getting out of her bed.

"It's Dad, Tess. He fell and hurt his back. We're at the hospital now, and he'll be going in for surgery in the morning."

"Oh, I'm sorry," Tess said. She felt a momentary twinge of guilt, worried that her words were nothing but an expected and polite gesture, without any meaning behind them. But she wasn't lying. She rarely saw her family and carefully arranged her life to maintain a distance, but she was honestly relieved that Kelly's news wasn't worse.

"We're going to need you to come home, Tess."

She was wrong. Kelly's news was worse than she had originally thought.

"Well, first of all, I am already home." She had moved away from her family and their small coastal town over a decade ago, when she had left for college, and she had only been back twice since then. She wasn't planning to go now. "School starts soon, but I'll try to get up there to visit him, if I can. Or I'll just send flowers."

"That's not what I meant, Tess."

"No flowers? Okay, how about a Beer-of-the-Month subscription? A stripper?"

Tess laughed, trying to prove she was just teasing and trying to keep talking so her sister couldn't get a word in and explain what she really had meant.

"Listen to me. I talked to the doctor, and Dad will be laid up for several months. There's no way Mom is strong enough to take care of him, so they'll need you to stay here for a while."

"What about you?" Even as she said the words, Tess knew what Kelly's response would be. She had a five-year-old son and was four months pregnant. She had taken over the role of caretaker for their aging parents and sole actively involved daughter when Tess had left, but she couldn't possibly be expected to give their father the physical assistance he would need while he recuperated from back surgery. "Sorry. I wasn't thinking. But we have other options. Won't their insurance pay for home care help? Or for a nursing home?"

Tess heard a quiet tap on the bathroom door before Lydia let herself in. She mouthed something that Tess interpreted as *Is everything all right?* She nodded, hoping to be left in private to deal with this situation, but Lydia came over to her and stood close, putting her hand on Tess's shoulder in what was likely meant as a gesture of comfort, even though it felt claustrophobic. Tess got tense whenever she had to deal with family matters, and she just wanted to be off the phone and alone in a dark room.

She refocused on Kelly's voice, tuning out the heavily synthetic scent of Lydia's expensive perfume.

"You know their coverage isn't great," Kelly said. Tess actually had no idea about her parents' health care situation, but Kelly seemed to be well versed in the subject. "They have a massive deductible, and they'll be stretching themselves far enough with hospital costs. Besides, Dad wouldn't want a stranger in the home, taking care of him in such a personal way."

Yeah, but he'd be thrilled to have his lesbian daughter who worked at the extremely liberal Evergreen College help him walk to the bathroom. He had never approved of who she was or any of the choices she had made, and he seemed happy enough to have her out of town and out of his life. He wouldn't want her around now, especially if he was feeling weak and vulnerable. She couldn't suggest that her mom take care of him alone, since she wasn't in much better health than her injured husband. She had been using a walker the last time Tess had seen her. Tess sighed and heard an echoing one come from Kelly. She made decent money as a professor, but her modern apartment in downtown Olympia wasn't cheap, and she wasn't exactly the frugal type. She'd offer to cover the expenses of a nurse or a home, but she wasn't sure she'd be able to afford it. Not that she could afford to take several months off work, either…

"He'll be in the hospital for a week after surgery," Kelly said. "Then another two weeks at least in convalescent care. That gives you time to either figure out another solution or find a way to come home and take care of your family. Let me know what you decide."

Kelly ended the call without a sound, probably wishing she had a receiver to slam down. Tess remained motionless with her phone still clutched against her ear, afraid that if she made a single move, she'd end up screaming and throwing her phone against the granite-topped vanity. Lydia was stroking her hair, but the sensation wasn't calming.

Finally, she took a deep breath and slowly set the cell on the edge of the bathtub, next to her leg.

"What's wrong, sweetheart?" Lydia asked, sitting next to Tess and wrapping her in a tight hug. "You look sick."

"My dad," Tess said. The words came out in a raspy way, and she cleared her throat. "He hurt his back. That was my sister, letting me know."

"Is he going to be okay? Do they live near here? What will—"

Tess held up her hand to stop the flow of questions. "Can we not talk about it right now? I just…I need to process this and make some decisions." She rubbed her forehead and felt Lydia stiffen slightly. Her words had sounded harsh. She didn't want to be rude, but she also wasn't prepared to share her personal history with someone she barely knew. Tess's closest friends knew little about her past life, and she didn't even like to think about her family inside her own head. She ran her hand over her face and let it drop onto her lap before smiling at Lydia.

"You're sweet to care. It's just a shock, you know, getting one of those middle-of-the-night calls. Let's get back in bed."

She lifted her hand again and brushed it through Lydia's rumpled blond hair. Lydia dropped her head on Tess's shoulder, relaxing into her again.

"Are you sure you don't want to talk about it?" she asked. "I can help if you need to make plans, or I can call the hospital and find out what's going on."

She's just being nice, Tess repeated to herself to keep from pushing Lydia away, physically and emotionally. She hoped the damsel in distress moment wasn't turning what had been a mutually agreed upon fling into something deeper on Lydia's part.

"I'm fine," she insisted, standing up and pulling Lydia along with her. "Thank you, though."

She kept a smile on her face and a touch of lightness in her voice even though her mind was reeling. She led them back to her bed, and Lydia immediately cuddled close, with her head resting on Tess's shoulder and their legs entwined.

"Shall I distract you instead?" Lydia asked, kissing her way along Tess's collarbone and rubbing her hand over Tess's belly.

"Talk to me," Tess said, covering Lydia's hand with hers to still its motion. "I can't…not right now. Tell me about your work."

She felt Lydia's shrug. "Okay. Whatever will help you. So, I've been drafting a proposal for a noise ordinance…"

Lydia sounded wide-awake and happy to talk, and Tess let herself subside into a brooding silence, punctuated by occasional sounds of interest in the topic at hand. Her thoughts, however, were far from this bed and the legislation being discussed in it.

Even while she was desperately searching for a solution to the home care issue, part of her mind was resigned to the fact that she would need to go back to her parents' house for a while. Anything longer than a day or two was painful to envision, so she focused on the logistics instead. She had no doubt that Evergreen would take care of her and grant her emergency leave. Her course load for the upcoming semester wasn't heavy, and her colleagues would be able to cover for her. She had a miniscule amount of savings that should get her through the few months she'd be on the coast, but she'd probably need to look into getting a job while she was there. After the first few weeks, her dad might be getting mobile enough that she could move out of her childhood home and rent a place of her own—the town had plenty of places that would be sitting empty during the off-season.

"That's cool," she said when she noticed Lydia had paused in her monologue.

"Isn't it?" Lydia agreed. She continued talking, and Tess breathed a soft sigh of relief because she had apparently given an appropriate response. She tried to pay better attention, but her mind wandered back to the coast. There was a small marine research facility near Forks, the decrepit old town in which she had grown up. Maybe she could do some work with them. Hopefully paid work, but she'd even consider volunteering if it would give her a chance to escape from her parents now and again and give her a way to keep her mind involved in the subject she loved so dearly.

The gray whales would be migrating soon, heading south for the winter. She'd be there in plenty of time to see them, and then maybe to watch as they passed by in a few more months on their trek back from Baja to Alaska. She'd possibly have a chance to see some humpbacks or some of the offshore killer whales, giving her a respite from her diligent and depressing focus on the dwindling resident orca pods in Puget Sound. No matter what issues Tess had with her family and her upbringing, she loved the rough northern coast of Washington. The views were spectacular, and the opportunities to study marine life were unparalleled, even though the barely populated towns bored the hell out of her. Teeming ocean life made up for the dull life on shore.

She had first discovered her passion for whales and dolphins when she was barely five and had run away from home with all the indignation a small child could muster. She had made it to a bluff where she had sat, transfixed by the arcing movements of regal black fins through the churning waves, until her mother tracked her down and brought her home again. Tess hadn't run away again—until she finished high school. She had channeled her energy away from home and into school, determined to learn as much as she could about the beautiful creatures she had seen. They had saved her then and would continue to do so if she had to go back to the coast.

Lydia finally drifted back to sleep, but Tess lay quietly, still unable to relax and calm her mind. Somewhere in the night, she had come to terms with the inevitable. She had a responsibility to her family, no matter whether she liked them all that much. She'd find a way to be close to her beloved orcas while she was exiled, and they would make the Forks prison sentence bearable. She'd focus on research, studying and observing as much as she could, and she'd return to Evergreen for the spring semester with a mind full of new ideas to share with her students. She'd find a way to convince Cara and Lenae to visit, to ease her boredom for a few days. And maybe she'd find an attractive and willing woman to share her bed during those cold, bleak winter nights.

Unlikely. She snorted softly, careful not to wake Lydia. She'd be on her own in her parents' spare bedroom, crossing the days off on a calendar until she could reenter civilization. Just trying to get through the days without any of the horrible arguments she and her father had had while she was growing up.

Tess stared at the ceiling until morning.

CHAPTER TWO

B rittany James sat on a hard wooden bench in the courtroom. She didn't fidget or shift in her seat, although both her restless mind and almost numb rear end cried out for movement. The routine of the trial and her impending testimony were comfortable to her, even if the bench wasn't. She let her mind skim through the research she had done to prepare for this case but was careful not to memorize phrases or answers to the expected questions she would be asked. She wanted to sound natural and unrehearsed. Genuine.

Britt let the sounds of the trial blur into a distant drone while she mentally scanned a list of bullet points she wanted to be sure to mention. Although she loved her daily work in the lab, she felt more present and alive during these occasional trials, as if every part of her brain was needed to help her through her time on the stand. Logic and creativity; preparation and spontaneity. She was damned good at what she did and somehow felt more engaged in the courtroom than anywhere else.

She glanced at the plaintiff's attorney's easel as he flipped to a large photo of a tiny dead bird, making a terrifyingly unexpected contrast with her internal thoughts about how alive and smart and wonderful she was feeling. Britt felt the smooth varnished wood slide under her sweaty palm as she gripped the edge of her seat, trying to confine all the tension she suddenly felt inside to one hand, one set of clenched fingers, instead of letting it show in her body or on her face. Where was her air? She had been breathing just fine only a moment ago, and now she felt a desperate need to gasp for oxygen to fill her strangely hollow chest. She forced herself instead to watch the endless parade of photos without showing any of her internal agitation or closing her eyes to keep out the horrifying images.

From the outside, she knew she must look cold and controlled, with her auburn hair tamed in a tight chignon and her body squeezed into a pale green suit jacket and pencil skirt. She had been as carefully dressed as she had been mentally prepped for her testimony in the case against her company. She had been here before, almost a dozen times in the decade she had been employed by Randall Chemical. Just last year, she had sat in this very courtroom and had coolly delivered her expert testimony after a small explosion had rocked her lab and several local residents claimed they'd gotten sick from the resulting fumes. She knew she had played a big role in swaying the jury to see Randall in a more personal way—she was the face of the company in the courtroom, and she helped shift the jurors' impression of the R&D firm, until they saw it not as an evil, poisonous corporation, but as a progressive, beneficial family of chemists who were deeply sorry for the pain the plaintiffs were suffering.

Randall had still lost the case, as they had expected, but the payout was significantly lower than the worst-case scenario. As in millions of dollars lower. Britt had received a good chunk of the company's savings in her holiday bonus check, as she had in all the previous cases.

This one was no different, she told herself sternly. She was here to protect her livelihood. Accidents happened in every workplace, and although a small number of those unforeseen incidences at Randall were potentially more harmful than ones that occurred at a florist shop or a manufacturing plant, they shouldn't be punished all the way out of business because of them. The benefits they provided, the products they discovered that greatly enhanced the lives of everyday people, more than made up for a few mishaps along the way.

Britt gripped her hands together in her lap, feeling the slickness of sweat on her palms. Photo after photo of the damaged local pond and the birds that had lived near it flashed in front of her, but she couldn't let the jury see her respond in any way. She felt their eyes flick toward her every once in a while, but she kept her composure. Her only allowed motion was the occasional shake of her head, as if she was aggrieved by the obvious exaggeration on the part of the plaintiff.

Eventually, the barrage of visuals was over, and she was next to be called to the stand. She looked over at her boss and saw him watching her with a frown. He leaned toward the company's lawyer and whispered something to him, apparently telling him to call for a short recess because he immediately stood and did so. Britt got up as the judge left the courtroom, and then she calmly made her way over to her employer. She was shaken—unexpectedly and uncomfortably shaken—but she was too professional to let her emotions show.

She thought. Ben, Randall's lawyer, motioned for her to take his seat, next to her boss, and he casually positioned himself so he was blocking her from the opposing lawyer's sight.

David Randall smiled at her, with his normal toothy grin. "What's going on, Brittany?" His voice was tight and quiet. "You looked like you were seeing pictures of a child up there, not just some clumps of dead bushes and some obviously photoshopped birds."

Britt swallowed, her throat suddenly dry, and forced her mouth into a pleasant shape that felt completely unnatural and probably looked more like a grimace than a grin. Ben poured a glass of water and pushed it toward her. She gratefully took a sip, but it made her think about the spoiled pond water and all the animals that were forced to drink from it. She set the glass down again.

"I just feel—"

"No. You don't *feel*, Brittany. You think," he said. The strands of his argument tightened around Britt's neck and chest until she could barely breathe. "You weigh costs and benefits like a scientist, like you do every day at work and every time you testify for us. You understand the importance of the product our company has created, and you share that with the jury because they're the ones whose lives will be enhanced by the amazing advancements you created in your lab."

"*Paint*," Britt said in a whisper that sounded like a hiss. "We made paint that is less likely to chip. How is it possibly worth all the damage we caused?"

David and Ben exchanged a glance, but Britt couldn't read their expressions well enough to tell if they were angry or worried or merely indulgent.

"Paint that will save homeowners thousands of dollars because it will last longer," David said, patting her on the shoulder.

"We just dumped all the chemicals behind the warehouse, and they leached into the soil. We killed that pond and everything in it."

"We had issues with disposal of some by-products, but those problems have now been solved. We personally examined the pond and made sure any trace contaminants were completely removed."

Ben tapped on the table to get Britt's attention. She looked up at him, hoping her eyes weren't as red with restrained tears as she thought they might be.

"Britt, you know the truth is somewhere in the middle. Think long term, not short. Do you really want Randall Chemical to shut down because of a tiny pond? We'll make it better, we'll clean up our messes. And next week you'll be back at work, inventing some brilliant new kind of tape or the best latte flavoring I've ever had. But if you crash right now, there won't be a next week for Randall."

"Besides, our employees enjoyed cleaning the pond area so much that we're planning to have our company picnic there next month," David reminded her. "We have a personal stake in it now, sort of like an adopt-a-highway kind of thing."

Britt rolled her eyes, and David dropped his jovial tone.

"You need to stop thinking about those photos and start thinking about your colleagues. Your friends. What are you going to tell them next week? That you choked on the stand and now the company will go bankrupt? They'll lose their jobs, Brittany. Maybe even their homes."

Britt put a hand on her stomach, feeling a rising lump of tension building and moving upward. Soon it would completely fill her throat, preventing her from speaking. But she had to form words and sentences and protect not only her job, but those of her coworkers.

She couldn't selfishly let a momentary, emotional reaction to some pictures destroy the livelihoods of Randall's employees, could she?

"Maybe we shouldn't call her to the stand—" Ben started, but David waved off his concerns with a relaxed smile on his face. He had read Britt's expression perfectly.

"She'll be just fine. Randall Chemical is a family, and Brittany won't let her family down."

Britt silently got up and walked back to her seat, feeling as stiff and lifeless as the bench beneath her. She had too many thoughts spinning through her mind to accurately separate and analyze them, and she had no way to stop time and get them in order. Before she knew it, she was on the stand and performing her act flawlessly. Instinctively. She smiled, she sighed with compassionate but detached concern, and she extolled the wonderful work done in Randall's labs. She could see the jury's response every time she made eye contact with them, and she knew she had managed to fool everyone in the room except Ben and David. And herself.

When the ordeal was finally over, she walked calmly out of the courtroom and to her car. The day was still young, and she had plenty of time to drive back to the lab and get some work done on her current project. Or she could go home and rest. Think. Try to draw a full breath.

She normally appreciated the beauty of Seattle's downtown area, with its mix of art deco and modern glass buildings that reflected a rainbow of colors in the late summer sunshine, but today she felt hemmed in by steel and concrete. She inched through traffic, concentrating on driving and putting aside her experience in the courtroom for the time being. She had always found that to be her best course of action when she struggled to solve a particularly difficult question, whether in school or at work in the lab. Input the information and then let it simmer in her mind until a clear answer presented itself. She wasn't sure why she had been so moved by the photos of the pond and its creatures. And without understanding her reaction, she couldn't figure out what she needed to do about it.

She sped up as soon as she was past the city limits and the traffic on I-5 thinned out. She passed the exit that would take her to Federal

Way, where just last week she had toured and fallen in love with the home she planned to buy with her trial bonuses. The thought of stepping inside the home—the gorgeous and huge suburban house that would have been paid for by Randall Chemical—made her feel queasy again. If she'd had the cash in her hands, she would have thrown it out the window, but how could she get rid of thousands of dollars from her bank account? She jerked her car to the right, off the ramp and into a rest stop, waving a weak apology to the cars honking behind her. She parked and fumbled for her phone, googling the first name that came to mind and typing in the number with shaking fingers.

"Cathy Linwood."

The voice on the other end of the line was as confident and competent as Britt remembered from the trial two years ago, when Cathy had represented a group of citizens who had experienced severe allergic reactions after using one of Randall's products. She had won the case, but Britt had been instrumental in keeping the payout reasonably low.

"Hi, Cathy. Or Ms. Linwood." Brittany's own voice was anything but controlled. It sounded as shaky as her hands were. "Um, I'm not sure if you remember me, but my name is Brittany James and I—"

"Randall Chemical. Yes, I remember you."

Britt sighed at the suddenly cold tone, wondering if her phone could withstand the ice bath it was getting from Cathy's end of the line.

"I have money that I want to give away, as soon as possible," Britt continued. She hadn't thought this through before calling, but her mind seemed to be continuing to work even though her lungs and other body parts were threatening to shut down. "A grant, maybe? Yes, a grant. For someone doing something good for the environment."

"That's vague, but I can work with it," Cathy said, with a noticeable thaw in her voice. "How much money?"

Cathy swore audibly when Britt mentioned the amount, but she recovered quickly and outlined a plan for them to get started. She seemed as anxious to move forward with the grant as Britt was, probably to keep Britt from having time to change her mind. Britt wouldn't change her mind about this—she might be rattled and confused about everything else right now, but she had no doubt she was doing the right thing with her money. She'd grasp at that while she figured out the rest.

After giving Cathy her contact information, Britt eased her car toward the freeway again. Now what? Back to Seattle? She felt marginally better now that the money was, in essence, out of her hands, but she wasn't ready to go back. She decided to simply drive for the time being.

She headed south again and took the exit for Highway 16 when she reached Tacoma. Once she crossed the Narrows Bridge, tall fir trees encroached on the highway in place of businesses and homes. She felt her shoulders relax a fraction, and her breathing loosened as well. She wasn't completely at ease, but she was headed in the right direction. Soon she would identify the trigger that had upset her during the trial, and she would plan a further course of action. Maybe she needed to pick up trash in a park or put out birdseed in her backyard or volunteer somewhere.

For now, she would keep going. She rolled down her window a few inches and let the high-speed wind pull her hair out of its careful arrangement, strand by strand. She was feeling better with each mile, and soon she'd be able to turn around and drive back to her old life.

She thought.

Over three hours later, Britt pulled off the road and parked in a small lot near several other cars. She started walking along the trail that led to Cape Flattery. She had heard it mentioned before, by friends who had vacationed on the Olympic Peninsula, but it had never been on her radar as a place to visit. Still, here she was.

She wasn't dressed for hiking, and her cream-colored silk-covered shoes were ruined before she had walked a quarter of a mile through the dust and fallen fir needles. At least the heels were low enough to be comfortable on the well-maintained path. She couldn't say the same thing for her ridiculously snug skirt, and she spent most of the hike tugging it back in place every time it inched up her thighs. If she had known she'd be running away from home today, she'd have brought a change of clothes.

She passed a few other people who were on the return trip from the cape, all wearing layers of flannel and wool, with suitable footwear. She ignored their curious stares, just like she ignored the scenery around her. She was walking for its own sake, just as she had driven aimlessly until she got to this place. Her mind was too distracted to pay attention to her surroundings.

She spent most of her waking hours in the lab, bent over a microscope, and she was woefully out of shape. Only one mile along the gradually inclining trail, and she was gasping for breath and could feel the heated flush of exertion. She had a painful blister developing on her left heel, and her lower back muscles were aching with a steady thrum. The discomfort was welcome, oddly enough, keeping her present and aware of every step.

Heavy winds buffeted her as she neared the end of the trail, and her lightweight wool suit jacket was ineffective against the wild sea air. Britt wrapped her arms around her middle, flicking her head now and again to get her loose hair out of her eyes. She skipped the first two viewpoints and climbed the narrow rungs of a stepladder leading to a small platform on the third. She walked over to the railing and made a quiet sound of awe at the view before her. She was at the northwest tip of the contiguous United States, the very edge of her small part of the world.

The ocean was far below her, but she could see birds riding the waves and the occasional glimpse of a seal's head breaking the surface. The surf was powerful here, matching the winds in energy and force. The rocky cliffs were carved by eons of contact with the water, and evergreens framed the scene with a colorful contrast.

Britt sighed, and the sound was lost in the noise of the chaotic waves. She could breathe again. The scents of tangy salt and musty ferns, overlaid with the sweetness of sap, filled the empty space in her lungs. A small lighthouse stood on Tatoosh Island across a channel from her. The perfect place to rest and think. Maybe she could rent a room there and stay for a week or so. Or longer.

How could she have changed so drastically in the course of a single day? The realization that she might not be able to slip back into her old life—and that she really wasn't sure if she wanted to— came closer to knocking her over than the strong winds did. She leaned on the railing and started to unravel the tangled ball of the day's experiences. Every strand she pulled went deeper than this morning's court session, though. She might have been snared by a need to escape today, but she had been weaving the noose for a long time, without realizing it.

After more than an hour, she finally turned away from the view and walked back down the steps, hoping she could make the two-mile journey to the trailhead before it got too dark to see. Getting back to nature was one thing, but stumbling through the woods at night wearing an impractical suit was something else entirely.

Her Lexus was the only vehicle left in the parking lot when she got back. Dusk turned quickly to darkness out here where the tall trees blocked the last glimmers of sunlight. Britt got in the car and turned the heater on high as she drove back down the highway a few miles to the town of Neah Bay. She stopped at the motel she had seen on her way past just a few hours ago. A towering wood-carved thunderbird—its red, black, and white paint chipped but still bright—loomed near the glass door leading to the office.

Tomorrow she would buy a sweater and some jeans. She'd find a place to rent for a while, and call David and tell him she wouldn't be in the lab for a couple of weeks. All she needed was a little time to get her shit together. She tried to ignore the nagging question: Would she ever go back? Something had broken inside her today, and she wasn't certain she wanted to fix it. Maybe a part of her had needed to break.

CHAPTER THREE

Tess clicked her windshield wipers to a higher setting. When she had left Olympia this morning, a fine mist had seasoned the air around her. The minute droplets joined together into larger and larger raindrops the farther she drove along Highway 101. Although people across the country were aware of Washington's high amount of rainfall—every time Tess traveled and told people where she was from, she heard the inevitable question *Doesn't it rain* all *the time there?*—no one but locals truly understood how varied rain could be from region to region in the state.

The eastern edge of the Peninsula, along with about a third of the northern coast, benefitted from the rain shadow effect cast by the Olympic Range. The western side suffered from the opposite, and the buildup of marine clouds along the mountains made Tess's childhood home of Forks one of the rainiest spots in a rainy state. A couple hundred days a year with measurable accumulation wasn't unusual.

Tess loved it.

Relentlessly gray skies and damp air depressed some people, but not her. Perennial sunshine sounded too boring for words—the world was much more interesting when overcast. Not to mention, the bleak weather discouraged overpopulation, and the Peninsula had a much more appealing ratio of wildlife to humans than the urban areas where Tess had gone to school and now worked.

It helped that most of the Olympic Peninsula was protected as a national park. Coastal, alpine, and old-growth forest ecosystems shared this space, along with the temperate Hoh Rainforest that was yet another testament to the perks of a wet climate. And off the shoreline was the protected marine sanctuary where Tess would find minke whales, seals, dolphins, and her beloved orcas. She eased up on the gas and slowed down until she was reasonably close to the speed limit. The coast and its creatures pulled her forward like nothing else could do.

She followed the winding highway as it skirted the southern tip of Lake Quinault. She was tempted to stop at the lodge for lunch even though she had gotten a breakfast sandwich and an enormous coffee less than two hours ago, but she knew she was only trying to delay the inevitable arrival at her parents' house. As much as the landscape around her felt like home, and as much as she wanted to get to the ocean, the actual place where she'd spent her childhood—and the family with whom she spent it—seemed alien to her. She wasn't looking forward to being back in their world. When she was small, she had suspected that she didn't really belong with them. She must have washed up on shore one day, part sea creature and part human, and her parents had grudgingly taken her in and raised her. Tess wasn't sure she had ever stopped believing in this myth, and she wouldn't be at all surprised to look in a mirror one day and see gills on her neck or the beginnings of a dorsal fin forming along her spine.

Once she reached Queets and the highway turned up the coast, Tess pulled out the chocolate croissant she had bought along with her breakfast and munched on it as she drove. While she was in Forks, the nearest Starbucks would be more than two hours away, so she had taken full advantage of her visit there this morning. She tried to focus more on the pastry than on the ocean view to her left, but she hit the brakes hard when she thought she saw a seal bobbing on the waves and jammed chocolate and crumbs on her steering wheel. She pulled over and did her best to clean the mess with bottled water and paper napkins before resuming her trip.

Luckily, the road took her east again, inland and away from the distracting ocean. She had been away from the sea too long. She loved her work at Evergreen's marine lab, and she spent most of her days either on the water or within a few yards of it, but the tame Puget Sound couldn't compete with the wild, beautiful expanse of the Pacific Ocean. She had been away from her family even longer, but when the highway cut directly through Forks, she passed by her turn and kept driving until she crossed the border and entered the Quileute Reservation. She parked in the public lot in La Push and got out of her car. She just needed a moment here to feel the sea tugging at her bare feet and the wave-smoothed rocks under her soles. Then she would be able to begin her prison sentence.

Only two other cars were in the lot with hers. The weather was unseasonably cold and seemed even wetter than unusual—Tess wasn't sure why, but some rain was wetter than other rain—and most of the tourists had packed up and gone home by now. She walked to the edge of the concrete and jumped down onto a large driftwood trunk. She sat down and pulled off her shoes and socks, reveling in the smell of briny seaweed and the heavy wind gusting through her short, already soaked hair. The public beach access brought her to a small inlet, but there were no soft buffers of sand or shallow harbor waves to separate her from the fierce beauty of the place. Steep cliffs topped with towering fir trees curved inward, separating this section of the coast from neighboring ones. Huge hunks of driftwood that would cost fifty dollars in the city littered the beach. The surface was made of rough bits of shell and rock, as well as smoother, more weathered pieces, so the process of erosion seemed to be taking place right before her eyes.

Tess hobbled toward the jagged edge of sea foam that marked the reach of incoming waves. Her feet were too soft after months wearing rubber boots and shoes, and she winced with every step, relishing each sharp jab she felt as she walked. The pain disappeared almost instantly when her feet came in contact with the frigid water, but even the risk of hypothermia wasn't enough to wipe away the grin Tess felt spreading across the tense muscles of her jaw and cheekbones. She closed her eyes, letting the sounds of the ocean ease her worries. The waves pounded with rhythmic force close to her, but the beats blended together into a constant hum farther from shore. Whitecaps splashed in between, nearly drowning out the screeches of glaucous-winged gulls. She imagined she could hear the grunts and whistles of killer whales calling to her.

She raised her arms slightly, tempted to dive into the ocean and find them, but she opened her eyes instead and laughed at the resurgence of her childhood fantasy of merging with sea life, letting her adult mind resurface and assess the situation. She was standing in two inches of water, so a dive would be more of a splat onto the pebbled beach. And if she waded farther out before starting to swim, the ocean temps would take their toll and she wouldn't make it past the curved arms of the inlet before she lost all use of her limbs. Too bad, since she knew her real family was out there somewhere and would welcome her with open fins…

Tess stepped out of the water and turned back toward her car, nearly jumping back into the ocean in surprise when she found herself face-to-face with a woman. A gorgeous woman, with shiny auburn hair forcefully tamed in a strict-looking braid that was managing to withstand the buffeting winds. Her eyes were enchanting. They were the color of sea kelp, Tess thought, swallowing with a suddenly dry throat. Greenish brown and glistening, shifting colors as clouds skirted across the sky and changed the light. The woman looked as startled as Tess felt, even though they were standing on a wide-open beach and shouldn't have been able to sneak up on each other. How long had Tess been standing there with her eyes closed?

"Where did you come from?" she asked. She smiled again for the second time since she had come to the beach—probably the second time since she had gotten Kelly's phone call—but this one felt different. Relaxing. Easy. "Out of the ocean? You're a selkie, aren't you? I've always wanted to meet one."

Calling her a selkie was better than likening her eyes to kelp, even though the seaweed reference was a high compliment coming from Tess. She had learned the hard way to refrain from comparing women to anything she'd find in a tide pool.

The woman gestured toward the parking lot, then seemed to notice the price tag still attached to the cuff of her flannel shirt's sleeve.

"Damn," she said softly, tugging the tag and breaking its plastic string. She tucked it into the pocket of her jeans which looked new and still creased from being folded in a store. "I came from the parking lot. Or Seattle, depending on what you meant by the question. I came over to see if you needed help because you looked like you were about to jump. Not that you were on a cliff or anything, but the water is…cold."

She looked flustered, and Tess figured she had come to Tess's aid without thinking it through. She had seen someone who might need help and had instinctively stepped forward. Beauty and substance. Maybe Tess's exile wouldn't be as bad as she had thought. For a few days, at least, until the woman—clearly defined as a tourist and not a local by her appearance even more than her words—returned to Seattle.

Tess laughed. "I was thinking about jumping, but not in a suicidal way. I live too far away from the ocean now and only get back here for brief visits. I'm just staying on the coast for a short time, and I thought I'd stop for a quick feel of the water."

"Ah. Did you grow up around here?"

Tess gestured vaguely toward the south with her head. "Yes, nearby. Until I went to college. I'm Tess, by the way."

"Brittany. Well, as long as you're all right…"

"Wait, don't go yet," Tess said, stalling for time until she could transition from her childlike wonder at being back by the sea and return to her adult role as seducer of women. She hadn't expected to meet someone like Brittany so soon after arriving on the coast. Or *at all* while she was on the Peninsula. She couldn't let her slip away as mysteriously as she had appeared. "The Fates brought you here to rescue me, so apparently we're meeting for a reason."

"Fates, selkies…you're mixing your mythologies." Brittany smiled, though, and didn't walk away. The top of her flannel top billowed open in a sudden gust of wind, and Tess got a glimpse of a silky, pale green dress shirt underneath. The contrast between elegance and roughness was mesmerizing to Tess. Everything about Brittany, aside from her outer layer of clothes, seemed careful and cultured. Definitely more Seattle than Forks. She wasn't going to be here long, and that suited Tess just fine. She'd be a taste of the world Tess had left behind, but with no threat of commitment.

"Give me time and I'll figure out a way to work the Hammer of Thor into our conversation." Tess paused, feeling oddly uncomfortable launching into her usual seduction scene. Was it because she was standing on the beach, too close to the magic of the ocean? Or because she was expected at her parents' house and really shouldn't be trying to arrange a date with a stranger? Whatever the reason, she felt an almost desperate need to push past her reservations, either because of her attraction to Brittany or due to her driving need to delay the onset of a barren and lonely few months in Forks. She wasn't sure which, but both of them seemed important. "Maybe over dinner tonight?"

Brittany took a step back. The move seemed involuntary, triggered most likely by surprise, judging by the expression on her face. Tess sighed. Smooth.

"Or any time, I mean," she added, trying to soften the awkward way she had asked Brittany for a date. "Since we're both transients in the area. And there's really not much else to do around here. Not that I was only asking because—"

Brittany laughed and held up her hands. Tess stopped talking, relieved to have Brittany interrupt a flow of words that was becoming less manageable and coherent by the minute.

"I'm flattered, Tess, but I'm not a quick fling kind of person. I came here because I needed space while I figure out some career stuff." She frowned and averted her eyes, looking toward the parking lot. "Oh, and I guess the main reason is that I have a girlfriend."

Interesting. Brittany's inflection made the addendum sound more like a question than a statement. Tess was going to comment on her tone when she registered the first part of Brittany's rebuff. "Wait, what makes you think *I'm* a quick fling kind of person?"

Brittany looked at Tess again, an amused-looking smile replacing her frown. "You have a lot of tells. For starters, you introduced yourself with only your first name. And in our five-minute conversation, you used at least three synonyms for the word *temporary*. Plus, you were vague when you answered my question about where you grew up."

"Forks," Tess said with a sharpness in her tone. She had been trying to avoid talking about her childhood home for personal reasons, not to hold Brittany at arm's length. Maybe. "Do you want the address?"

"No, thanks. I'm not criticizing you. I just didn't get the impression that you were looking for a meaningful relationship, and there's nothing wrong with knowing exactly what you want."

Well, that was irritating. Tess didn't respond for a moment, taking a few seconds to unclench her jaw and get control over the indignation that was bubbling to the surface of her mind. Brittany was right, of course, and Tess prided herself on making expectations clear at the beginning of any flirtation. She would never promise more than she was willing to offer, but she usually made her feelings known with subtlety and finesse, not in the clumsy way she'd done today. Establishing the parameters of a mutually beneficial and short-lived connection was one thing. Bumbling along with overt warnings not to expect her to stick around was something else entirely.

She fought back the desire to snap at Brittany. Tess was angry at herself for letting this sojourn with her parents affect her so deeply, and disappointed because she had blown her chances with Brittany, who seemed to embody an enticing blend of chaos and control. In another time or place, with a better delivery of what Tess had to offer, they might have shared something explosive and wonderful. If the girlfriend was out of the picture, of course. Tess shook her head. There were too many *if only*s in that scenario.

She wanted to stay by the ocean longer, letting the waves stabilize her and wash away the impressions left by this conversation before she went back to Forks, but she backed a few steps toward the parking lot instead.

"You read me well, Brittany," she said, flashing what she hoped looked like a cocky smile, but probably just looked a little sad. "I'm not in the market for anything permanent. I hope you enjoy your stay here and that you find the answers you're looking for."

Brittany visibly sighed. "I hope I can figure out the right questions, at least. Good-bye, Tess."

Tess walked a few steps toward her car, and then turned around. Brittany was already facing away from her and staring at the ocean like Tess had been when they first met.

"Hansen," she called, raising her voice to carry over the distance and the sound of the waves.

Brittany looked over her shoulder with a puzzled expression on her face. "What?"

"Tess Hansen. My last name."

Brittany grinned. "Brittany James."

Tess felt an answering smile relax her tight jaw. Not a cocky smile, or a sad one. Something calmer than both of those. She nodded a good-bye toward Brittany and left the beach.

CHAPTER FOUR

B ritt stood at the edge of the water, willing herself not to turn and watch Tess walk away. Not to run after her and say yes to dinner. To whatever short-term, temporary affair Tess had offered. She was here for soul-searching and for contemplating major changes in her life. What could be further from her usual routine than sex with Tess in the back seat of her car in a public La Push parking lot?

Britt laughed at the fantasy and stepped into the ripple of a departing wave with her brand-new shoes. They were advertised as waterproof, but Britt wasn't sure she'd trust the health of her toes on footwear she'd bought in a Neah Bay general store. Still, she'd submerge in the chilly water if she needed to—anything to help her retain at least some sense of self while she felt her old world crumbling to the ground.

She had stopped in this tiny coastal town for two reasons. First, the woman who owned the hotel she had stayed in the night before had recommended her cousin's resort as an ideal place for an isolated getaway. Second, it was the closest Britt could come to being in the center of the northern stretch of Highway 101. If she turned back, she would come to the more civilized, hip towns of Sequim and Port Townsend. If she went forward, she'd either turn inland toward Olympia or reach the popular tourist areas of the southern Washington Coast. Either option would give her the opportunity to think about her future with the benefits of coffee shops, decent clothing stores, and quaint B and B accommodations. They'd also put her closer to Seattle and the temptation of her familiar life.

She had thought she'd be better off here, where she wouldn't be able to distract herself from her thoughts with wine tastings or movies. Of course, she had decided on this before she met Tess. An even more alluring distraction than anything civilization could offer.

Brittany trudged along the shore, fighting against the harsh wind. Whoever said the ocean was a calming place hadn't been to this particular stretch of beach, with its rough pebbles that slid under her feet, making walking difficult, and the gusty breeze that threatened to blow her hair out of its braid and completely off her scalp. She could jog on her treadmill for miles, but a hundred yards on this coast left her out of breath. As soon as she was sure Tess had had enough time to get in her car and leave the parking lot, Britt turned around and headed back.

She climbed onto a driftwood tree trunk and scrambled up to the cement lot, hoping no one in the row of tiny cabins along the bluff was watching her ungraceful ascent. Those cabins had been her original destination, but now she stood between her car and the resort, unsure how to proceed. She had spent her life making decisions quickly and efficiently and then sticking to them, but she had felt uncertain and shaky since she had been on the stand in the courthouse yesterday. She had drifted to Neah Bay, and now to this godforsaken place. She had nearly come to tears in a small diner this morning because she couldn't decide whether to have eggs or French toast. After breakfast, she had finally settled on a short stay in La Push, but now Tess had caused her to question her choice yet again.

Tess. Britt shook her head in amazement. Who would expect to randomly meet someone like her on this beach? She was stunning, with her dark hair curling wildly in the breeze and her gaze that was as intense and powerful as the ocean. When Britt had seen her standing by the water, poised as if to jump into the sea like a porpoise, she had been drawn forward almost against her will. She had sensed something frantic, like Tess was running from something the same way she was. And something beautiful, as if Tess knew where to go to escape.

But no matter how tempted she was, Britt hadn't been lying when she said she had a girlfriend. She was pretty sure she still did, at least, though she had cringed inwardly when she heard her voice betray her uncertainty to Tess. Cammie hadn't sounded thrilled with Britt's impromptu disappearance when Britt had called her from the hotel last night. She obviously didn't understand why Britt had felt the need to leave home while she thought through her next moves. She had sighed audibly and said, *Call me when you cool off.* Britt was sure she heard the phrase *come to your senses* echoing behind the words Cammie had actually said.

Britt turned toward the resort as resolutely as she could manage. She was tempted to stay because of Tess and tempted to leave the area for the same reason. But she was here for herself and would stick with the original plan. Or at least the one she had sort of decided upon while eating the pancakes she had finally chosen for breakfast. She would stay here for a few days. Come to her senses.

She hurried to the main entrance of the large, run-down lodge before she could change her mind yet again, or just stand in place for days, paralyzed by indecision.

Britt paused just inside the doorway, jarred out of her self-obsessed thoughts by the lodge's great room. She hadn't been expecting anything fancy, given the outside of the building and the fact that it had been recommended by last night's landlady who had questionable taste when it came to decor, but the lodge was magnificent. One entire wall was a mosaic of large smooth stones surrounding a huge fireplace. A series of baskets—some taller than Britt—were displayed on a wide mantel of interlocking pieces of driftwood. They appeared handwoven based on their irregular shapes, but the patterns on them were harmonious and intricate. A mural covered the expanse of the wall facing the fireplace, with two wolves baying at a full moon. The picture was made up of geometric patterns and bold black, red, and white colors.

No one was at the front desk, but two older men who looked like they should be in a theater heckling Muppets were sitting at one of the tables near the fireplace, playing Scrabble. Neither one acknowledged her as she walked over to them.

"Hello," she said. She didn't get a response, so she cleared her throat and spoke louder in case they were hard of hearing. "Does either of you work here?"

"No."

"You don't need to shout."

Britt sighed before trying again in a normal voice. "Does anybody work here?"

"Fifteen seconds, Jim," the man closest to the window said, practically cackling with glee as the other shuffled through his tiles, muttering softly to himself. Britt leaned over Jim's shoulder and picked up several of them, laying *D-A-V-E-N* in front of the word *port* along the left edge of the board.

"Now will you help me?" she asked, crossing her arms over her chest.

"Ha! Triple word score." He added up his total and then looked up at Brittany. "Thank you. I'll go get Chris if you guard my tiles and don't let Alec look at them."

"Those points don't count," Alec yelled at Jim's retreating back before turning to glare at Brittany. "That's cheating."

Nothing like angering the locals. Brittany was about to apologize when Jim and another man—presumably Chris—came back into the room. Chris was about her age, with black hair and a gaze that seemed to excavate her thoughts. He was wearing a flannel shirt and jeans, clothes nearly identical to hers minus the green silk shirt she had been wearing with her suit yesterday, but he looked comfortable in his while she felt like an imposter.

"Brittany James, right? I've been expecting you," he said, sliding a ledger along the top of the counter toward her.

"Oh, um, you have?" Britt stuttered, wondering how he knew who she was. Had he really been able to read her mind?

"My cousin Nan called and said she sent you here. Betty told me you left the diner at ten, so I thought you'd be here earlier, but Alec saw you heading toward the beach."

"Okay, that's a little creepy," Britt said quietly to herself as she walked over to the desk, relieved that her thoughts were still personal even though her whereabouts weren't. Apparently she was now part of the coastal grapevine. "Do you know what I had for breakfast?"

"Pancakes," Chris said without missing a beat. "Good choice, although I would have gone for the French toast instead. I was going to put you in one of the rooms here in the main lodge, but Nan thought you might want more privacy, so I had our finest cabin cleaned for you."

Privacy seemed to be a relative term in La Push. Britt was about to comment on that, but she was distracted by Alec's derisive snort.

"Hey, why did he make that noise when you mentioned the cabin?"

Chris waved off her question. "You'll love it. All the modern amenities."

"When you say amenities, do you mean an espresso machine and a jetted tub?" she asked.

"Amenities like running water and a roof," Alec said, not taking his eyes off the tiles he was rearranging.

Chris shook his head and pulled the ledger back across the desk as soon as Britt finished writing the *S* of her last name. She didn't have time to lift the pen, and she left a line of ink across the page as he moved it. He handed her a narrow rectangle of wood with *cabin 6* painted on it and a key attached to one end. Britt accepted it reluctantly. It didn't bode well for the condition of the cabin that it looked like the type of key she'd get if she asked to use a gas station bathroom.

"Do you need my credit card number, or did Betty already give it to you?"

Chris laughed. "Of course not. You can pay when you're ready to leave. I trust you."

Alec snorted again. "Fool. She cheats at Scrabble."

Britt rolled her eyes and left with a quick wave at Jim. This wasn't anything like the experience she had the last time she had checked into a hotel. She was quite certain the clerk at the Four Seasons hadn't known what she had eaten for breakfast, and no one in the lobby there had implied that she might abscond without paying her bill.

She walked away from the lodge and along the row of small cabins that followed the curve of the shoreline. Hers was at the end farthest from the public parking lot. Between Alec's scoffing and the gorgeous appearance of the lodge's main room, she had no idea what to expect when she went inside. She thought she'd find either something horribly decrepit or something beautifully decorated, but the reality was a lot plainer.

She stood inside the empty cabin and wondered what the hell she was doing there. The room was nothing more than a small box, with unadorned walls, a small bed, and a teeny kitchen. A door led to the bare bathroom. Was Cammie right? Did she really need to leave the comforts of her roomy apartment and her bright white, ultra-modern kitchen to figure out what to do with her life?

A plaid curtain covered the sliding glass door at the back of the room, and Britt walked over to it with low expectations. She probably had a view of the lodge's garbage bin or something equally unappealing. She pulled the curtain aside and gasped at the view. The fir-covered cliff rose sharply on the left side. She was closer to the edge of the bluff than she had realized, and the gray-green ocean seemed about to flow right into the cabin. She felt small in the presence of the immense sea and the cliff but protected and sheltered at the same time.

She left the curtain open and sat on the edge of the bed, suddenly sure that she was in the exact right place for what she needed to do.

❖

Later in the evening, when it had gotten too dark to see more than the occasional tinge of a whitecap outside her window, she sat at the little table and arranged several notebooks, pens, and a bowl of canned soup in front of her. She had bought everything at the grocery store, including a thick sweatshirt to supplement the flannel shirt and jeans she had found in Neah Bay.

She tested her new pen on the receipt to make sure the ink

was flowing before turning to the first empty page in one of the notebooks. She was in a beautiful, inspiring setting, and she had the time and space to think. She would simply tackle this problem the same way she confronted any other issue in her life. Lists of pros and cons for taking a sabbatical and staying at her job versus quitting. Mind maps to determine possible routes to take with her future. Brainstorm pages and formal outlines with bullet points. The answer would be in there somewhere, and she just had to use a variety of methods to ferret it out.

She started with the pros and cons for running away from home, even though she had already done it. She figured she was still in the grace period and could slip back into her life without much of a fuss if she went back soon. She filled an entire column with sensible reasons to go back to Seattle, while the only reasons to stay were facetious. *Signs of instability will be a good bargaining chip when asking for more vacation time* and *This will make an interesting chapter in my memoir after I win the Nobel Prize in Chemistry*. She had a hard time articulating the real reasons to stay here and think because they were too connected to feelings and not to logic.

She tossed that page aside and started a mind map with all the ways she had violated the environment. She sometimes paid the extra five cents for a plastic grocery bag because she routinely forgot to bring her reusable ones to the store. She ate meat, she had never rescued a homeless animal, and she didn't have a compost heap in her backyard. Just last week she had thrown away a stack of old magazines instead of recycling them. Not to mention being complicit in the indiscriminate dumping of hazardous chemical waste.

Britt crumpled the page. How could she right every wrong? She didn't even know where to start. She got a fresh piece of paper and wrote *Pros and Cons: Having a fling with Tess Hansen. Hanson?* The con side was obvious. Cammie. Common sense. She added the fact that she had already said no and wouldn't be able to find Tess even if she changed her mind, but she knew it wasn't true. Chris and Betty probably knew everything about Tess, too, from her current address to her cholesterol level.

The pros were a fun fantasy, and Britt allowed herself to indulge in them for a few minutes. Those deep blue eyes. Her silky-looking hair. That body...

Eventually the Tess list was scrunched up and added to the growing pile of paper balls. Britt gathered them up with a sigh, mentally adding *wasting precious resources by making useless lists* to her mind map. Her soup had long since grown cold, and she heated it up again, glad that the cabin's amenities included a miniature microwave.

CHAPTER FIVE

Tess barely noticed the gloomy scenery as she drove inland from La Push to Forks, but she couldn't escape it once she entered the town. Forks had once been a thriving foresting community—well before Tess was born—but now it was as bleak and depressing as the gray cloud cover. A short section of the main road contained a connected downtown area, housing a few stores and the town's tiny library, but most of the businesses were separate. Tess passed hotels, a dentist's office, an antique store, and a bakery that all looked exactly the same. Box-shaped buildings covered with yellowing white paint and with blinking *Open* signs in the windows, tied to the electrical grid with tangles of aboveground wires. No personality or individuality. Just a barren sameness. Exactly what Tess had run from when she reached eighteen.

As she passed the hospital, she saw a tour bus stopped along the curb with a handful of passengers on board. They held cell phones out the bus windows, most likely snapping photos of the place where a fictional vampire doctor worked. Tess shook her head. Even decades after the book series had been released, the desperate town was still holding tight to its connection to sparkly vampires as a way to bolster the economy. On her way to La Push, Tess had noticed signs warning vampires to stay out of werewolf territory. It was kind of cute, but ties to an ephemeral pop culture franchise wouldn't create a lasting source of revenue for a community like Forks.

Tess turned off the main road and passed her high school, hating the sense of traveling through time and turning back into her teenage self. She had been as awkward with Brittany today as she had been when asking out her first crush. Not to mention, she had been turned down in both cases. Yeah, she definitely wasn't going to mention that. During college, she had spent nearly as much time studying her interactions with women as she had marine biology, carefully honing her skills until she was adept at establishing distance while closing the gap between her and a potential date. It was tricky business, setting boundaries and initiating intimacy at the same time, but Tess was very good at it. Usually.

She blamed her family for the failure, of course. Being forced to come back here, where she had felt unaccepted, un-nurtured, and bored out of her mind, had transformed her into a sulky teen again. Her inability to smoothly ask Brittany on a casual date—that would end in amazing, but casual, sex—had nothing to do with Brittany herself. Nothing at all.

Well, maybe a little. Tess had been bemoaning the fact that she hadn't met an unattached Brittany under different circumstances, but she was probably better off meeting her in this dead-end place. Brittany intrigued her. She seemed kind and intelligent, but Tess was accustomed to finding both of those traits in women. Somehow, though, Brittany oozed with juxtapositions, and Tess wanted to figure them out. Her fiercely tamed hair, her silk blouse, her brand-new beach-appropriate clothes. The odd inflection in her voice when she mentioned the girlfriend. Brittany was full of question marks, and Tess wanted to take the time to find the answers.

Well, she wouldn't find them here. Even if Brittany hadn't shot her down—Tess couldn't seem to keep her promise not to mention that fact in her mind—she couldn't imagine dating Brittany in the context of her childhood home. Would she take her to a diner in Forks? Sit on a tour bus, holding hands as they followed a sparkly vampire trail? Ludicrous. Tess was alone in her exile.

She pulled into the driveway of her childhood home and sat in the car with her engine idling. The two-story house was a plain, postwar box that had always been easy for her to draw when she was young—an upended rectangle with a triangle on top. Nothing special, but her parents had always taken care of the property because they had what Tess, when she was a know-it-all teenager, had considered to be an excessively bourgeois concern for what their neighbors thought of them. Her mother had tended her flowering shrubs and rosebushes, turning their garden into something worthy of an English estate. Her dad had painted the house—always slate blue with dark gray trim—as soon as the old coat showed signs of chipping or fading. Now her mother's beautiful flower beds were overrun with weeds, and the house paint had weathered to a powdery light blue.

Tess sighed and shut off her car. She had managed to make a three-and-a-half-hour trip last more than six hours with all her detours, but she had only delayed the inevitable. She got her small suitcase out of the trunk and walked up the cracked cement path leading to the front door. She wasn't sure if she should knock or just walk inside, but her sister opened the door before she made a choice, and Tess had the eerie feeling of coming face-to-face with herself. She and Kelly had often been mistaken as twins, and the similarities between them had only grown more pronounced as they had gotten older. Kelly's dark hair was longer than Tess's and tied in a ponytail, but it was the same dark sable and framed the same bright blue eyes. Her belly was slightly rounded from her pregnancy, but otherwise she was as slim and angular as Tess. They were even wearing similar cable-knit sweaters, for God's sake. Tess fought the childish urge to strip down to the tank top she was wearing underneath.

"Dad won't take his pain pills. Where have you been? We expected you hours ago."

So much for a warm welcome home. Tess hadn't expected a banquet in her honor, but she hadn't thought she'd be met with the same hostility from Kelly that she felt inside herself.

"Hey, Kelly, great to see you, too," Tess said, hesitating on the porch before she stepped inside the house. Nearly every surface was covered with something crocheted, and Tess wondered if her mother was putting all her old gardening energy into the less strenuous needlework.

"Hello, Tess. Glad you could finally make it."

The disapproving-older-sister expression on Kelly's face was probably almost identical to the rebellious-younger-sister look Tess gave as her response. They both got a lot of mileage out of the two-year age difference between them.

"Tess? Is that you?" Tess's mom, Edith, came out of the kitchen. She was using a walker, but once she saw Tess, she set it aside and came over to her with a halting step. Tess met her halfway across the room and stooped down to hug her. Her body felt smaller, frailer than Tess remembered, but her arms gripped Tess tightly enough to make a wave of guilt flow through her because she had been away so long. She shook off the feeling. She would be going away again, as soon as her parents were able to handle her father's injury without her help.

She looked over her mom's shoulder and saw Kelly's son Justin hovering in the doorway between the kitchen and the living room. He wouldn't meet her eyes, and his hands flapped almost imperceptibly against his thighs. She untangled herself from her mom's grip and knelt down, reaching into her backpack for the plastic dinosaur she had brought.

"Hi, Justin," she said. "Remember Aunt Tess? I brought you something."

He came toward her with hesitating steps and reached for the toy. He turned it over a few times in his hands, still not looking directly at her, and then launched himself at her neck. The hug was brief, but tight, and Tess dropped one hand to the floor behind her to keep from falling over. The physical movement seemed to loosen something inside Justin, and he started to speak rapidly.

"It's a Tyrannosaurus rex, from the Cretaceous period. They sometimes weighed more than ten tons and ate…"

Tess sat back on her heels and listened in amazement as Justin rattled off an impressive array of facts about dinosaurs for such a young boy. When she had last seen him, he still hadn't started to speak, and Tess knew from infrequent phone conversations with her mom that he had been slower to develop than other children his age.

He was apparently trying to catch up by fitting as many words into each breath as he could, and she loved it.

Kelly must have heard enough of those words by now to have lost some of her excitement about them because she came over and put her hands on her son's shoulders. "Okay, Justin, enough for now. You can tell Tess all about dinosaurs over lunch, but right now she needs to take care of Grandpa."

This last bit was directed at Tess with a sharp nod toward the ground floor spare bedroom. She sighed and got to her feet.

"At least take your bag to your room first," Edith said. "Get settled in."

"Dad should have taken his pain pill two hours ago, Mom. Tess needs to take care of him right now."

"But she just got here, and..."

Tess shook her head and left the two of them bickering in the living room. She tapped on the open door of the bedroom where her dad was staying because the trip upstairs was probably too much for him right now. She didn't get a response, so she stepped inside. Her dad was propped on the bed in an upright position, staring at the television screen where robots, elves, and humans seemed locked in some sort of sci-fi or fantasy battle. Her dad had a game controller in his hands, but Tess couldn't tell which of the characters he was.

"Hi, Dad."

He glanced at her, and then refocused on the television with a grunt. "Tess," he said in his usual brief way of acknowledging her presence.

She walked over to his bedside table and looked through the array of pill bottles before finding the right one. She tipped one pill into her palm and held it toward him. "You need to take this."

He disengaged one hand from the controller and waved dismissively at her. "I don't hurt. Besides, I don't want to risk getting addicted to those damned things."

Tess stood silently for a few moments, watching her father play his game and noticing the occasional wince when he got too aggressive with the controls and probably felt the movement in his back. She had been dreading seeing him again, and it was almost comforting to have him focused on the game instead of her and her life choices. She was tempted to let him suffer for being so stubborn, but she couldn't.

"Look, Dad, you need these pills to help your body relax and heal. If you keep fighting through pain, you'll be in bed longer, and then I'll be here longer. Neither of us wants that, do we?"

He looked at the pill as if nearly swayed by her argument, but then shook his head. "Just leave it on the table. I'll take it when I need it. Whoa! Did you see that? I just took out two cyborgs at once."

Tess closed her eyes and mentally transported herself back to her bedroom in Olympia. She was safe and warm, with a woman's leg draped over her thigh and delicate fingertips trailing over her stomach. Kelly's damned phone call never came, and Tess, roused from sleep, looked over and saw…Brittany. Not Lydia. Where had she come from? She heard Brittany's laugh as she answered. *The parking lot. Seattle. The sea?*

Tess opened her eyes, shaken by the daydream. She snatched the controller out of her dad's hands.

"Hey! I was about to level up. Give it back."

"Take your pill, and then you can play your game," Tess said. She had to get the hell out of this place before she went mad, and she would do whatever it took to get her dad well.

He grumbled but took the pill and drank from the glass of water she handed him next. He muttered under his breath about being treated like a child while she straightened the items on his table, making as much noise as she could in the process.

"Well, if you insist on acting like one, it's how you'll be treated," she said. She hesitated with a plastic pink water carafe—probably brought from the hospital—in her hand, and then set it gently and deliberately on the bedside table. Their angry words were echoes from the past, but their roles had reversed. Weird. Her dad still stared at the television, but his hands weren't moving on the controls. She wondered if he'd noticed the same thing. Tess cleared her throat.

"Do you need anything else?" she asked in a somewhat softer tone.

"Ginger ale would be good. If we have any."

"Fine."

"Thanks."

Snippy, but not angry. A real breakthrough moment. Tess took a deep breath and left the room. She picked up her bag from the living room floor.

"We saved some lunch for you," Edith said, coming out of the kitchen. Justin stood next to her, leaning against her legs. "Are you hungry?"

Tess wasn't, but she nodded anyway. Easier to eat something than to get into a long discussion about it.

"I'll be right there. Don't let T-Rex eat my lunch before I get back, okay, Justin?"

He giggled and ran back into the kitchen, where he would probably take a dinosaur-sized bite of her sandwich.

She grinned and carried her suitcase to her old room on the third floor. Everything looked exactly the same as it had when she was in high school, complete with taped-up posters and a dusty collection of shells on the windowsill. She figured the utter absence of change had less to do with her parents keeping a shrine to her and more to do with their lack of imagination. To them, her room was simply her room and they probably couldn't conceive of it being used for anything else.

Tess tried to stretch out her moment of solitude, but it only took her a few seconds to toss her clothes into an empty dresser drawer. She changed out of her warm sweater and into a long-sleeved T-shirt before going back to get her dad some ginger ale and eat a lunch she didn't want.

CHAPTER SIX

Tess backed out of her parents' driveway and paused at the four-way stop for a few minutes, drumming her fingers on the steering wheel, even though there were no other cars on the road. She should be relieved to get out of the house—time off for reasonably good behavior—but somehow going to the grocery store was even worse than sitting at home with her family. At first, she had jumped at the chance to get away and had leapt into her car the moment her dad or Justin mentioned an item that wasn't in the pantry. After three days, though, the relief of being out of the house had been eclipsed by the turmoil of emotions she felt walking through the damned grocery aisles, and she would rather have stayed in her old room. But the precedent had been set, and now her family assumed she'd eagerly fly out of the house whenever a sudden yearning for a particular food or drink was expressed.

She sat at the intersection and contemplated her options. She could flee back to Olympia. Take a long detour to a store in Port Townsend and not get back until well after dark. Drive off the bluff and into the ocean...

Okay, the last option was a bit drastic. Tess turned left, aiming toward the center of Forks instead of toward a chilly plunge into the sea. She wasn't sure why the prospect of a shopping trip had become so daunting in such a short period of time, but it had. Something about the mundanity of the errand made her feel trapped in this town and this lifestyle more than anything else had. Taking care of her father was strange and unlike anything she had experienced in her childhood. Going to the store, however, was a normal, familiar task. She had met several of her classmates from high school on previous trips. They had been friendly, but oddly unsurprised to see her again after so many years. They acted as if they had been together in homeroom or biology class just the day before, and their acceptance of her reappearance as something unremarkable made her feel the same sense of suffocation and yearning to be far, far away she had felt as a teenager.

Being here and thrust into the unwanted role of caretaker was one thing. Settling into the routine of daily life in Forks was something else entirely, and she hated it. She felt trapped, and the grocery store had become her prison yard where she was sent for daily exercise.

She drove slowly, caught between feeling sorry for herself and realizing how ridiculous her self-pity actually was. She was an adult, with a job and life waiting for her in Olympia, and she needed to stop reverting to a stage of adolescent claustrophobia.

Or, she thought as she pulled suddenly off the road and cringed at the grating sound of her hubcap brushing the cement curb, she needed to find a way to distract herself from it.

She let the car idle while she looked in her rearview mirror at the reason for her abrupt stop. A cream-colored Lexus, looking out of place on Forks' nearly empty main street. One of the cars that had been in the La Push lot when she had first arrived and gone to see the ocean. Of course, there was a chance it didn't belong to Brittany, but Tess shrugged off the possibility. Brittany had seemed out of her element in La Push, but she'd look right at home inside the elegant car. Tess stepped onto the cracked sidewalk and wandered along the street, peering into the stores and trying to look like she was casually window-shopping instead of Brittany-stalking.

Tess finally spotted her in a clothing shop. Her breath caught, and her thoughts started tumbling over themselves like her words had when she and Brittany had first met. What was her endgame here? Brittany was in some sort of relationship, and Tess was determined to avoid anything resembling a commitment. But Tess was feeling trapped in the quicksand of normalcy here in her hometown, while Brittany looked about as un-Forks as she could be, even dressed in a plain gray sweatshirt and jeans, with a small mountain of flannel draped over her arm. She had a quiet elegance about her that made her look as if she should be wearing a little black dress and sipping a latte in front of a Tiffany store rather than rummaging through racks of cotton and denim.

Tess shook off the vision of removing the imaginary silky black dress from Brittany's body and stepped resolutely through the door of the shop. She just wanted a short break from her regression into her past. What was the harm in saying hello?

Brittany yelped and spun around when Tess tapped her on the shoulder.

"Hey. I didn't mean to startle you," Tess said, bending down to pick up the bundle of heavy flannel shirts that Brittany had dropped. Her hands brushed against Brittany's when she handed her the clothes, and Tess took a step back. Maybe there *was* the potential for harm in saying hello. She was confused by the strength of her reaction to being this close to Brittany, and the sensible side of her wanted to get the hell away. The rest of her wanted to see what would happen if she got even closer, like a child who wouldn't stop playing with a light socket.

"Hello, Tess. I'm not usually this jumpy. I don't really know anyone around here, so I've kind of gotten lost in my own world." Brittany laughed and reached up to tuck her hair back in place as if it wasn't neatly braided and under control. Tess wanted to release it from its plait to give Brittany something to fidget with. And to give herself a chance to touch her.

She cleared her throat and gestured around at the clothes racks. The movement seemed a little frenzied, but she needed to occupy her hands in some way. "I just came in to buy a few things and saw you, so I thought I'd say hello."

"Really. You're buying clothes here."

Tess followed Brittany's gaze and looked down at what she was wearing. She was casually dressed, but her dark jeans had a designer label and her sweater was cashmere. Nothing overly fancy, but she didn't look like she tended to go for the casual beachcomber look that was prevalent in Forks.

Brittany shook her head with a rueful sounding sigh. "You're dressed like someone who's been to a city with a population larger than three hundred. And someone who lives in a house with insulation in the walls."

Tess laughed, eager to move the conversation away from the question of why she was really in the store. "What are your walls made of?"

"The plywood equivalent of twenty-pound bond paper."

"Oh. Then you might want to get one of these." Tess picked up a hunter-orange flannel hat, complete with earflaps and a sherpa fleece lining, and set it on top of Brittany's armful of shirts.

Brittany balanced her load of clothes in one hand and used the other to pluck the hat from the pile and put it on her head. She tugged on the strings to tighten the flaps. "Mm. Warm. I don't care how much you laugh at me, but I'm buying it."

Tess was too busy thinking of all the ways she could keep Brittany warm on these cold autumn nights to do much laughing. She was feeling a definite rise in her own body temperature and she looked around for something else to distract herself from dwelling on her attraction to Brittany since the funny hat idea had backfired so alarmingly.

"Come on, Britt," she said, leading her to the back of the store. "We'll have you looking like a local in no time. The hat helps, but it's just a start."

"You don't look like a local," Brittany said, pulling off the hat and smoothing her hair down as she followed Tess. "Why should I listen to your fashion advice? Aside from the brilliant hat suggestion, of course."

Tess sorted through a rack of dresses. "I'm a Forks expert. I spent my entire life studying what the locals wear and how they act so I could do the exact opposite once I escaped this town."

Britt sighed and dropped into a nearby chair, her flannel shirts clutched in her lap. "I escaped *to* this place, and you seem eager to escape *from* it again."

Tess paused in her search and glanced over at Brittany. Her expression was softening from laughter to sadness, and Tess struggled to find the right response that would make Britt cheerful again. They might have come to the Peninsula with separate agendas and drastically different viewpoints about being here, but they could certainly work together to improve their situations. For a short time, they could add some much-needed fun and laughter to each other's lives. Some companionship. A lot of heat. But what she saw as a positive—their fleeting connection as fellow transients—was likely a negative for Britt. And would be further proof to her that Tess was the casual-fling type, just like Brittany had identified her at their first meeting.

Tess didn't want to give Brittany more reasons to think of her as someone immune to serious relationships, but she wasn't about to proclaim the opposite, either. She decided to keep her thoughts to herself. For now, at least.

She pulled a dress from the rack and held it up for Brittany. It looked like a pair of denim overalls, but with a skirt instead of pants and embroidered red flowers on the bib. White long sleeves and a collar were sewn onto the denim. "How about this?" she asked.

"For what? Herding cows through an Alpine village?"

Tess held the dress in front of herself and pulled the skirt out to one side, as if she was about to curtsy. "For dates with your girlfriend."

Britt gave a snort of laughter and tossed her hat at Tess's head. "Are you purposefully trying to break us up?"

Yes. "Of course not," Tess said, hanging the dress back on the rack. "You laugh now, but you'll be back for it once you're fully assimilated into the Forks community."

Brittany shook her head, still grinning at the imagined look on Cammie's face if Britt showed up for a date wearing anything resembling overalls. The plaid shirts and thick sweatpants she was planning to buy wouldn't suit Cammie's tastes, either, and Britt would definitely *not* wear the earflapped hat when—if?—Cammie came to visit. Unless it was really cold, of course.

Britt got up and dumped her clothes into Tess's arms. "Here

you go. I think you'll be more useful as a shopping cart than as a fashion consultant."

She walked over to a wall of socks and chose the thickest, warmest looking pair. How many pairs should she get? One? Twenty? She stared at the overwhelming number of wooly, multicolored socks and felt the now-familiar sense of unreality slide over her, disconnecting her from her surroundings until she felt as if she was watching a show instead of experiencing the shopping trip in person. Cammie was the trigger this time, but any number of reminders of the life she had left behind would do the same thing.

They had spoken on the phone several times. Stilted, awkward conversations in which Britt was unable to clearly articulate what she was looking for in La Push. Cammie never gave her an ultimatum, but Britt heard one in every sentence she spoke. Britt knew she had plenty of options when it came to her future even though she didn't know what to choose right now. But when it came to Cammie, Britt had only two choices. She could return to Seattle and act like normal, whether at her old job or in a new one, thereby giving their relationship a chance. Or she could continue her course and make drastic changes to herself and her way of life, reducing her chance of remaining with Cammie to somewhere near nonexistent. There was a ticking clock on the decision, too, because Cammie wouldn't wait around forever. She'd already mentioned nights out with friends, conversations with other women from work, and Britt hadn't even been gone a week. Cammie's life was moving forward on its regular schedule while Britt had interrupted hers abruptly. She struggled to take a deep breath. If she couldn't make a decision about her future and her girlfriend, how could she decide how many fucking socks to buy?

She was building toward a full-blown panic attack when Tess jostled her back to reality. She pulled the socks out of Britt's clenched fist and hung them up again, selecting a pair of emerald-green ones instead.

"These are just as warm, but not as bulky, so they'll be more comfortable. Plus, they're better at wicking moisture away from your skin, which is helpful if you spend a lot of time in the rain or near the ocean, and both are givens if you live around here."

Britt wasn't sure how much of her inner turmoil had been obvious in her expression, but Tess's voice had been less playful and quieter than before, almost soothing. Britt reached out with a hand that was only slightly shaky and took the socks.

"Thank you," she said, covering the sock advice and Tess's friendliness with one simple phrase.

Tess bumped her with her shoulder. "See? I'm more than a shopping cart."

Britt smiled, firmly back in Forks again. She added a half dozen pairs of the green socks to her pile of clothing. "You truly are. My ears and toes will be eternally grateful for your fashion tips."

Tess paused, as if considering her next words, before saying in a rush, "I'm a good listener, too, if you ever need to talk. I really just mean talking, since you have a girlfriend, and I'm not suggesting anything…you know…inappropriate, or not in public."

"Well, I appreciate you not suggesting anything not in public," Britt said, repeating Tess's odd phrasing and smiling when Tess blushed.

Tess rubbed a hand over her eyes. "You know what I mean."

"I do, and thank you," Britt said, careful not to go beyond simple gratitude and ask for Tess's phone number or for a public meeting for coffee and a chat. Not because she doubted Tess's words—she seemed to be honestly offering a friendly ear without any strings attached—but because Britt was tempted by the endearingly and awkwardly presented offer. She'd never cheat on Cammie, of course, but she felt the void of having no friends or family to talk to about her thoughts and options. Hours of making lists and debating with herself about her career and future were lonely, but necessary right now, no matter how much she'd rather her days were filled with friends and her nights were filled with sex. She couldn't allow herself to picture Tess fulfilling either one of those roles. Tess had put the ball in her court by extending an offer of friendship, and Britt had to intentionally let it drop.

"Well, okay." Tess cleared her throat and shifted the clothes back into Britt's arms. "I should get to the grocery store and back home. I'm glad we ran into each other again."

"Me, too," Britt said. She had been planning to go buy groceries while she was in Forks, as well, but she decided to change her plans and stop by La Push's tiny market on her way back to the cabin. She wanted to roam the grocery aisles with Tess, making jokes and having fun. She wanted to spend time with Tess more than she should. Instead, she would put on her new hat and socks and about four layers of clothes and walk on the beach until she froze the image of Tess's beautiful eyes and the warmth of her smile right out of herself.

Tess put the hat back on Brittany's head and tugged on the earflaps. "Bye, Britt," she said.

"Bye, Tess."

CHAPTER SEVEN

Tess aimed her car south and breathed a sigh of happiness as she left Forks behind. She pretended she was heading back to Olympia and home for a few glorious miles, until she turned onto the small road leading west toward the coast.

She hadn't been able to get away from the house for over a week except to go to the store, and the stress of life there was exhausting. Every attempt to help her dad had been a struggle at first, turning even the simplest tasks into argumentative ordeals. After each barrier was breached, however, it became part of their daily routine. Now her dad took his pills when she reminded him, he ate the food she brought, and he let her support him whenever he needed to leave his bed. Still, he would fight each new step as a matter of pride, and she expected a battle tomorrow when they had to begin doing the physical therapy exercises his doctor had prescribed.

Tess turned south again, crossing onto the Hoh Reservation. As annoying as her dad was, she knew she would be an equally difficult patient. She hated to admit it, but she had inherited his stubborn pride and independence. Sometimes the only thing keeping her from running out of the house and going home was understanding how hard it would be if she was in the same situation herself—forced to have her parents taking care of her because she was injured and helpless. She would hate it, too.

She had found ways to cope with her exile, and the week hadn't been as terrible as she had expected. Spending time with Justin was great, and part of her was already sad that he'd be left behind when she finally was free to go. She'd have to convince Kelly to let him visit her in Olympia, and she vowed to make more of an effort to visit him. Tess and her mom had gotten along fine, but they had so little in common that meals and evenings were largely spent in a reasonably companionable silence, neither wanting to say something wrong and break the fragile sense of peace.

Even though Tess hadn't seen Britt since the clothing store, she had been on Tess's mind more than was comfortable. During her brief excursions around Forks, she was constantly on alert for the sight of a Lexus or a glimpse of Britt walking along the sidewalk. During the silent meals at home, she spent most of her time wishing she was able to have conversations with Britt about something, nothing, anything. And especially at night, in her old room, enveloped by the sleepy creakiness of the old house, Britt was there. Then her imaginary interactions with Brittany had less to do with talking than with fantasies of exploration and silent connections.

But Britt had made it quite clear that she wasn't interested in what Tess had to offer—not a casual fling and not even friendship. So Tess made a determined effort to forget about Britt. When she spotted her car, Tess immediately turned in the opposite direction. When Britt was too present in her thoughts, she'd initiate conversations with her mom about innocuous topics like crocheting, or with Justin about the infinitely more interesting dinosaurs. And at night…well, sometimes her efforts to put Britt out of her mind were more futile than at other times.

Tess nearly missed the turnoff for the Hoh Marine Center, but no one was behind her and she was able to back up and get on the private road. She parked in the lot next to a dilapidated pickup and an ancient Volkswagen, both rusty from age and constant exposure to salty sea air. The Center was made up of a square building with several additions that didn't match the main unit in either color or architectural style. Each new wing looked like it had been designed on a whim, by a different person, and the result was rambling and lopsided. Tess got out of her car, drawn to the sea, and walked past the building and out to the water, where a Zodiac and a large fishing boat bobbed in the waves.

The Center was located in a deep inlet, protecting it somewhat from the battering ocean waves. Instead of a beach, the shore was lined with huge basalt boulders, and the tide was just going out. Tess dropped over the side of a cement retaining wall until she was standing just above the waterline, on a rock still wet from high tide. A bed of rockweed waved at her like hundreds of tiny hands in the retreating sea. Tess bent down and reached into the water, moving aside a few fronds of the seaweed and exposing some little conical limpets and curling snails stuck to the rock underneath. She ran her fingers gently over a bumpy limpet shell, feeling the strength of its muscular foot as it pulled back from her touch. She carefully covered the creatures again and stood up, wiping her hand on her jeans. She spotted an otter a few yards out to sea, performing its ritual of ablutions in the surf. It rubbed its face thoroughly with its front paws before swirling around and dunking itself in the water. As soon as it resurfaced, it began scrubbing again. It shook its head, fluffing out its brown fur and twitching its whiskers as it noticed Tess watching.

She laughed happily, watching the small acrobat twist and turn in the water. She hadn't been back to the ocean since meeting Brittany in La Push. At first it had been because she was needed at home, but after the clothing store she hadn't wanted to run into Britt again and possibly have her unaccustomed awkwardness reassert itself. And once she figured it was safe to go back—surely Brittany had been driven back to Seattle by boredom after a few days spent in the lonely little town and her freezing-cold cabin?—she couldn't face going to the beach and not seeing her there. None of it made sense to Tess. Brittany had been on her mind longer than most women spent there.

Now Brittany was back home, most likely, and Tess's dad was improving a little and could do without her for part of the day. The ocean was hers again. She waved good-bye to her otter friend and clambered back up to the parking lot.

Tess went to the front door of the Center and stepped inside. A small, empty desk sat to her right, and a coatrack and fake potted plant, thick with dust, were on her left. Pamphlets on tides and marine animals were scattered in messy piles across every surface. The place felt deserted.

"Hello?" A door led from the reception area and into a long hallway. Tess looked both ways, unsure where to find actual people. She opted for going to the right, careful not to trip over the three-inch rise that must be where one of the additions connected to the main building. She found a kitchenette with a dorm-room sized fridge, several more fake and dusty plants, and a coffeepot that was opaque from hard water stains. She absolutely did not want to look in the microwave. She was sure it had years' worth of spills inside.

She went back toward the front door and continued along the hallway in the other direction, stepping up again at another join in the flooring. At the end of this route, she came into a large, open room. The walls were covered with charts and maps interspersed with posters advertising marine conferences and rock concerts from the past three decades. Books and skeletal bits of sea creatures battled for space on sagging shelves. Several radios were playing at once—one with classic rock music and the others with updates on whale sightings along the coast and the inside passages of Puget Sound and Canada. A fourth speaker relayed sounds that must be coming from an underwater microphone in the bay outside.

Tess felt a wave of homesickness as the familiar sights and sounds washed over her. The lab was very similar to her own at Evergreen College, although hers was much cleaner and busier with a constant stream of students coming to study and work. It was good for her to be in a place like this, where she could get back to the research that gave her life meaning and the passion that filled her soul. Lately, she had been focused on unproductive passions—the passion for avoiding family closeness and a growing passion for a woman who didn't reciprocate the feeling. Here, among the charts and photos of killer whales and the radio voices of other like-minded enthusiasts, she could finally be herself. She easily picked out individual discussions from the cacophony of sound, and when she heard someone call in a sighting of her J pod whales, she moved closer to the desk where the radio was sitting.

A young woman—barely older than Tess's students—stood up suddenly and yelped when she saw Tess standing right by her desk. Tess startled, too, and nearly knocked over a tall lamp that was inexplicably unplugged and standing in the middle of the room.

"Hey," Tess said, righting the lamp and gesturing toward the foyer. "Sorry to startle you, but no one was at the front desk, so I came back here."

The woman looked in the direction Tess indicated with a small frown, as if she had forgotten they had a reception desk at all. "Oh, yeah. We don't get visitors much, so no one sits out there. I was cleaning some coffee I spilled under my desk and didn't hear you. Um, we don't do whale watching tours here."

She sat at the desk and turned her attention to a chart of whale sounds. She was wearing one of those knit hats, with cat ears and ties hanging longer than her straight brown hair, that Tess thought had gone out of style years ago unless the wearers were under the age of ten. She said she had been cleaning coffee, but she hadn't emerged with either an empty cup or dirty paper towels. Tess added the underside of the woman's desk to the inside of the microwave on a running list of places she didn't want to examine up close.

Tess sighed and started again. "I'm Tess Hansen. I teach at Evergreen, but I'm on sabbatical in Forks for a few months, and I was wondering if you needed any help while I'm here."

"Tess Hansen? *The* Tess Hansen?" A man who looked to be in his forties came out from behind a rack covered with large yellow rain slickers. Had he been hiding back there, waiting for her to leave? These two didn't seem accustomed to much socializing.

"Well, I consider myself *the* Tess Hansen, but I'm sure there are others."

"Jake. Jake Fisher." He came over and shook her hand enthusiastically. "Melissa, this is Tess Hansen from Evergreen College."

Melissa had grabbed a book off one of the shelves—remarkably quick to find the one she wanted amidst the mess—and looked at the back. Tess groaned inwardly as she recognized the green cover and the title *Fading Song*.

"It *is* you," Melissa said, looking from Tess's picture to her and back. "Will you sign this for me?"

"Hey, it's my book," Jake said.

Tess felt awkward from the attention. This out-of-the-way marine research center was one of the only places in the world where she would be considered a major celebrity based on her work, and she wasn't accustomed to being singled out because of her book.

"So I guess we can use the book as my résumé," she said, trying to make a joke and ease the intensity with which they were staring at her. "I don't suppose you have any openings for part-time help?"

"We wish," Melissa said, propping her hip on the edge of the desk and hugging Tess's book to her chest. "We're studying the communication patterns of a pod of offshore whales right now. When we can find them on the open sea, that is. We sure could use your help comparing their songs to those of the Southern Residents."

"But we can't pay much," Jake said. "Well, not anything at all. The Center is pretty much broke."

Tess had been ensnared from the phrase *offshore whales*. She really could use a paycheck and she didn't have time to spend doing volunteer work, but she was hopelessly lost once she heard about the opportunity to study the offshore orcas. Little was known about them compared to the residents and transients that lived, bred, and fed closer to shore. Maybe she would learn something she could use to help in the continual—and seemingly futile—quest to save her local pods.

"Hey, what about the new grant?" Melissa asked.

"Ooh, yes. A grant. Tell me more," Tess said. She had been about to offer to pay them for the chance to hang out at their Center, but this was even better. She was nearly as good at getting grants as she was at getting dates. Well, not counting Britt. She didn't help Tess's stats, especially since she had rejected her twice so far. Tess definitely wouldn't ask a third time, either for friendship or a date. Probably. She winced and turned her attention back to Jake and away from her admitted weakness for making a fool of herself in front of Britt.

"We just heard about it last week. It's pretty good money and restricted to local applicants. I have the form here somewhere."

Jake rummaged through the jumble of papers on his desk. No wonder the Center was low on funds if juicy grant applications were hidden in all this chaos. Step one if Tess came here to work—or volunteer, or just hang around like an orca groupie—was to organize the place and extricate every potential source of funding from these black hole desktops.

"Is it a foundation or an individual?" she asked Melissa while Jake searched.

"Some woman with money to spare. The requirements are pretty vague. The recipient just needs to be doing something to help animals or the environment. If we say you'll be doing research with us and connect it to the Southern Residents, we'd have a great chance to get the money and use it as your pay."

"Some of it, maybe. I wouldn't take it all."

"Here it is," Jake said, waving a piece of paper like a flag of surrender before handing it to her. "Of course the money would be yours. If you publish your findings, we'll get some good exposure. Besides, we won't stand a chance of getting the grant if you don't do the application."

"And the personal interview," Melissa added, making a retching expression. "Jake and I don't do well at those."

Tess wanted to argue with her statement just to be polite, but she had a feeling Melissa wasn't exaggerating. They seemed to be happy working in isolation and disorder, but those traits wouldn't help them impress people with money to give. Attracting grants and other funds required diplomacy, flattery, and persistence. Tess possessed those qualities in abundance, although Brittany might disagree with all but the third one.

"I can schmooze with the best of them," she said, skimming over the application. "And I can teach you a thing or two about it while I'm here. For starters, the person giving this grant has a personal stake in the process. Look at the wording in this first section, and here, where the decision-making process is discussed."

"What difference does it make?" Melissa asked, reading over her shoulder.

"We'll phrase our proposal to match the tone of the grant description. It'll be less formal than something we'd send to a large foundation or corporation. We'll be more…touchy-feely, I guess."

Tess flipped over the page, mentally forming sentences that would make her application irresistible. The money wasn't about her anymore, or even about the Center. It was about her local killer whales, and the frightening prospect of their extinction in the near future.

She closed her eyes at the thought, calming herself with deep breaths until the threat of tears passed. Her problem wouldn't be forming an emotional case in order to win this grant. Instead, it would be trying to keep her feelings in check so she didn't lose control when she had to talk to the donor.

She opened her eyes again and focused on her surroundings, on something she could actually change.

"We'll need to clean this place before she tours it," she said. "Not too neat and sterile, but tidier. And maybe we should change the name of your boat."

"The *Delta Flyer*?" Jake asked with a horrified expression. "She's named after the fastest shuttlecraft on *Star Trek: Voyager*."

"I recognized the reference," Tess said. "But the donor probably won't. She seems to have a vague desire to save the planet, but no real direction for doing it. She's an idealist, and maybe we can come up with a less esoteric name she'll relate to, like the *Whale Saver* or something."

"No way. I will clean my desk if I have to, but I will not paint over our ship's name." Melissa's voice rose dramatically, and Jake nodded in agreement, stepping closer to her and crossing his arms over his chest.

Tess rolled her eyes. This wasn't going to be easy. "Fine. The name stays. Now, tell me what else you know about this donor. How did she make her money and why does she want to give it away?"

Jake shrugged. "We've asked, but no one seems to know. Our best guess is she's a famous Hollywood star using a fake name. Once the grant is given, she'll reveal herself."

"Big publicity stunt," Melissa said with a nod.

Tess resisted the urge to roll her eyes again. "What's her name? Or fake name? It isn't listed on here."

"It's on the cover letter," Jake said, going back to his desk and flipping through another stack of papers. "Here it is. She's calling herself Brittany James."

CHAPTER EIGHT

W e've tried doing anagrams to figure out her real name, if she really is a movie star, but we haven't succeeded yet," Jake continued.

Tess took the letter from him with suddenly shaky hands and read through it. Brittany. She had said she was making some major career decisions while staying in La Push. Finding someone to take a wad of her cash seemed to be one of those big decisions. Tess felt an unexpected wave of claustrophobia and she was tempted to find an excuse to leave even though only moments before she had been ready to do anything she could to stay and help with research at the Center.

She had been confident in her fundraising abilities, sure she would be able to get the grant, but now she wondered if Melissa and Jake might be better on their own. Brittany had called her out as a player when they'd met on the beach and had thwarted Tess's awkward attempt at initiating a friendship with her. Now she was looking to fund someone who was devoted to a cause, and Tess wasn't sure she could convince Brittany to trust her with the money. She wasn't even an employee here, and she doubted Brittany would believe she'd stick around long enough to put the funds to good use.

She rested her hand on Melissa's desk, seeking some sort of stability while her thoughts ran rampant. She knew Brittany's assessment of her was fair on one level. She didn't want a permanent relationship. But when it came to her killer whales, she was the poster child of steadfastness. Still, she wouldn't jeopardize the Center's chances. She'd help them write the proposal and make the building presentable, but she'd leave the personal interactions with Brittany to Melissa and Jake. She sighed, already feeling a sense of longing because she wouldn't be the one to talk to Brittany. Her reaction made it even more clear how poorly suited she was for the task—what if she embarrassed herself and the Center by asking Brittany on another public date during the grant interview? She didn't seem able to muster her usual control and suave casualness when Brittany was around. She seemed to have left them behind in Olympia.

She stood upright again, ready to renegotiate her part in the grant writing, when a nearby orca sighting came out on the radio. All three of them stiffened, listening past the music and static from the other speakers to focus on the information they were always attuned to hear. Tess immediately started to rummage through the piles on Melissa's desk, searching for a pen and paper to record the coordinates.

Jake and Melissa, however, were sprinting toward the door before Tess found a legal pad and pencil. Melissa paused in the doorway.

"Aren't you coming?" she asked.

Tess shook her head, more at her own reaction to the sighting than in answer to Melissa's question. She was used to recording data as soon as she heard it and studying it later since she was usually too far south in the Sound to reach the locations mentioned. Now she was only steps away from the inlet, yards away from the open ocean. "Of course I'm coming," she said. The quiver of anticipation she felt as she followed them out to the dock more than compensated for the sorrowful realization that she was—in career and apparently in reflexes—an academic, and not a true field researcher.

"Hydrophone's in the Zodiac," Jake said, leaping off the dock and into the boat. Tess was relieved when he bounced into a seat near the engine rather than bursting right through the bottom of the small craft. She and Melissa waited a few precious seconds until the Zodiac stabilized again before joining him.

Tess sat down, reluctantly playing the part of observer as Melissa and Jake moved through a dance choreographed during long hours working together. If they had been half a second out of sync, Jake would have been steering the Zodiac toward the mouth of the inlet before Melissa unmoored them, but the entire procedure was performed seamlessly, with no wasted moments.

And then she was out at sea. Tess had been tempted to jump in when she had merely been standing on the shore with her toes in the water, but now the urge strengthened exponentially. Spray from the waves coated her face and hair with salty droplets, and she was immersed in a breeze thick with brine and cedar. She clutched her pencil and paper with one hand and the edge of her bench with the other, keeping herself from leaping out of the boat. After all, Brittany wasn't here to save her this time.

She tried to keep her mind off Brittany, instead concentrating on Jake and Melissa as they led them on the search for the orcas. Melissa was wearing headphones, most likely listening to the same radio frequency they had heard in the office, and every few moments she would tap Jake on the shoulder and shout new coordinates. Tess had briefly considered this kind of life in the field, but she had taken the laboratory route instead. The fragile killer whale pods needed both types of people—those who spent long hours at sea and in isolation, and those like Tess. She brought the orca plight to the attention of the general public and her students, through her writing, the classes she taught in conjunction with other departments at Evergreen, and the research she did as she analyzed and interpreted data collected by Jake and Melissa and others like them at research stations. Tess had made the right choice for herself. She was good at her job and she loved Olympia. She still had plenty of opportunities to spend time outdoors and on the Sound, as well as occasional chances to take extended trips to study the resident pods along Washington's and British Columbia's coastlines.

She sometimes regretted not choosing this life, though.

She was relieved when Melissa handed her a pair of binoculars and she was able to feel useful by scanning the horizon once they got close to the last-mentioned location of the orcas.

"Have the two of you always worked at research stations?" Tess raised her voice to be heard over the rumbling motor.

"After the Coast Guard, I spent a few years on research vessels in the Atlantic," Jake said. "I wanted to be land-based again, and I have family in the Northwest, so I came here about a year ago."

"I interned in the Queen Charlottes while I was finishing my thesis," Melissa added. "I came here about a month before Jake."

Tess sighed. She had spent three wonderful weeks in Haida Gwaii, or the Queen Charlotte Islands, several summers ago. The archipelago just north of Vancouver Island was a local mecca for killer whale biologists. She wasn't going to deny the twinge of jealousy she felt for the lives Jake and Melissa led, although she probably would choose the same course if she had a chance to do it over again. Living in the city, she had access to better restaurants and a more abundant dating pool—although if Brittany was an example of the type of tourists they got around here, she'd have to reconsider whether she really had the better deal in Olympia. Tess was determined to make the most of her time while she was here, throwing herself into the life of a field researcher as much as her family duties would allow.

The three of them continued to stare through their binoculars even while they shared stories about graduate school and research topics. Tess was fooled by splashes of churning water several times—wishful thinking, more than because they were anything that actually resembled the breathing spray of an orca—before she spotted what she had been longing to see. She watched for a few moments to make certain she wasn't falling for one of the ocean's many tricks, savoring the moment when she recognized a black fin, tiny at this distance, breaking the surface of the water.

The passionate and personal wording from the grant came to mind suddenly, and she imagined Brittany's expression if she had been here, getting what would probably be Brittany's first glimpse of orcas in the wild. She guessed Brittany's face would mirror her own sense of awe and excitement, and she unexpectedly wished Brittany was here to experience this with her. Tess's relationship to her killer whales was too personal to share, usually, and she had never wanted to bring a current girlfriend on a whale-studying trip because she knew she would reveal too much of herself when she was at sea and around her orcas. She didn't mind having other scientists along because they usually felt the same as Tess and were focused on observing the whales and not her.

Tess blinked away the image of Brittany as if she was nothing more than cold drops of sea spray and tapped Jake on the shoulder, pointing toward the horizon. He nodded and steered them in the new direction with one hand, while holding his binoculars to his eyes with the other.

Melissa spotted them and whooped loudly, doing a little dance at the prow. "Have you been studying news about the offshores lately?" she asked Tess.

Tess shook her head. She'd spent the week before she left Olympia in meetings with various members of Evergreen's faculty, trying to make the transition to her semester away as smooth as she could and barely having time to look over the resident pod sightings when she had some spare minutes to spend in her lab. She knew about the offshore whales, of course. Or, at least, as much as had been learned about these more elusive cousins of the resident pods.

"I've been out of touch for a while," she said. For much too long. "I was hoping to get a chance to see them while I was here, but I thought my chances of spotting offshore orcas this close to the coast were slim, at best."

"Normally, you'd have been right." Melissa spoke to her, but kept her binoculars trained on the approaching whales. "But we've spotted this pod four times recently. Very unusual."

"And that's not the only thing different about them," Jake said, with an air of mystery in his voice. "I can't wait to hear your interpretation of what's going on."

Jake brought them within several hundred yards of the whales and slowed the Zodiac's speed to match that of the pod, careful not to encroach on their territory. The whales were obviously aware of their presence, though, and began to double back. Jake cut the engine, and the small boat bobbed on swells high enough to block the fins from sight when the Zodiac was in a trough. On the next swell, Tess gasped because the orcas were nearly upon them. She should have been scared shitless as the pod circled the boat, surfacing to stare at the humans through intelligent dark eyes and swimming nearly close enough for Tess to reach out and touch them. Jake had carefully observed the distance boaters were required to keep between themselves and whales, but the orcas didn't follow the same rules. This was their ocean, and if they wanted to check out the Zodiac, they were going to do it. One playful toss of a head or a too-close breach, and the Zodiac could be destroyed, and the logical part of Tess's mind at least acknowledged the potential danger the whales posed. The majority of her orca-obsessed brain, however, thought the chance of being flung from the boat was a small price to pay for the thrill of being part of a pod for even a brief time.

Melissa hastily lowered the hydrophone, and soon the sounds of descending whistles and clicks were coming from the speakers. Tess blinked away tears, as emotional as she was every time she heard whale song right at the source and not through a recording. For too many seconds, she just sat and stared, drinking in the sight of angular black fins and the sound of complex chattering, before she kicked back into scientist mode and started systematically observing the pod.

Count the whales. Five. Scan for defining features, from the shape of the dorsal fins to the shape and coloration of the saddle markings. Wait. Count again.

"Five?" Tess yelled the question above the cacophony from the hydrophone and the suction-like splash when the whales surfaced. Offshores were usually found in pods ranging from twenty to fifty whales, unlike the smaller family groupings of resident and transient orcas. These were definitely offshore whales, though, with their taller dorsal fins that were straighter and less gracefully arched than the residents'. They were notched and nicked, probably due to exposure to harsher elements in the open ocean than the residents faced in Puget Sound and the inside passages of British Columbia's coast.

"Five," Melissa said, sharing a triumphant look with Jake before returning to her work.

They seemed thrilled to have surprised her, and Tess couldn't blame them. Her mind was spinning with the implications. Why was this offshore pod living in a family group similar to a resident one? Was it a reaction to something negative, such as a decrease in food sources? Or was it a positive evolutionary step? Tess couldn't begin to come up with answers yet, and she was too busy filling the pages of the legal pad with notes to form sufficient questions. Those would come later, but for now she had to transcribe everything before she forgot any tiny detail.

She didn't know the designations for the whales, so she gave them temporary names to distinguish them in her mind. The matriarch was Juno, and her two boisterous sons were Mars and Vulcan. Juno's daughter, Bellona, had a sturdy baby at her side. Tess kept her cell phone propped on the pad and made note of every movement of the whales she could, along with the exact time it occurred. Later, she would replay the sound recordings in slow speed, comparing the behavior she was observing with the sounds the orcas were making. Melissa was likely doing the same thing, speaking into a handheld recorder. Jake seemed to be the designated photographer, and he alternated between taking still shots and filming footage, often trying to do both at the same time with his two cameras. Tess shook out an annoying hand cramp and resumed her frantic writing. The three of them should have the encounter well documented once they combined their notes and images.

Juno and Mars seemed to be the most interested in checking out the Zodiac, swimming close enough to break up the smooth ocean swells into choppy, short waves. Tess was glad she'd never had issues with seasickness, because the rough, arrhythmic movement would have been enough to make most people queasy. All she felt was the need to grab her seat several times to keep from being tipped out of it. Vulcan didn't come as close as his mother and brother, choosing instead to swim in circles around the boat, breaching unexpectedly now and again and making the Zodiac rock wildly. Tess's notes were punctuated with long streaks of ink caused by his sudden leaps.

Bellona protectively kept between her calf and the boat, but Tess had plenty of chances to observe the baby as he attempted to dart by her and get close to the new object in his world. The family unit would spend its entire life together, rarely if ever moving out of physical and acoustic range from each other. Tess smiled as she recorded Bellona's movements. She often thought it was funny how she had chosen to study a species that lived in such close proximity to family members, when she had spent her whole life trying to put distance between herself and her own.

As quickly as they had arrived alongside the Zodiac, the whales turned in unison and started swimming toward the west, deeper into the ocean. After the chaotic swirling around the boat, their smooth transition to synchronous surfacing and diving was beautiful to watch. Tess lowered her pen and let herself simply enjoy the sight until the orca fins were barely discernible from the dark undersides of the ocean swells. She wanted to yell at Jake to keep following them, not to let them out of sight, but she was surprised to realize that it was nearly dusk. They wouldn't want to be caught this far from the shore once night fell.

The three of them settled into an easy silence as they made the trip back to the inlet. Later, they would talk about what they had observed and speculate about the reasons behind this offshore pod's size and behavior, but for now Jake and Melissa seemed to share Tess's need to quietly process the overwhelming experience of being surrounded by wild killer whales. Tess felt Brittany on the edge of her consciousness, though, giving her the sensation of not being as truly alone with her thoughts and emotions as she usually was after an encounter like this. Even while she had been focusing on capturing every detail on paper, she had been formulating ways to describe what she was seeing to Brittany.

She took a deep breath, filling her lungs with sea air. Her pride was still wounded after her awkward encounters with Brittany, but she would put that aside and apply for the grant anyway. She would meet with Brittany and convince her to give money to the Center, even promising not to take a cent of it for herself if necessary. These offshore orcas might hold some key to helping her resident whales, and Tess would never let her ego get in the way of her research.

More than the money and the research, though, she wanted to share this day with Brittany. She made excuses for her irrational desire by reminding herself that she was stuck with her nonunderstanding family and exiled from her Evergreen colleagues. She was merely trying to reach out to someone, *anyone*, because she had been moved by what she had seen and heard. Her explanation didn't take into account her new but comfortable connection with Jake and Melissa, who seemed to have been as emotionally affected as she was. She chose, however, to ignore the seeming contradiction. The alternative was that she wanted to form a deeper connection with Brittany, despite her insistence on casual definitions of dates and friendships—and aside from a meeting about the grant, nothing like that was going to happen. Brittany had made her feelings about Tess perfectly clear. All Tess really had to do now was make Brittany care about the killer whales, not about her.

CHAPTER NINE

B ritt sat at her usual booth in the La Push diner, sifting through paperwork. Once she had made the decision to give away what was left from her courtroom bonuses, she hadn't been able to rest until she got the money out of her account and into the hands of her lawyer. Cathy Linwood had been a wonderful find, and she had enthusiastically responded to Brittany's ideas for the money. The process of establishing guidelines for the grant and sending information to local agencies had been amazingly fast and had given Britt a sense of purpose. She had finally made a decision about something, *anything*.

Unfortunately, she didn't have enough money to spend the rest of her life doling out cash to worthy charities just to make herself feel better. This was a one-time grant, unless she could find a way to fund and set up a charitable trust, and the process of choosing the recipient would be over soon. She would eventually need to make more decisions, and the next ones would likely change the course of her life. The thought threatened to paralyze her again, the same way she had felt when facing the wall of socks in Forks. Then, Tess had managed to help and had shaken Britt out of her internal spiral of pros and cons. Now, Britt was tempted to find her again. To accept her offer of friendship and enlist her as an ally in this confusing time. Taking advice about socks was one thing, but letting someone else's opinions sway her decisions about the future was something else. Something Britt couldn't afford to risk. For now, she would focus on her grant and get as much mileage out of the experience as she could. Then she would tackle the next step.

She had received a surprising number of proposals given the quick deadline for the grant. Some of them seemed like stock applications—probably written for other grants and hastily adapted to the one she was offering. Four of them were carefully written and seemed more in line with her vision for the money. She was meeting with the first one today, someone named Melissa who studied killer whales.

Britt took a sip of her Coke and watched the door. She wasn't sure what she was expecting from Melissa, whether she would be wind-roughened and wearing a ragged Greenpeace T-shirt or more of a gentle hippie, but she knew one thing for sure. She hadn't expected her to look exactly like Tess Hansen.

But Tess was the one who walked through the door of the diner and came directly over to Britt. Tess hadn't been far from her thoughts since they last saw each other, and Britt had wondered if she had been gradually embellishing the reality of her, until the Tess she imagined no longer resembled the real woman. She was wrong. Tess was just as strong and beautiful and poised as she had been in Britt's dreams. Damn it.

"Hi, Brittany," Tess said, resting her fingertips on the table. "I know you're expecting Melissa, but I work with her at the marine center. I'm actually the one who wrote the proposal."

"Oh," Britt said. She reached for something else to say, but her mind was an uncooperative blank. Finally she gestured at the bench seat across from her. "Why did you use her name on the form and not yours?"

Tess gave her a sheepish-looking, lopsided smile and sat down. "I wasn't sure if you'd reject the application because you saw my name on it. You didn't seem interested in seeing me again."

Britt laughed. She wasn't about to tell Tess how many times she had been tempted to search for her contact information online. Or use Chris as an access point for the coastal grapevine. She would have gotten faster results from him than her internet connection. It was highly unlikely she would have turned down a chance to see Tess a third time. Although now, being close and feeling the returning wave of attraction she had felt for her, she wondered if she really might have chickened out and torn up the application if she'd known who had written it.

"Besides," Tess continued, "I don't officially work at the Center. I'm on sabbatical from Evergreen College and wanted to do some research while I'm staying in the area. The Center studies a variety of sea life, but the grant money would be devoted to research I would do with the team, studying communication in a pod of offshore killer whales. The work we do might give us more insight into the species and could possibly enhance our ability to protect other endangered pods in the Northwest."

"I see." Britt nodded, distracted by this new version of Tess. Professional, articulate, sexy. Britt had taken a moment to catch up to this unexpected twist in her grant plans, but she was fine now. Really. She could be professional, too. She shook her head with a guilty laugh and decided to start fresh. "Actually, I don't see. I'm a little confused by all this. For starters, you only wrote about them as killer whales. Am I not supposed to call them orcas anymore? Is it not PC?"

Tess laughed along with her. "Their binomial is *Orcinus orca*, but some people don't like the negative connotations of connecting them to Orcus, a Roman god of punishment in the underworld."

"Do they think killer whale sounds cuddlier?"

Tess grinned. "Right? And another issue is they're not even whales but are actually the largest member of the dolphin family, *Delphinidae*. I like the mythological connections with Orcus, so I tend to use the terms interchangeably when I talk, but usually not when I'm writing. I'll also call them blackfish, which is the name most of the local tribes used for them."

They paused to give their order to Karla. Britt watched Tess's hands as she opened a packet of sugar and sprinkled it in her coffee. She seemed to move with purpose no matter what she was doing, whether stirring coffee or standing poised in front of the ocean. Britt, in contrast, had felt an untethered energy seething under her skin since her court appearance. Her fingers always seemed to be itching to do something—fidget, write lists, destroy napkins into paper rubble—and being close to Tess added a whole new dimension to Britt's agitation. She forced herself to focus on the paperwork in front of her. Part of the reason she had decided to create this grant was to expose herself to the different ways people were helping the environment. She wanted to learn, and Tess seemed to have knowledge to offer. Britt would think of her as a teacher. Nothing more. And she would be teacher's pet…

She shook her head, veering off the dangerous path her daydream had just taken. She looked up and saw Tess watching her with a frown.

"Is everything all right? You sort of zoned out for a minute."

Britt waved her hand and took a drink of her Coke, feeling the rough edges of the straw against her lips. She had been gnawing on it before Tess arrived—yet another of her newly discovered fidgety habits.

"I'm fine. I was just thinking of my next questions. So, can you tell me more about the pods? You talk about different types of killer whales, and I'm not sure I'm following."

"We have three types around Washington, the offshores, residents, and Bigg's, or transients. The residents eat mainly salmon. The transients eat mammals like seals. These feeding patterns affect everything else about the whales, from communication to movement. Residents are chattier and more boisterous when they swim and play. The transients hunt more intelligent prey, so they're stealthier and quieter. Offshore whales haven't been studied as thoroughly, but they eat fish and even sharks. There's a lot of debate going on right now about whether they are three distinct species or just variations on a single one."

Tess propped her elbows on the table and gestured as she spoke. Britt figured she was catching a glimpse of Tess's teaching style. She was casual and comfortable speaking about the topic, but Britt felt something more underneath Tess's calm delivery of information. Passion and enthusiasm radiated from her, even though her demeanor remained calm on the surface. She reminded Britt of the way she used to talk about chemistry and her work at the lab.

"What side are you on?"

"The right one, of course," Tess said with a wink.

Britt laughed. "Very diplomatic of you."

"You never know. Your decision about the grant might hinge on your deeply held belief that we're dealing with either orca species or subspecies."

"I'll be sure to take your tact into consideration."

"Thank you. I'm nothing if not tactful." She paused. "Well, most of the time, anyway."

Tess's cheeks turned a deeper shade of pink, matching the warm blush Britt felt spreading across her own face. She guessed Tess was referring to the not-so-subtle way she had asked Britt on a date, and then a *public* friendship. Luckily, the grant changed their relationship dynamic, and Britt wouldn't have to find out if she could muster the resolve to say no to Tess a third time. Tess turned away and moved them past an awkward moment when she pulled a dark blue binder out of her messenger bag. It was filled with plastic sheet protectors, each holding several photos of orca fins. Britt watched her flip through the pages, apparently noticing something about them Britt was missing because they looked like duplicates of the same photo to her.

Tess moved the Coke out of the way and set the open binder in front of Britt. She tapped the plastic-covered photo. "This is a picture of one of the offshore whales. See the shape of the dorsal fin, and all the nicks along the edge?"

Britt nodded, silently repeating the mantra: *Do not stare at her fingers. Do not stare at her fingers.*

Tess turned to a different page. "Here's a male transient, and here's a female. The fin shape is similar to an offshore, and both are taller and more angular than the resident whales. Here are the Southern Residents. Their territory reaches into Puget Sound and through the inlets and waterways of the San Juans and some of British Columbia. These are pictures of the whales from the J, K, and L pods. We use the shape of the dorsal fin and the pattern of this gray area on the back, called the saddle, to help us identify individual whales. Each is as unique as a fingerprint."

Britt had admittedly been paying more attention to Tess's hands as they turned pages and traced the outlines of the whale photos, but when she turned to the pictures of the residents, her voice changed and became softer, with almost a reverent hush. Britt was startled by the sudden shift and finally looked more closely at the photos.

"Hey, I can tell them apart," she said, surprised when the group of monotonous photos—all showing the dorsal fin and back of a whale's left side as it arched out of the water—transformed into a series of individual shots. "Look at this one, didn't we see it already in a group shot?"

"Good memory," Tess said with a smile.

Britt felt warm with pride, the way she always did when she mastered a tough equation or new skill. Somehow, sharing the process with Tess made it even more satisfying.

"So you work with the resident pods." Even if Tess hadn't mentioned it at the beginning of their conversation, Britt would have been able to guess which whales were personally important to her by tone of voice alone.

"Yes. I've spent most of my career studying their communication patterns."

"Are you trying to talk to them?"

Tess closed the binder and set it on the bench seat next to her, out of the way of the plates of food Karla delivered to them. Her movements were deliberate again, as if she was giving herself time to phrase her answer the way she wanted. Britt picked up a triangle of grilled cheese and tried not to sigh too loudly as she took what seemed to be her twelve thousandth bite of pasty white bread and sticky American cheese. She had jumped from decision to decision in her mind, even though her daily actions were minimal and ordered, and one of the ways she had decided to atone for her part in the ecological harm her company had done was to become a vegetarian. This sandwich was the closest thing she had been able to find on the menu to her new diet plan, besides the ketchup on the hamburgers. She was searching for a cause to champion, and the destruction of every prepackaged slice of fake orange cheese might be the life's mission she was looking for. Tess took a huge bite of her cheeseburger and Britt resisted the urge to throw a pickle at her.

"I don't know if it's possible for either orcas or humans to reproduce the sounds required for direct communication with each other. Maybe someday, with the use of computers, we could carry on a conversation with them, but our methods of creating, hearing, and processing sounds are anatomically dissimilar. It goes far beyond learning a new language." She paused and ate one of her fries. "But what really matters to me is exposing the complexity of whale songs and sounds to the public. Pods have distinct dialects and accents, depending on their group and location. Whale language varies across distance and outside families."

She chewed another fry, looking absently out the window as if she could see a killer whale breaching in the parking lot, but then her focus shifted back to Britt with a sudden intensity that made her startle.

"It's the same thing that happened when you looked through the photos. At first, they were just generic whales, weren't they? And then you really looked at them, noticed what made each one unique. Then they became individuals. People are more likely to fight to protect individuals than nonspecific groups."

Britt ate another triangle of her sandwich, barely registering the taste as she watched Tess talk. Her application for the marine center had been impressive, but watching her discuss these creatures she loved was something else entirely. Britt wondered how many other impassioned stories were hidden in the bland scientific language of these grant forms. Would one of them inspire the same sense of passion in Britt, giving her the key to her future? She hoped so. The grant process was about more than the money now—it was a way for Britt to get a backstage pass to this new world she so desperately wanted to be part of.

Tess continued, "Just think about how your perception of someone changes between the moment when you see them as a stranger across a room and when you interact and hear them talk about their lives or families. I see whale communication the same way. I don't think it's important for people to understand exactly what whales are saying, but they absolutely need to realize that whales are communicating in a sophisticated, individual way. Then more people might believe they're worth saving."

Tess ended her speech with a shrug, as if she was pushing the emotion she had shown back into a private place inside her. She had been very professional at first, reciting information like…well, a walking grant proposal, but now she seemed more like the Tess Britt had met near the ocean. More human. And more tempting.

Britt knew exactly what Tess was trying to convey because it matched what she was experiencing. At first, Tess had been a stranger at the beach. Then she had talked to Britt—asking her out while making sure Britt wouldn't be surprised if Tess didn't even hang around for an entire meal. Now, she was sharing her passion through her words, body language, and voice. With each step, Britt was drawn further in, wanting to learn more about her, wanting to find out what Tess would say or do next. But Tess's love of whales aside, she was still temporarily on the coast, at the marine center, and in Britt's life.

No matter if Britt had been tempted to accept Tess's terms. The moment of opportunity had passed, and they were meeting in a professional way now. Plus, Britt was aware of how desperately she needed to find stability. The grant work was fun and gave her something positive to do, but she needed to reestablish the security and solidity she had felt in her old job and home. Probably not back at Randall Chemical and maybe not with Cammie, but somewhere else. As much as she might have wanted to give in to the feelings she had for Tess in another time or place, right now she couldn't stand the thought of falling too deeply and losing yet another piece of herself.

Britt continued to eat while Tess moved on to the less personally exposing details about the marine center's equipment and research projects. She seemed particularly animated when she started describing an offshore pod that was behaving like a resident one—or was it the other way around? Britt was rather shamefully aware that more of her attention was on Tess and her expressions than on the information she was sharing. Britt would make sure to study killer whales more in depth once Tess herself wasn't around to distract her. One thing nagged at her, even though she should be putting her interest in Tess the woman aside and seeing her only as Tess the marine biologist. Tess had made it clear what she wanted in a relationship, but she seemed completely different when talking about her work. She had spent her life caring about these killer whales, studying them with single-minded focus, and fighting to protect them. Was she really two people—one a carefree lover and the other a devoted, loyal scientist?

Britt wiped her greasy fingers on her napkin and left the crumpled ball on her plate. She had enough to worry about in her life without spending too much time trying to figure out the enigma that was Tess. Or wondering if anyone would ever make Tess feel as passionate about a relationship and love as she did about her career. She was working so hard at not thinking about any of those things that she didn't realize Tess had asked her a question until she caught her expectant look.

"What? Sorry, I was thinking about killer whales. And dorsal fins."

Tess pushed her empty plate aside. "I just asked what the story is with this grant. Do you have any specific objectives, or are you interested in environmental research in general?"

"Oh, um, I guess the second one," Britt stammered, clawing her way out of her daydreams and back to the conversation. She hated to tell Tess how random the decision to create a grant had been—along with the random decisions to flee Seattle, drive to the middle of nowhere, and rent a cabin in La Push—when Tess was so thoughtful and future-oriented about her career. "I suppose I'm using the money in the same way the recipient will. As research."

Tess cradled her coffee mug in her hands, waiting patiently while Brittany clearly struggled to express what she wanted to say. Tess was ready to take a back seat in the conversation. She was used to talking about herself and her lab in this type of interview, but she didn't feel as comfortable as usual today. Still, she had made it this far without making any embarrassing overtures toward Britt—despite how much she wanted to—and she only needed to hold herself together long enough to wrap up the interview. In normal situations, this would have been easy for her to do, but her every nerve fiber seemed to be on high alert these days, even as she felt herself growing almost eerily calm on the surface. The pressure of interacting with her family, the longing to be back in Olympia at her lab, the discouraging talk about trying to save pods of whales that seemed destined to disappear forever. Adding Brittany's focused way of watching her—as if every word was being internalized, processed, compared, and contrasted—Tess felt ready to snap.

"What are you researching?" she asked, when Brittany didn't seem about to elaborate.

"I think I told you I was considering a career change, didn't I? I guess I thought it would be helpful to talk to other people who are working in environmental fields. See what some of my options are."

Tess leaned across the table and spoke in a loud whisper. "I'll let you in on a little secret. Most environmentalists are happy to talk about the work they're doing. You don't need to bribe us with grants."

Brittany smiled. "I know. But I wanted to get rid of this money, and I thought it would be a good thing if I did both at the same time. Help a researcher and explore some directions I could possibly take on my own. Or at least learn about the processes involved with this type of work."

Brittany had reduced both hers and Tess's napkins to shreds while she spoke, and she gathered up the confetti and piled it on her plate with an apologetic-looking smile when the server came to get their dishes. She had an anxious energy about her, especially when she talked about her career, and Tess wanted to calm her by touching her restless hand. By stroking her beautiful hair, which was loose and wavy today. By kissing her…

No kissing, Tess reminded herself. She had been given another chance to get to know Brittany without the possibility of sex or anything personal between them because their relationship was a professional one now. She could satisfy her curiosity about this woman who intrigued and surprised her. Spend time encouraging her to laugh and smile, with no worries about entanglements or awkward dating conversations. Now if only Tess could keep herself from thinking about kissing Brittany, the situation would be ideal.

"Must be nice," she said, taking a sip of her newly refilled and hot coffee, "having money you're just itching to get rid of."

Brittany shrugged. "It's not like I'm a millionaire with more cash than I can spend. I'm just not really proud of the way I earned this money."

"Ponzi scheme? Drug dealing?"

Brittany tossed a wadded-up straw wrapper at her. "No. I am... was...am a chemist. When my company would make mistakes— spills or products that might have caused unexpected problems—I was the one they'd put on the stand to represent the plant. I wanted to do something good with the bonuses I got from testifying in those cases."

"Blood money," Tess said. She felt the pressure of her hands tightening, and she set the coffee mug on the table before she shattered it. Thoughts of kissing Brittany disappeared, replaced by images of her beloved orcas slowly strangling in chemical-filled water.

"That's how it started to feel," Brittany said, continuing her story, seemingly unaware of Tess's spiking blood pressure. She must be better at maintaining a calm facade than she had thought.

"Anyway, after this last trial, I couldn't stand it anymore. I left the courthouse and started driving, without any real direction. Somehow, I ended up on the beach in La Push, where we met. I'm trying to figure out what to do next, making a real plan instead of drifting. All my friends think I'm crazy, though, and expect me to go back to my old life."

"Maybe you need different friends." Tess heard the ice crystals forming on her words, and Brittany looked away from the window and at her with a shocked expression.

"What?"

"Friends who don't think you're insane for deciding to help the environment and not destroy it. Seems to me the thing they should be saying is *What took you so long?*"

"Whoa, Tess, I'm trying to make it better."

Tess shook her head. This was too much for her to process. "Those pictures I showed you are whales that might be the last of their kind. In our lifetimes, the Southern Residents could become nothing more than a memory. A few photos, the echoes of their songs. All because of depleted and damaged ecosystems, polluted water. I don't know if I could even consider using this money to help them when it represents what put them in danger in the first place."

"Randall Chemical was never even near the Sound. They...*we* didn't hurt your whales."

Tess was aware of the way her voice had risen in volume during her last speech and she made an effort to get control again. "It's all connected, Brittany. Remember that, even if you learn nothing more from playing around with these grant applications. Everything is connected."

Tess was finished, and she wasn't about to let her lunch be provided by Brittany's chemical company. She dug in her pocket for a couple of twenties and tossed them on the table before walking out of the diner.

❖

Tess pulled over twice on her way back to Forks, idling on the side of the road and waiting for her hands to stop shaking. She couldn't untangle the emotions she was feeling. The knot had started the night Kelly had called, and Brittany's betrayal had been the final tug of the thread, making it nearly impossible to undo.

The grant had seemed ideal on the surface. It offered her a chance to do some good while she was exiled from the home and job she loved. It was an opportunity to remove herself from her parents' house and the company of her family, and it would have given her some money to both subsidize a term away from work and support the needy marine center. But the grant was nothing more than a guilt offering, as bad as those offered by oil companies after spills, as if they could wipe away all the death and destruction they had caused if they funded an artist who took photos of seagulls.

Okay, Brittany wasn't *that* bad. At least, Tess didn't think she was. She merged back onto the highway—if she could even call it merging when there was no other traffic in sight—and replayed the conversation in her head, trying to distance herself from the personal feelings involved. She hadn't given Brittany a chance to explain what her company had done, but judging by the amount of money she was offering from her bonuses, the damage to the environment must have been significant.

Tess had thought Brittany was something special. She had been attracted to her, of course, but it went deeper than anything physical. She had been drawn to her as a person, for the intelligent and kind traits she seemed to possess, and Tess had been happy when they had smoothly transitioned into a comfortable relationship while talking about the grant, when all possibility of a romantic relationship was removed.

And the moment Brittany proved she was an imperfect human, Tess had stormed away.

She parked in her parents' driveway and turned off the engine. She stood by her belief in what she had said in the diner, but she could have handled the situation better. Brittany was looking at the grant applicants as mentors, in a way, and Tess had shut her down completely. If she really was honest about wanting to get to know Britt—and wasn't just expecting her to be an ideal woman to fantasize over—then she had to accept Britt where she was and who she was. Someone who acknowledged the negative aspects of her past and was determined to change them.

Tess went into the house reluctantly. Everything had happened too quickly after Kelly's initial call to allow her to really think through each step of what had changed in her life. She decided that today, for once, she would give in to her dad's constant efforts to rush through his exercises, letting him hurry back to his video game and her back to her room where she could think.

Her family seemed to have other plans. When she walked into the living room, she saw everyone but her father settled in for the afternoon. Kelly was sitting on the couch with a guitar, of all things. Justin was next to her, bouncing on the seat cushion as if in anticipation of some music. Her mom was on the recliner, crocheting something that looked like a sweater in the exact shade of dark green she always loved Tess to wear. *Please don't let it be a sweater for me.*

Worst of all was her dad's exercise mat, unfolded and spread across the center of the room.

"Hey," Kelly said. "Dad's been asking me to play the guitar for him, and I thought we could bribe him with music to make him do his exercises without fighting you."

Tess hesitated in the doorway. It was about the friendliest thing Kelly had said to her in years, and she suspected a trap was about to be sprung. She glanced at her mom, who ignored her and concentrated on the shiny blue crochet hook as it poked in and out of the green mass of yarn. She must have told Kelly about the arguments she and her dad had been getting into about his physical therapy.

"Um, okay," Tess said, finally moving all the way into the room and shutting the front door behind her. "Do you play well enough to function as a bribe?"

Kelly smirked. "Of course I do."

Tess wasn't sure what *of course* there was about it. Neither of them had ever displayed any musical talents while growing up. Kelly had always had the ability to be extraordinarily self-confident, though, so maybe her smugness passed as skill.

"I'll get Dad."

He was waiting for her with the television turned off. She helped him into a warm sweatshirt, expecting a complaint about the exercises or her rough way of tugging shirts over his head or *something*, but none came.

"Is Kelly really good on the guitar?" she asked, puffing slightly as she supported most of her dad's considerable weight and helped him stand. He was taller than she was, and more muscular even after idle weeks of bed rest. Helping him was proving a more effective workout than exercising at the gym, but these repetitions increased her stress level, so it wasn't much of a tradeoff.

"You haven't heard her play before? Yeah, she's great."

Tess's parents both seemed to be constantly surprised when reminded of her long absences. It sometimes seemed as if they still thought she was around, visiting relatives with them or listening to Kelly's impromptu concerts. *Oh, I forgot you didn't go with us to see Uncle Billy in Kansas. That's right, you weren't at your sister's latest guitar recital.* Tess, on the other hand, felt as if she had never really existed in this world. She woke up every morning surprised to be in her old bed.

Tess carefully lowered her dad to the floor in the living room and started gently warming up his back muscles by bending his knees one at a time. Kelly strummed the open strings of her guitar a few times before launching into her first piece. Tess almost dropped her dad's ankle when she heard the first notes of what sounded to her like something by Bach. She had been expecting the guitar equivalent of "Chopsticks," not anything classical.

It was by far the strangest concert Tess had ever attended, what with the crocheting and physical therapy. Her dad was soothed like a savage beast, and because he was relaxed, the exercises were easier on both of them. Kelly moved on to a new piece, and Tess helped her dad into a straight-backed chair near the couch. She sat next to Justin, and he scooted over and curled against her side.

Tess's childhood had left her battle-scarred. She had fought with her parents over every detail of her life from the time she was a toddler, over everything from what she wore to whom she dated. Her liberal views about the environment and animal rights had been the main wedge between her and her dad, though, and they had never been able to get past a fundamental difference of opinion. He was a logger, the son and grandson of loggers, and Tess hadn't been tactful in her denouncement of his career. She had come at her parents with all the self-righteousness of a budding teen activist, but the truth was, she was being supported by her dad's money. Until she got out on her own.

Should she be judged because she stayed as long as she did instead of setting out on her own at the age of fourteen? Criticized for letting financial reasons keep her with her family until she started college? No. But today she had done the same thing to Brittany. Instead of supporting her as she made a serious financial sacrifice—if the amount of the grant was any indication—and started life on a new trajectory, Tess had told her she should have changed sooner. Tess's experience had taught her activists were made, not born, and something had happened to Brittany to make her want to change. Tess should have honored the reason behind the transformation, and not dismissed it. Every year, she saw students change while at Evergreen, growing as their world views expanded. Was Brittany a bad person because she was older than a college student when she decided to make a difference? Or older than Tess had been? Of course not.

Tess felt ashamed as she sat with her arm around her nephew, letting the soothing notes wash over her and start to heal some of the pain she had been carrying around. She didn't own environmentalism or make decisions about who was worthy to join the fight. Brittany had deserved more from her today. She wondered if she could get another chance to make this right, and if she would ever find a way to relate to Brittany somewhere in between hitting on her and yelling at her.

Kelly stopped playing, and Tess realized Justin was almost falling asleep against her.

"I should get him home," Kelly said softly. "He didn't sleep well last night and needs a quiet evening before I put him to bed."

"I should put Dad to bed soon, too," Tess said. "Those six pain pills I gave him should be kicking in soon, and he'll be passing out any moment now."

"Very funny," Roland said. "I'd like to see you try."

Tess and Kelly laughed, and Tess tried to remember the last time they had done so at the same time. She couldn't come up with a memory of laughter unless she hunted in the deep past, and she covered up the discomfort of that realization by gesturing toward the guitar Kelly held loosely in her lap.

"You play beautifully," she said. "What was the last piece? I thought I recognized it."

"Thank you. It was part of Vivaldi's *Four Seasons*. The third movement of 'Spring.' It's one of Justin's favorites."

Tess watched the way Kelly looked at her son. She hadn't left town or pursued a career like Tess's, but she had obviously found her own passion in life. She somehow recognized the connection between Justin and Kelly's music. "Is he why you play?"

"Yes," Kelly said, with obvious surprise in her voice. "How did you know?"

Tess waggled her finger back and forth between them. "Sisterly bond. Two hearts beating as one, and all that."

"Gag. Anyway, when Justin was a baby, he didn't respond much to verbal or visual cues. Not like other children did. But when he heard music, he'd get transfixed by it. Very calm. Josh and I played recordings for him, but when I was looking for ways to connect with him I tried singing and then the guitar. It's one of the best ways to dissipate a meltdown."

Tess knew Justin must be a challenge at times for Kelly, especially since her fisherman husband was at sea for long periods of time. "Could you teach me? I've always wanted to learn an instrument."

Kelly looked skeptical. "Since when?"

"Since always," Tess said indignantly. "Or at least since I learned you're really good. I can't let you win."

"I've heard you sing. I don't know if adding a poorly played instrument to the mix is a good idea."

"Hey, I have a great voice."

Kelly made a scoffing noise.

"Play nice, you two," Edith said.

"Listen to your mother," Roland added.

"Oh my God," Tess said at exactly the same time as Kelly.

They laughed again. If this got to be a habit, Tess was going to have to leave Forks sooner than expected. She'd find some way to pay for her dad's private nurse.

"I guess we can try a few lessons," Kelly said. "But if you break my guitar, I'll kill you."

"I'd like to see you try," Tess said, mimicking her dad's voice. If Kelly could soothe Justin's meltdowns with music, maybe she could teach Tess a song that would make Brittany forgive her and give the marine center a second chance at the grant.

CHAPTER TEN

B rittany locked the door to the tiny cabin behind her when she left, even though she seriously doubted a thief would want to bother stealing her meager belongings. She had bought plenty of warm clothing since her green suit wasn't useful out here in the middle of nowhere, but no one would risk breaking into a cabin for some flannel shirts and a pair of Levi's. Besides, given how thin the cabin walls were, a locked door wasn't going to deter an ambitious squirrel, let alone a human bent on ransacking her near-empty drawers.

But force of habit made her lock the door, just as it had forced her to establish a daily routine that was as rigid as hers had been when she was back in her old life, with her full schedule of work, dating, and research. She had spent the past two decades pursuing degrees and career advancements, with days filled to the gills, and the sudden spate of empty time cried out to be filled somehow. Making lists and contemplating her future took up surprisingly little time and didn't seem to be getting her anywhere. After her encounter with Tess and her righteous anger, Britt was beginning to wonder if anything she did would possibly make up for her past actions.

She kept plugging along in her new life, though. Already this morning, she had gotten up at sunrise for some yoga stretches. She had been taking classes at a gym near the plant for years but had always followed whatever the instructor told her to do while most of her mind was focused on the day's work ahead of her. Now she didn't have anything pulling her attention away from her clumsy attempts to string together half-remembered poses into a reasonable daily practice.

After yoga, she ate breakfast. Cereal. Then she walked on the beach. Now she was on her way to lunch at the local diner—not necessarily because she was hungry, but because she was accustomed to going after the walk. Everything she had done on her first full day here in La Push had become a routine. Set in stone. Tess had provided some of Britt's only breaks from her predictable days, and the emotions she inspired in Britt were far too intense to be comfortable.

Britt walked the two miles between her cabin and the diner. She wished she had been wearing her pedometer when she had run away from Seattle, because she was racking up an admirable number of steps every day, mostly because there was little to do besides walk. On the beach, to the restaurant, to the little grocery store.

She knew her routine—more religiously followed than any other she had ever created—was as much a response to the stress she was feeling as to a real need to have scheduled days, when she had no real purpose in life anymore. The schedule gave her some sense of normalcy and comfort, and she was going to grab on to both of those feelings wherever she could find them until she figured out what her future held. David had willingly given her as much time as she needed, and she had weeks of unused vacation time coming to her, so she wasn't in a hurry to make any more challenging decisions than whether to turn right or left when she got to the beach every morning.

He had seemed unfazed when she had called and told him she had driven randomly to the coast and would be staying for an undetermined amount of time. He had seen it before, given their high-stress job and clients who wanted the impossible accomplished by improbable deadlines. He said she wasn't the first employee to need a forced holiday after suffering from a mental schism.

Mental schism. His phrase had made her laugh when they were talking, but more because she was disturbed by how accurately it described what she was feeling than because she thought it was funny. She added the phrase to other terms that had come to mind as she had driven away from her old world and toward something unknown. She was adrift. Out of focus.

Her life had been routine, successful, predictable. Now it was nothing but metaphors.

She pushed through the glass door of the diner and waved at Karla before sitting at her usual booth in the far corner. She had considered switching seats because this one was filled with Tess's presence now, but she didn't. As much as Tess's words had stung, they had given Britt a much-needed reality check and a different perspective on the choices she was facing. As soon as she sat down, Karla was at her table with a grilled cheese sandwich and a Coke. Brittany thanked her and put a napkin in her lap before picking up a piece of the sandwich. It had been cut in four triangles for her. She had cut it across both diagonals before eating it for about three days before Karla and the chef noticed her habit and started cutting it for her. She bit into the melted American cheese and felt it coat the roof of her mouth with the tenacity that only highly processed foods can have.

After she ate and paid her bill—leaving her usual generous tip that might be part of the reason these locals were so attentive to the needs of a potentially crazy tourist—she went to the La Push grocery store to buy food for dinner. Most of her time seemed to be spent either eating or preparing meals, or walking the miles needed to burn them off. Tonight would be different, though. A break in her routine, a change of pace that would have nothing to do with Tess. Tonight, she would have company. Cammie would finally be here, and Britt would have someone to talk to about her future. Someone to help her sort through the confusion she felt. And—most important—someone to hold her and banish Tess from her dreams.

Britt pushed her cart through the store, checking first to see if any new magazines or books had come in since she had been in the day before. She was quickly running out of reading material and would either need to drive to a town large enough to have a bookstore—at least a three-hour trip in any given direction—or she would need to make an online order. At least she had her laptop with her, in her heavy work briefcase, but the internet connection in this area was a technological step backward from the telegraph machine.

She moved through the rest of the store and decided what she'd cook for dinner based on what looked freshest. She was accustomed to making huge casseroles back home, and then scooping some out every night during her busy weeks. She was trying to adapt her familiar recipes to make them vegetarian, but when she took the hamburger or chicken out, she was left with nothing but bland fillers like pasta and cream of mushroom soup. She added a cookbook to her mental book-buying list, but for tonight, she chose local salmon for Cammie, plus the rice and broccoli she would eat, too. She put a bottle of soy sauce and some brown sugar in her cart to make a glaze for the salmon and a sauce for the rice. Oreos were Cammie's favorites, so they would have to suffice for dessert since Brittany wasn't much of a baker and she hadn't noticed any Michelin-starred pastry chefs in town.

She got back to her cabin and hurried to put the food away, hoping to have time to squeeze in her afternoon walk and let the wind gusting off the ocean clear her head and help her prepare to talk to Cammie. She was about to walk out the door when she saw a sleek black Jaguar pull into the driveway behind her Lexus. Camilla Grayson stepped out and stood in place for a moment, studying the scenery around her.

Britt looked around, too, trying to see the place through Cammie's eyes. The setting was gorgeous—even Cammie would have to admit to that. The bluff overlooking the ocean was only yards away, and the huge inlet was bounded by a steep basalt cliff projecting out into the water on one side and a long spit made of huge granite boulders on the other.

The resort grounds were simpler than its lobby, but there wasn't a real need for fancy landscaping when the majestic Pacific Ocean was right there to overshadow anything human-made. The main building was a brown rectangle, with peeling paint and a crooked handrail leading to the front office. The smaller cabins were lined up to the right, like a flock of square brown chicks following their mother hen. She kept telling herself the La Push cabin had turned out to be exactly what she needed for the time being, but she didn't feel any closer to figuring out her life than she had been when she first checked in. Still, it was cheap at this time of year, clean, and within walking distance of everything in town, which wasn't saying much, but still…

Cammie sighed deeply—visibly to Britt, who stood on the porch—and walked to the cabin.

Britt met her halfway, overwhelmingly happy to see someone from her regular life, even though she hadn't been gone long, and even though she wasn't certain how she and Cammie would work through this new paradigm. When she had mentioned Cammie to Tess, all her doubts about their relationship had been painfully clear in her voice. She and Cammie had been dating for almost six months, but in some ways, they seemed to barely know each other. And what had Tess said about people in Britt's life—like Cammie—who found her sudden life-changing shift crazy? Oh, right—she needed to make better friends. Britt liked Cammie and respected Tess, but she needed to listen to her own heart and not let either one of those two strong, opinionated women take control over the decisions she was going to have to make in the coming days. Britt hoped she and Cammie could work this out together, in a bit, but for now, Britt was just wholeheartedly glad to see her.

She and Cammie fell into a tight hug. Cammie pulled back and tucked a piece of Brittany's hair behind her ear. "Are you okay? Really okay?"

"Of course," Britt assured her, but she shook her head at the same time, betraying her uncertainty to herself and surely to Cammie. "I just had to get away. To think."

Cammie sighed and draped her arm over Britt's shoulder, leading her toward the cabin as if she was the host and Britt the visitor. "You think all the time, Brittany. And now you've isolated yourself in the wilderness to think even more? It's not healthy."

Britt opened the cabin door, and Cammie paused to look around again, with another heavy sigh. "I'm sure the brochure advertises this as rustic charm, but come on, Brittany. You've got enough money to stay somewhere besides an old shack while you're doing this soul-searching business. I'll bet a massage in the Hyatt's spa would unkink those knots in your head."

"I like it," Britt protested, surprising herself by how much she meant the words. "It's simple and basic."

Cammie went over and sat on the sofa. The plaid upholstery was faded and worn and the cushions were lumpy, but Cammie somehow elevated the piece of furniture to showroom status. Ratty and possibly bug-ridden became shabby, but chic, when she sat there and crossed her long legs, one arm laid across the back of the couch. She was wearing jeans and a thick sweater, with her glossy hair pulled in a ponytail and sturdy hiking boots on her feet. Britt wasn't surprised to see her as appropriately dressed as she was, and although she had never seen any of these items of clothing on Cammie before, nothing looked oddly brand-new or stiff. Cammie fit everywhere she went, no matter how fancy or unsophisticated the setting, and she wore this beachcomber outfit as easily as she would wear something suitable for a black-tie event.

In contrast, Britt had shown up on the coast wearing her court attire. Cammie would never run away without packing the right clothes first. She sighed and sat on the sofa, half turned so she was facing Cammie.

"I brought some clothes and books from your house," Cammie said. "Plenty of things to get you through another week or three up here. Are you sure you want me to have the movers pack the rest of your things and ship them here? Why not wait awhile, give yourself time to…" Her voice trailed off.

"Come to my senses?" Britt suggested. She expected to feel angry because Cammie didn't really understand her, or even cherished because Cammie was as generously giving her space to figure out what was happening inside as David had. Instead she felt distant, as if she was watching the conversation from the chair on the other side of the room. She pretended to have an itch on her cheek as she tried to hide her smile. Another schism, just like David had said. Now she was imagining herself in two places at once.

Cammie shrugged. "Your words, not mine. Why don't you tell me what's really going on? Help me understand this, Brittany."

Britt shifted uneasily, her smile fading away. "I don't understand myself, yet. I guess it's been building for a while, this feeling that I'm doing something wrong when I help defend the company. Or even by working there, when I know they sometimes take the easy and cheap route when disposing of chemicals, instead of spending the time and money needed to do it right."

Britt paused, hating to admit the next part. It was something she hadn't dared mention to Tess. But dredging up her guilt out loud seemed easier somehow than dwelling on it internally. "I always managed to get through the trials, though. I'd prepare the best way to phrase my argument, and how long to maintain eye contact with the jurors. Some of it was rehearsed, but most of it felt real. I enjoyed being on the stand, sharing my knowledge and research, but I was only focusing on one side of the situation. But this time...I couldn't ignore what the other side was saying this time."

Cammie shook her head. "You don't work for an evil company, Brittany. It's not like they're dumping tons of toxic waste in a schoolyard. They make some mistakes now and then, but they pay for them. I'll bet David would even be willing to make changes, try harder, if it meant you coming back."

"No." Britt frowned, feeling the tension in her mind taking physical form as the muscles on her face tightened. She hadn't realized how much more relaxed she was as a rule here, until the stress of her old life came back full force. "I can't be part of it anymore. I never believed it would make a difference if I quit, or stopped doing the trials, and maybe it won't. David will get someone else to testify, and the company will still take shortcuts sometimes." She leaned forward, with her elbows balanced on her knees, hoping Cammie understood what she was about to say and wishing Tess was here to hear it, too.

"It won't make a significant difference in the fate of the earth or the future of humankind if I stay or if I leave. But whatever I decide now will make a difference to my soul, to who I am as a person."

Cammie was silent for a long time, sitting very still. "Where do you expect me to fit in with this epiphany, or breakdown, or whatever we're calling it?" she finally asked.

Britt wasn't sure if she was hearing anger or irritation in Cammie's voice, since her placid expression wasn't giving any clues. She'd much rather have Cammie express her anger honestly, like Tess had. Tess's words had hurt, but they had come from an authentic place. "I don't know, Cammie. Maybe we can take it slowly, not make any quick decisions until I have this figured out."

"No quick decisions. Like the one you made when you ran away."

"Yes. I didn't handle it right, I know that now. I couldn't breathe, so I drove until I could. But there must be some way we can make this work. Let's have dinner first, let everything settle, and then we can talk again. You'll love sleeping here, and hearing the waves." She was rambling, not really convinced that Cammie would enjoy hearing the ocean all night or if it would only annoy her. But if she stopped talking, everything else would stop.

Cammie looked at her elegant gold wristwatch, the only thing about her that was out of place in this setting. "If I leave now, I'll be back in Seattle before the Thai Ginger closes. You can come with me if you want, but I'd rather not stay here."

The flatness in her tone had a finality to it that Brittany could hear loud and clear. She paused, recognizing this as her point of no return. She could stop this right now. Tell Cammie she was through with her schism and they could go back to Seattle together, either tonight, or tomorrow if she could convince Cammie to stay for a meal and a night together in the cabin. Apologize to David and thank him for the short-notice vacation time. Go back to her old job or look for something different in Seattle. She wasn't convinced she could make things better, and Tess didn't have faith in her either, so why try when it was so hard and meant giving up so much?

Brittany took a deep breath, careful not to disturb the air around her any more than she had to while she gave herself a moment to think, to decide. Of course she could return to Seattle anytime in the future, but this was her chance to put everything she had broken back together again, with only the tiniest of cracks to show where the breaks had been.

But those cracks would split again, shattering her peace of mind or her career or her relationships.

She spread her hands in a gesture of helpless hopelessness, and Cammie nodded.

"All right, then. Let's get your boxes unloaded, and I'll be on my way." She reached over and smoothed her hand over Britt's windblown hair. "Good luck, sweetheart. If you come back, and if I'm not seeing anyone…"

Britt nodded, but they both seemed aware that it wasn't going to happen. Even if Brittany did go back someday, she wouldn't contact Cammie. And Cammie wouldn't be likely to take her back.

They unloaded Cammie's trunk and moved the boxes into the cabin, setting them against the wall next to the couch. Cammie kissed her good-bye, with affection, but no real passion. Passion had never been the driving force behind their relationship, but what little they had shared was gone now.

Britt sat on the porch long after Cammie's car was out of sight, listening to the rhythmic surf and wondering at the small flame of relief she felt burning deep in her heart. She should be crying right now, sobbing tears of regret, but she only felt hungry. Her scheduled dinnertime was still hours away, but she was famished. She finally gave in and went inside to cook Cammie's salmon—since Cammie wouldn't be eating it. She'd be a better vegetarian starting tomorrow. And a better environmentalist, in some way. She'd prove it to herself and to everyone who doubted her. Starting tomorrow. For now, she was just going to eat.

CHAPTER ELEVEN

Tess got up early the next Saturday and hurried her dad through his morning routine of breakfast and exercises. He grumbled about her haste, until he was settled for the rest of the day with his game controller in hand. She grabbed the grocery list off the fridge and told her mom she'd be back in a few hours.

Tess knew all her hurrying about might be for nothing. She had tried to call Brittany over the past few days, ever since their disastrous lunch, but she had been sent to voicemail each time. She had finally left a professionally polite message saying she apologized for her outburst and hoped they would still see her at the Center for her tour. Tess had no idea if Brittany would arrive at the time they had prearranged when she had originally called to schedule the interview at the diner.

The rushed feeling of the morning stuck with her, and Tess was a bundle of nervous energy at the lab. She hated to disappoint Melissa and Jake by suggesting Brittany might not come, so she focused instead on cleaning every crevice in the building. They had followed most of her suggestions, and their desks were at least presentable, but Tess went on a dusting binge and had every fake plant in the place shining by the time she was finished.

She stepped out the back door to make sure the grounds were in order, but the outside of the Center was gorgeous without needing any help from her. The tide was low, revealing a larger variety of sea life than Tess had seen during her higher tide visit. Clusters of gray-tipped mussels covered the exposed rocks, and just under the surface of the water, Tess could see colonies of aggregating sea anemones waving languidly in the gentle surf. Meager autumn sunlight splashed the water with daubs of gold.

Tess hadn't been surprised to find the boathouse lab in much more presentable condition than the work areas inside the Center. The delicate equipment provided the means for communicating with the ocean world, and Melissa and Jake kept everything spotless and carefully stowed. Salt water was a harsh medium, and the gear and delicate instruments wouldn't survive long if not tended properly. The same level of care obviously didn't extend to desktops and microwaves.

The Center's two boats were old, but well tended, and Tess noticed the *Delta Flyer*'s name had been freshly repainted in a bright neon orange. She couldn't do anything but admire such pigheadedness. The name of the boat seemed inconsequential now, anyway. Insulting the donor was probably higher on the list of reasons to be denied a grant than choosing a potentially wrong name for a trawler.

Tess stood balanced on one of the shore's highest boulders, reluctant to leave her oceanfront perch and return to the parking lot. She had to go soon, though, because Brittany's tour was scheduled to start in fifteen minutes. Tess sighed, about to turn away from the water.

"Are you planning to jump?" The voice startled her. "I might not try to talk you out of it this time."

"Brittany. You came." Tess jumped off the rock and her momentum carried her almost into Brittany's arms. Not that she looked like she was about to reach out and catch her.

"Obviously. And let's go back to Britt. Brittany is too formal if we're on an insulting-each-other basis."

Tess did her best to look abashed, but she could tell Britt was trying to hide a smile. "I'm sorry, Britt. I was rude, and I should have given you more time to explain. When I start thinking about what's happening with the whales, I get out of control sometimes."

Britt shook her head. "You could possibly have phrased your comments in a kinder way, but what you said was true." She paused and looked with unfocused eyes at the ocean over Tess's shoulder. "I had a hard time admitting this to myself, but I was starting to think I was some sort of hero, gallantly tossing aside my home and job to do something noble. Corny and self-centered, I know, but sometimes it's been the only thing keeping me going forward and not back."

Britt had been beautiful to Tess from the start, standing on the beach when they'd first met, but now it seemed as if her openness and determination and intelligence were adding planes and angles to her appearance, giving her a depth of attractiveness that took Tess's breath away. "You *are* brave. I know exactly how hard it can be to follow your own path and not the one your family or boss has chosen for you. You should be proud of what you're doing."

"I don't know. Maybe I need a good dose of humility instead of pride." She turned her gaze back to Tess. "I've been doing some research since our...meeting. I didn't have time to really study each grant topic before, but I have been reading about the Southern Residents. I hadn't realized how bad the situation was for them, and I don't blame you for being as reactive as you were. Randall Chemical wasn't dumping PCBs in the Sound, but they were getting away with minor spills and accidents. If that becomes acceptable and defensible, then it's a small step to allowing larger companies to do the same thing on a more devastating scale. It's why I left, Tess. I was looking at a picture of a tiny dead bird, and suddenly I saw the bigger context."

Tess took a deep breath and pushed away the despair she felt when she or anyone else brought up the endangered orca pods. Her feelings were compounded by her relief at her restored relationship with Britt. She was about to move them past the uncomfortable emotional part of the day and suggest they start the tour of the Center when Britt made a hissing *shh* sound and pointed toward the water.

"Don't turn around too fast, but there's a thing out there. An animal, I mean. Don't scare it away."

Britt watched in fascination as the furry creature balanced a red, spiky shell on its belly and ate out of it while watching her and Tess. "It looks like it's at a movie, eating from a bucket of popcorn."

Tess laughed. "And we're the main feature. *Apologies at the Seashore*. Rated two flippers up."

"What is it?" Britt asked. "Some kind of seal?"

"A sea otter. I've seen the same one out there almost every time I've come to the Center. Lots of good eats in this inlet, like that sea urchin."

"Oh, of course." Britt chided herself for not recognizing the animal. Her perspective was different out here, seeing creatures in their element and not in artificial ponds and streams. "I've seen them at the aquarium before, but never up close like this, out in nature." She took a step back from Tess. "Are you going to go ballistic because I've been to an aquarium before? I can add it to my offenses against nature. I've got quite a list going."

"Some aquariums have educational and research value," Tess said with a mock serious frown. "I'll refrain from scolding you until I administer a test and find out how much you learned while you were there." Her expression softened into something sad. "Don't feel you have to be careful about everything you say and do around me. I'm far from perfect and I won't get judgmental with you again. Okay?"

"Okay." Britt smiled as the otter finished his meal and began to wash its face with frantic swipes of its paws. She gestured toward it. "I suppose seeing animals like this is commonplace to you."

"Are you kidding?" Tess turned toward her, and Britt recognized the flare of excitement in her blue eyes. "I will never take this for granted. Did you know sea otters were completely eradicated from this shoreline by 1910? All gone, shot for their fur. But in the seventies, some were captured in the Aleutians and reintroduced along the Washington coast. They're classified as endangered because of their limited range and susceptibility to oil spills, but they're here and the population has been slowly growing. It's always special to see them."

Britt watched the otter flip over and plunge out of sight. "What a shame if they had disappeared forever."

"Yes, and not just on an individual species level," Tess said, moving into full teacher mode. She walked over to the edge of the boulder-covered shoreline and pointed at a mass of nondescript looking seaweed. "One of the sea otter's favorite foods is the sea urchin, like the one we just saw that little guy eating, and sea urchins love to eat kelp. Without the otters here to keep the urchin population in check, they devastated the kelp beds. Kelp isn't as cute as an otter, so that might not seem like a bad thing, but it is. Hundreds of little crabs and fish and other creatures use kelp beds for shelter, food, places to reproduce. The loss of the otter had effects beyond the disappearance of one species."

Britt was slow to process the story Tess was telling because her delivery was impassioned and wonderful to watch. She was like a star going supernova when she got fired up about the sea creatures she loved so much. Once the full impact of her words registered in Britt's mind, though, she recognized a connection to other research she had been doing over the past few days.

"It's similar to hunting wolves to extinction in Yellowstone, isn't it? When they were no longer around to keep the elk populations in check, the elk ate and trampled most of the vegetation in the riparian areas, destroying the shady places where fish spawned and birds made their nests. I've seen photos taken before and after wolves were reintroduced to the park, and the difference is amazing."

"Exactly," Tess said, jumping off the boulder from which she had been orating and coming back to Britt's side. "The ramifications of losing a single species are often devastating to a carefully balanced ecosystem. You're interested in wolves, too?"

"Research. One of the other grant applicants is the Makah Wolf Sanctuary."

"Ah. Another worthy cause." Tess started walking toward the main building. "You seem to be getting a wide range of information from these grant proposals."

"Yes, but the more I study them, the more connections I see. I never would have expected wolves and sea otters to intersect like this before." Britt thought back to the times she had defended her company on the stand. She had been aware of linear cause and effect, of course. Dump harmful chemicals in a fish pond, the fish die. But the more she studied the different research groups that wanted her money, the more she saw nature as a web, not a straight line.

"It's all connected. I believe a very wise person once said that to you."

"*Yelled* it at me, is more like it. In the middle of a crowded restaurant."

Tess snorted as she opened the back door of the Center. "Nothing in La Push is crowded."

"Hey, there was a guy sitting at the counter. He was a crowd compared to other times I've been there."

Tess seemed about to respond, but once they got through the doorway, she stopped and Britt ran into her back. Britt heard a voice coming from the other side of the doorway, but she couldn't see who was speaking with Tess blocking her way.

"Hi, I'm Melissa, and this is Jake. Welcome to the Hoh Marine Center."

Britt walked around Tess, who seemed rooted in place. She was about to greet Melissa and shake her hand when she looked past her and saw what had likely made Tess stop so fast. A small shrine—there was no other word for it—had been set up on one of the bare desks with a propped-up book, a fake potted plant, and a framed photo of Tess that looked like it had been found online somewhere and printed out in black and white.

"It's you," she said, pointing at the photo and laughing at Tess's obvious embarrassment. She looked like she was about to hurl the plant at her coworkers. "You didn't mention that you wrote a book in the grant application."

"She's too modest," Melissa said.

"Yeah, modest. Exactly the way I'd describe her." Britt actually had a list of words to describe Tess back in her cabin. They ranged in nature from infuriating to admirable, and *modest* was distinctly absent.

"Hey," Tess said. "I'm the humblest person I know."

Britt grinned at her before picking up the book and flipping it over to look at the back cover. There were words describing what the book was about, but Britt only caught one or two of them. *Blah, blah, blah…killer whales…blah, blah, blah*. Britt was sure she would find the subject matter and writing of the book interesting at some point, but for now all her attention was engaged by the back-cover photo of Tess standing on a bluff, resting her hand on the gnarled trunk of a fir tree as she stared at the water below. Her curls were tousled by the wind, and the vivid colors of a sunset tinted her pale skin and blue eyes with shades of gold. Damn, she was hot. Britt was all too aware of Tess's attractiveness in person, but the photo captured something wild and precious below her surface. She knew she'd be ordering the book as soon as she got back to her computer.

Britt attempted to put the book back in its original position but knocked it over twice before she got it to stand upright. She had to pull herself together since she was here in a professional capacity and not as another Tess groupie. No drooling on the shrine.

"Do you mind if I look around?" she asked, raising her voice slightly to be heard over the several radios broadcasting throughout the room. Couldn't they agree on a station?

"Go right ahead," Tess said. She gestured at Melissa and Jake, obviously trying to get them to interact with Britt and show her around the lab, but neither one seemed inclined to act as tour guide. Melissa stood near the black-and-white photo of Tess, chewing on the fringed end of her cat-eared hat. Jake was hovering in between a rack of rain slickers and a desk, obviously prepared to dive behind either one of them if the need presented itself. Britt wondered if their shyness was the reason Tess had been chosen to meet her for the interview, or if Tess had wanted to see her, too.

"Why don't I give you a quick tour in here, and then we can go out and see the research equipment in the boathouse." Tess led Britt over to a series of whiteboards. "Melissa and Jake are tracking the reported positions of the local orcas. The T stands for transients, and you can see one of the transient pods was spotted in the Strait this morning, traveling east toward the San Juans."

Tess went on to describe the different pods and families, how many killer whales were in each one and where their preferred hunting grounds were located. Britt reached out and traced the morning route taken by the J pod. Somehow, they had transformed from a few photos in Tess's book to a living, loving family unit. Britt had gone from not knowing much about them and their situation to really caring about their survival. Tess's stories and descriptions had helped her understand, but Britt recognized that the depth of emotion she felt was her own. She wasn't following some whim or having a breakdown out here on the Peninsula; she was finally honoring a very real part of herself that had been buried too long.

She turned her attention back to the Center and her need to figure out the type of work they were trying to do. "If these pods are endangered, why can't you relocate other orcas to this area like they did with the sea otters?"

Tess sighed. "It just isn't feasible with killer whales. They live in matriarchal pods, and for the most part the children remain with their mothers for their entire lives. Strange killer whales would be isolated and wouldn't have much chance of being accepted into a family unit. Breed and release programs don't work either because captive breeding is a notorious failure when it comes to orcas."

"And the issues that made numbers begin to decline in the first place," Jake said, his voice coming from somewhere behind the slickers, "would still be present, so even if entire healthy pods were relocated to the Sound, they'd face the same problems as the residents—harassment from sightseeing boats, pollutants, declining Chinook salmon populations. Until those are…"

He stopped midsentence as he, Melissa, and Tess turned in sync toward one of the desks. "What is it?" Britt asked. "What's going on?"

"Did you hear them?" Tess asked, nodding at a radio. "They've spotted some offshores just a few nautical miles from here. Come on."

Did she hear what? Britt had heard a lot of noise—including an old Bon Jovi song and some staticky chatter, but she decided to take their word for it and follow. They ran out to the dock, and she noticed the name of the boat as Tess was reaching out a hand to pull her on board.

"What a cool name for a boat," she said, ready to go to warp speed after some killer whales. "*Voyager* is my second favorite *Star Trek* series."

"Put this on," Tess said, ignoring her comment and tossing

a life jacket in her direction. Melissa and Jake shared a high five behind Tess's back, and Britt wondered if it was some sort of pre-whale-seeking-expedition ritual.

Britt moved to the front of the old trawler and sat on a bench. The other three seemed to know what they were doing as they unmoored the boat and pulled away from the dock, and she didn't want to get in the way. She had been on a Caribbean cruise with Cammie last spring, but she had been bored by the vacation since there was nothing to do but eat, drink, and get herded along on rushed excursions. This promised to be much more thrilling, partly because she had a chance to see some killer whales up close and mostly because she didn't have much faith in the rusted old boat's ability to stay afloat in the ocean swells. She had come to the coast searching for change, and potentially drowning at sea was certainly different from anything else she had ever done.

As soon as they were under way, Tess came and sat beside her. "Are you okay? I didn't have a chance to ask if you get seasick or are scared of boats."

"Not scared, just excited," Britt said, feeling a heavy *whumph* as the boat passed out of the bay and onto the open ocean. A spray of water misted across her face, leaving a salty taste on her tongue. The wind tugged at her braid, and Tess reached over and tucked a loose strand behind her ear. Britt had started to shiver from cold, but Tess's touch left a trail of heat across her skin.

Tess let her fingers linger for a long moment before she moved her hand away. "I remember when we first met. You didn't have a single hair out of place, even on such a windy day."

Britt raised her hand and felt the side of her face where Tess had touched her. She expected to find blistered skin given the way Tess had spread warmth over her, but her skin felt as smooth as always. "The ocean and I spent some time fighting over my hair," she said. "I was so shaken by running away from home and my job that I needed to feel like I still had control over at least some small aspect of my life, and for some reason I fixated on keeping my hair from looking windblown. I didn't really care how it looked, I just wanted to be able to manage something. I eventually gave up, though, after reading about animal testing and how bad hairspray is for the environment."

Tess rested her arm along the back of the bench, alternating between looking at Britt and scanning the horizon, presumably for killer whale fins. She seemed unconcerned by the boat's shuddering progress as it picked up speed and left the shore far behind, and Britt decided to follow her lead and not worry about the boat disintegrating out from under her. Besides, she was far too distracted by Tess's arm lying within inches of her shoulders to care whether they capsized or not.

"You seem to have collected a lot of causes. Killer whales, wolves, the anti-hairspray movement. What else have you been contemplating?"

Britt pictured the mind map she had made to counteract her *Crimes I've Committed Against the Environment* list. Every time she tried to research one way she could make a difference, she found five more possibilities to explore.

"Well, when I finally leave La Push, I might buy a tiny home. I've kind of been living the lifestyle already since my cabin is maybe two hundred square feet. It might not count, though, since I still have all my furniture in my old house and I have a storage unit in Forks for most of my things. But I definitely plan to downsize. Reduce my carbon footprint. I've become a vegetarian, for the most part, and I want to try to be a vegan. And eat locally, even though it's pretty limiting in La Push. Oh, and go to one of those Slow Food meetings. I want to adopt a black dog, volunteer to play with the homeless cats at adoption centers, get a hybrid car, start composting once I get settled in a new home, and trade out all my cleaning supplies and cosmetics for non-animal-tested ones."

Britt paused and took a deep breath. The list was overwhelming, and she had barely covered one quarter of the ideas she had.

"Gee, is that all?" Tess asked. "I hope you don't need to work for a living, because you aren't going to have time to get a job."

Britt sighed and leaned her head back but bounced upright again when the nape of her neck came in contact with Tess's arm. "I figure it will get easier as I incorporate each step into my life. I

planned to start with one thing and add others once I'm accustomed to doing the first one, but they all seem important and I can't decide what to do first."

"Or you could decide what matters most to you and focus on it instead of trying to do everything. Unless you really want to be in your tiny house making slow vegan food for you and your dog. At least you'll be able to toss the meals you don't like onto your compost heap."

Britt laughed because Tess was joking, but she had identified one of Britt's main worries. She didn't seem to have a passion for anything. Not like Tess did, or the others who had applied for her grant. She thought killer whales and wolves were beautiful and important, but she didn't have a driving need to devote her life to them. She would be content doing so, but she would be taking on someone else's cause if she did. She doubted she'd ever find her own niche and would instead spend the rest of her life trying in vain to emulate everyone who did something positive for the environment.

Melissa came over to them, and Britt welcomed the interruption of their conversation. She liked talking to Tess, but she got tired just thinking of all the things she needed to be doing. Or to stop doing. She felt as if she needed to turn her life inside out to finally live the way she should, and she had to be careful not to be swayed by other people's agendas. She felt weirdly young and impressionable instead of competent and confident. She had always enjoyed the company of strong, opinionated people like Cammie and David and Tess because she had been focused and driven toward her own purpose. Now she had to protect her fledgling dreams in a way she hadn't experienced for a long time.

"We're at the coordinates, but we haven't seen any sign of the whales. No other reports have come in."

"Let's lower the hydrophone and listen for a bit. We probably missed them, though," Tess said. Melissa nodded and went back the way she had come. "I'm sorry, Britt. I was hoping to get a chance to show you the killer whales."

"It's okay. I had fun out here, anyway." She was surprised by how enjoyable the visit to the Center had been. She had been expecting an awkward encounter with Tess after their mess of an interview, but they had moved quickly past the apologies and back to companionship. She had learned more about killer whales and she would never look at sea otters the same way again. Unfortunately, she didn't feel any closer to discovering a clear direction for her life, aside from the realization that she liked being around Tess. She wouldn't have any excuse to see her again, though, since once she decided who would get the grant, their connection would be gone.

Melissa was sitting on the other side of the boat, wearing bulky headphones and an intense look of concentration on her face. She glanced at Tess and shook her head, giving her a thumbs-down sign.

"Does this happen a lot, where you follow sightings and just miss seeing the whales?"

"Sometimes. Especially with the offshore orcas because their patterns are still unpredictable to us and the area is so vast. It's easier to pinpoint the location of a pod in Puget Sound or the San Juans. This is part of the reason why we don't know as much about the offshore whales as the others. Well, I'll go help them pack up the equipment and we'll head back to the Center." Tess stood up but didn't leave right away. "I'm glad you came today, Britt."

"Me, too." Britt thought Tess was about to say something else, but she just smiled and headed back to where Melissa and Jake were working. Britt sighed and leaned back against the railing. For a second, she had thought Tess might be about to ask her out again, which was ridiculous. They couldn't date while the Center was in contention for the grant. Besides, Britt had already been clear about not wanting a no-strings relationship, and as far as Tess knew, she still had a girlfriend. But despite all the reasons to say no, she knew in her heart her answer would have been a foolish yes. Luckily, Tess hadn't asked.

Yeah. *Luckily*. She closed her eyes and let the steep rocking motion of the trawler ease her mind.

Chapter Twelve

Tess got back to the house and reached into the back seat of her car to get the grocery bags. She had spent the drive to Forks sorting through her feelings about the day. Nothing was on an even keel when it came to Britt. The abrupt swing from anger at the diner to relief when Britt arrived this morning was tiring on its own, but just the normal parts—when the two of them were talking and sharing ideas—were intense as well. Tess liked spending time with her, and she had almost caved at the end of the boat trip and asked Britt if they could see each other again, but she hadn't been able to think of a reasonable excuse for them to spend more time together.

She walked up to the porch and balanced two of the bags against her thigh while she struggled to get the key her mom had given her out of her jeans pocket. She eventually gave up and used her foot to bang on the door.

Kelly answered the door and crossed her arms over her chest. "There you are. Always keeping us waiting."

"A little help here?" Tess relinquished a few of the bags to Kelly and came inside, kicking the door shut behind her. "Does Dad need something? Or are we having another Hansen family fun night? Pictionary? Or s'mores and a sing-along in the backyard?"

"None of the above," Kelly said, putting her bags on the kitchen counter and rummaging through one for items for the refrigerator. "Mom took Justin shoe shopping, so it's time for your first guitar lesson."

"Really? I thought you'd back out of your promise to teach me." Her interest in learning to play had waned a bit in the past few days. She tended to go hot and cold with most pursuits, playing with hobbies and girlfriends for a short time before getting distracted by something new. Marine biology was one of the rare topics that held her attention on a permanent basis. Her friends were the same, and her affection for them never wavered. She wasn't overly eager to play an instrument anymore, or to spend quality sister time with Kelly, but at least the lesson offered to distract her from thoughts of Britt for a little while.

They quickly put the groceries away, and then Tess checked on her dad. He was taking a nap with the television still on and was resting peacefully for once. She knew the addition of physical therapy exercises had made him uncomfortably sore for a few days, especially because he had taken every pain pill she brought him without a peep. His body seemed to be adjusting to the new work, though. She refilled his water glass, setting it close by the bed on his nightstand, and quietly left the room, shutting the door behind her. She left the TV on because it would mask the sound of the guitar.

Kelly was in her usual place on the couch when Tess came in. As Tess sat down and watched her tune the guitar, she realized Kelly had been at the house nearly every day since Tess had arrived. Was she always here so often, or did she possibly—unbelievably—want to spend time with Tess? No way. The more likely explanation was Justin. He liked being around her, and Kelly probably came over here for his sake.

"Have you taken any music lessons before?"

"Nope. I listen to music all the time, though."

"Yay for you. We'll start from scratch, then. Hold the guitar on your lap like this…"

Kelly might be an annoying sister, but she made a decent teacher. Most of the stuff seemed fairly easy. Strumming, making chords. Tess listened with half her attention and used the rest to think about Britt. Did she play any instruments? She wouldn't have a chance to in the future if she kept up with her ridiculous plan to right every environmental wrong she had ever committed. She was going to burn herself out. Get so frustrated by her inability to be a superhuman that she'd decide to go back to the chemical plant...

"What are you doing? I just taught you the G chord, but your fingering is all wrong."

Tess wanted to tell her she could produce a dozen women who would say her fingering was just right, but Kelly didn't seem to be in the mood for jokes. "It was hard to keep my index finger way over there, so I just changed positions."

"You can't just decide where you want your fingers to go. Chords are specific, not random. Didn't you hear how out of tune you sounded?"

"Sure." Tess hesitated. "During what part?"

"You're hopeless," Kelly said, trying to pull the guitar out of Tess's hands, but Tess didn't want to let it go. "No wonder our sonar experiments didn't work."

Tess rubbed an imaginary sore spot on her forehead while still managing to keep the guitar out of Kelly's grasp. The two of them had spent weeks trying to use echolocation like dolphins, bumbling around the house with their eyes closed and emitting high pitched squeaks. Their mother had ended the game when Tess crashed into the corner of a shelf, shattering one of her grandmother's vases and getting bloodstains on the carpet. "I remember those experiments. They were your idea, not mine."

"If you're going to keep hold of the guitar, at least practice the chord again," Kelly said, manipulating Tess's fingers into an uncomfortable position on the fretboard of the guitar. "I know they were my idea. I was the one who got you interested in dolphins and killer whales because I liked them first. You copied me, like always."

"Did not," Tess said, grimacing at the babyish expression and tone of voice. She had fallen in love with the sea creatures on her own, when she had run away. Although those echolocation games had taken place before..."Hey, you did. I remember stealing your orca stuffed animal from your bed. You had such a fit, I figured it must be something special."

"And I used to read those Quileute blackfish myths to you by candlelight when the power was out, about the orcas using their songs to heal souls and bring rain." Kelly wrenched Tess's index finger back into place.

"Ow!" She examined the pads of her left-hand fingertips, where the steel strings had left red dents in her skin. She wasn't sure how she felt about sharing her love of killer whales with Kelly. They belonged to Tess, setting her apart from her family and making her unique. She kept her gaze on her hand, running her thumb over the small welts and not meeting Kelly's eyes. "Do you ever regret not making them your career like I did?"

"No," Kelly said, with no trace of doubt in her voice. "I love orcas in a more metaphysical way, not in a scientific way like you do. Although you seem to have both kinds of feelings for them, as you talked about in your book."

Tess looked at her in surprise. "You read my book?"

Kelly scowled and took advantage of Tess's lapse of attention, pulling the guitar away from her. "Yes. I still read, even though I'm a mom and wife. I read anything I can find about killer whales. Plus, you're my sister. Of course I read your book."

She plucked out a simple lullaby while Tess processed the conversation. Her book had been making a surprising number of appearances today, from the god-awful display Melissa and Jake had sprung on her to Kelly's revelation. She thought about the expression on Britt's face when she had been reading the back of the book. Tess wondered if Britt would get a copy and read it. She seemed to study every subject she came across in depth, and Tess wouldn't be surprised if she saw the book as another resource to help her make the decision about the grant. Britt would see more of Tess, too, in those pages. Although some of the book dealt with the harsh reality of the killer whale's history and current situation in the Northwest, most of it was Tess's personal and visceral ode to a vanishing species.

She watched Kelly softly strum the guitar, her loose dark hair falling over the side of her face and throwing her cheekbones into shadow. Tess had spent years trying to shield herself from her family, but she felt pleased—or maybe relieved—to know Kelly had seen the real Tess on those pages. And the thought of Britt reading her words and understanding her more deeply made something tremble inside her stomach.

Then Tess thought about the acknowledgments in her book, and the stories of her first encounters with killer whales. Kelly was nowhere to be found in there, and Tess had forgotten how much a part of the story she really was. Out of habit, she turned her guilt into an offensive attack, even though it was a half-hearted one.

"You've never come to see me at Evergreen," she said. "If you love killer whales so much, you might have been interested in coming to visit the lab."

Kelly stopped playing and glared at her. "Did you ever ask?"

"No. I would never have expected you to say yes."

Kelly shook her head and mumbled something that sounded suspiciously like *Such an idiot!*

Tess took a deep breath. The conversation had two possible routes to take. It could devolve into yet another petty argument between the sisters, or Tess could try a different tack.

"I've been working at the marine center. Well, volunteering for now. If you wanted to come out on the boat sometime, you're welcome to, and you could bring Justin. We might not see killer whales, but there are usually lots of seals and minke whales."

Her tone still sounded belligerent, but at least the words were nicer than her usual ones.

"I'd like that," Kelly answered with an equally quarrelsome tone that belied her words. "Thank you for *finally* asking."

Tess shook her head. Leave it to Kelly to keep the moment from getting too sappy.

Kelly handed her the guitar again. "Let's try those chords one more time. You can't be completely hopeless."

She took the instrument and attempted to stretch her fingers into the unnatural positions Kelly seemed to find comfortable and easy. Tess would have quit, but she had a sudden vision of herself serenading a potential lover. She was doing quite well in the romance department—when she wasn't in Forks, at least—but adding dreamy guitar playing to her seduction repertoire couldn't hurt. She did her

KARIS WALSH

best to ignore the image of Britt listening to her play, and watching her fingers gently strum the notes...

She and Kelly winced at the same time. "Well, at least I could tell I was playing the chord wrong that time," Tess said, struggling to get her fingers to cooperate. At this rate, she'd be attracting more howling coyotes than women, but practice would make perfect.

Chapter Thirteen

A s she headed into November, Britt had to make adjustments to her daily schedule. She tried to fit in her walks on the beach every day, but the weather rarely cooperated. She would valiantly struggle through at least a few minutes, stumbling along the pebbly coast and fighting to remain upright in the stiff winds. She had decided she needed to add meditation to the multitude of new habits she was trying to cultivate, and she thought of her beach time as a form of walking meditation. When it was too stormy to bear, she stayed inside and did a seated meditation instead, peeking at the clock on her phone every thirty seconds and getting absolutely nothing out of the practice except an increase in her fidgetiness.

She was working through her grant applications, and the time spent studying the applicants' topics had become the highlight of her days. She had two more research visits to do, and she was finding it challenging to choose among such worthy charities. They all needed her money and would do important work with it. She had been trying to find a way to prolong the process—both because she didn't want it to end and because she couldn't make up her mind— and Cathy had suggested hosting a cocktail party where she could chat with the top applicants in a more casual setting. Britt felt a little silly, like she was planning a reality show event, with her handing a red rose to the winning cause as the climax of the party, but she still had jumped at the idea. For all the right and honorable reasons, of course, and not just because she wanted to see Tess again. She had another week to make her final choice, and then the life decisions she had been avoiding would come front and center again, so she was going to make the most of it.

Britt got in her car and sat with the wipers blasting on full power, considering her options. She was already drenched, so a walk on the beach couldn't do more damage to her clothes and hair, but she could barely see three feet in front of her. The diner was a dry option, but she had already eaten lunch at Betty's restaurant in Neah Bay since she couldn't face another grilled cheese sandwich today, and Betty's iceberg lettuce and grated carrot salad had been a slight improvement. But she'd go stir crazy if she had to spend all afternoon inside her cabin.

She briefly thought about driving to Forks and cruising the streets, hoping for a sign of Tess. She could imagine what she would say if she did happen to find her. *Tess! What a surprise. I just happened to be prowling through the residential neighborhoods in Forks today. Wanna have sex?* She wasn't quite desperate enough for that. Yet.

She had one other choice, and she decided to take it even though it might cost her. She put her car in gear and drove past the general store to a small specialty shop she had seen when she first arrived. The sign claimed they sold items made by authentic Quileute artisans, and she usually avoided this type of boutique store unless she was surrounded by other tourists. She'd likely be the only customer they'd had in weeks since it was the off-season—and certainly the only one on a miserable day like today—and she would feel obligated to buy something more substantial than a key chain or refrigerator magnet. But it was either this place, or go to Forks and make a fool of herself. It was a toss-up, but she was already here, so the artisan store won.

Britt parked and ran across the lot to the door even though she was already soaked through. She pushed inside and stared at the scene in front of her. Had she been so confused by the obscuring rain that she had accidentally driven to the La Push lodge's reception room instead of the store she was aiming for? Not because the room looked the same—although some of the baskets and artwork mirrored what she had seen in the lodge—but because Chris was behind the counter and Alec and Jim were sitting at a table to her left. They were playing dominoes this time, but still…

Chris looked up from his laptop. "Brittany James. Good to see you. Did you enjoy your lunch today?"

Too weird. "Um, yes, thank you. Did Betty tell you I was coming here? Because I just decided on it about five minutes ago."

He laughed with the same booming sound that had space to echo in the great room of the lodge. In this tiny shop, it was loud enough to put the delicate glass sculptures at risk.

"No one said you'd be here." He gestured around him. "This is my store. I work here part-time and full-time at my lodge."

"So you own La Push."

"Not the grocery store. Yet. Look around, Brittany James. Find something that speaks to you."

She paused by the domino table. "Hi, Jim, Alec."

Alec made a *hmpf* sound in response.

"You're dripping on the floor," Jim said.

Britt looked down at the puddle forming around her feet. "It's raining."

Jim nodded thoughtfully, as if he was about to offer some sage advice. "It's always raining."

"Very wise," Britt said, forcing herself to wait until she had turned away before she rolled her eyes. She definitely had to buy something now, since she saw Chris almost daily at the lodge. She looked at some large and beautifully made baskets but was concerned by the lack of price tags on them. She didn't want to get to the counter and find out they cost hundreds of dollars. Besides, even one of them would significantly reduce her current living space.

She stopped next to a display of intricately carved totem animals, etched with geometric patterns and painted with bright reds, whites, and blacks, in a style similar to the mural in the lodge. She found a squat frog, a blackfish, a wolf. Each fit in the palm of her hand.

"Excellent choice," Chris said, speaking from directly behind her and making her startle. "My people believe we have a spirit animal that guides us throughout our lives, but people from all cultures sometimes feel a kinship with certain animals. Do you have a favorite animal from your childhood, or one that's been trying to get your attention since you've been on the coast?"

Britt sighed. She'd seen quite a few birds and animals since she'd left Seattle, and she'd read about others because of the grant. She was interested in all of them but hadn't found her personal equivalent of Tess's killer whales. Great. Another unknown to add to her list along with her passion, her destiny, and what she should do with the rest of her life. "No," she said. "Any thoughts?"

"Ask him which figurine is most expensive," Jim said. "You'll get the same answer."

"Snake," suggested Alec.

"No help from the peanut gallery," Britt said over her shoulder.

"Keep your eyes and heart open. Sometimes specific creatures appear frequently, especially when we are at a crossroads in life. It is our job to pay attention to what they are trying to tell us."

Britt couldn't believe she had so completely lost her way that she was hoping a raven or grizzly bear would show up at her cabin door and tell her what to do next. Could she have possibly moved any further from her logical nature?

Chris shook his head and took the little statue she was holding out of her hand and put it back on the display. "Not the eagle. Possibly a porcupine?"

"Like she's an eagle," Alec scoffed. "Maybe a rat."

Britt didn't turn around, but she raised her voice. "Next time, Jim, I'm finding you a word using Q, X, and Z."

"Hey," Alec said. "It won't count."

"Ignore them," Chris suggested, not very helpfully. "Now, where were we…oh yes. When you first arrived at the lodge, I could tell you were not quite right. Your soul has broken free and needs to be reintegrated into your body. I, as my tribe's shaman, could perform the necessary rituals."

No way was Britt going to let that happen, mainly because she was afraid Chris would tell her that her soul was too far gone to find again. Britt found herself wishing Tess was with her—not very unusual for her, but even more so this time. She was out of her element in a metaphysical discussion like this, but Tess would have been right at home. She would have been able to see the humor in the situation while still understanding the underlying truth behind what Chris was saying, and Britt figured the two of them would have been discussing the symbolic nature of killer whales and the ocean by now. Britt was simply trying to control her urge to throw a rat figurine at Alec's head.

"I'm not sure what you mean by *not quite right*, but it doesn't sound flattering."

Chris frowned as if he was deep in thought. "Perhaps unstable is a better word. I was able to sense this about you from the start."

"Of course she's unstable," Alec said. "She's been staying in La Push for over a month and eating nothing but grilled cheese sandwiches. You don't need to be a shaman to figure that out."

"Be sure to ask in advance how much it will cost to get your soul back. The name Chris in the Quileute language means Scams the Tourists," Jim said, setting down a domino and writing his score on a notepad.

Alec looked over as if checking to make sure Jim wasn't adding more points than he should. He turned back to Britt. "You can join our tribe, too. Your name will be Cheats at Scrabble."

"What does Alec mean in Quileute?" She returned his gibe. "Loses by Landslides?"

"Hardly. More like Conquers with Consonants."

Britt laughed, but quickly covered it with an attempt at a threatening expression. "That's it, Alec. You and me, tomorrow in the lodge. A Scrabble showdown."

"You're on. Winner gets to be shaman of the tribe since apparently anyone can claim the title."

"You think you have problems?" Chris asked Britt as she turned back to the display. "They follow me everywhere. Now, about the soul retrieval ritual."

"I'm sort of hoping it will wander back on its own, but thanks for the offer," Britt said. She picked up the blackfish figurine. "I'll take this one. And it's for a friend, so don't bother analyzing whether I'm worthy or not."

Chris laughed. "You're more than worthy of any of them. The trick is finding the right fit."

She wandered among the displays while he wrapped her orca. She had initially thought of giving it to Tess if she saw her again, but she probably had millions of killer whale knickknacks already. And she had been raised around here, where tribal art was plentiful. If she didn't have a chance to give the statue to Tess, she'd keep it for herself as a memento of her trip. A reminder of Tess, as if she needed anything tangible to keep her in her thoughts.

Chris handed her the package after she paid. "I put another one in there, just for you. On the house. It is an animal that offers protection during change."

Britt smiled. It sounded like exactly what she needed. "Thank you, Chris. I'll see you back at the lodge. Bye, Jim." She gave Alec a stern glare. "Until tomorrow."

He laughed. "You're going down."

"You bet. I'm going down in history with the highest Scrabble score ever."

She left before he could offer a retort and ran through the rain to her car. She started the engine and turned the heater on full blast. While she sat in the cocoon of dryness and let the waves of heat ease the chill out of her bones, she opened the package to see what animal Chris had given her. She unfolded the white tissue paper, and a seal sculpture rolled out and onto her palm. A protector during change, Chris had said. She frowned, knowing she had seen a seal recently, and grinned when she finally pulled the memory to the surface. The night she had run away from Seattle and had stumbled out to Cape Flattery in her completely unsuitable heels. She had stood on the bluff and watched a seal bobbing in the waves, far below her.

That night felt miles away, yet she was no closer to the revelations she sought. She had made a few changes, including quitting her job—although it didn't really count since David didn't believe her and she knew she could walk back to Randall Chemical tomorrow and no one would blink. She had funded a grant and had learned about sea otters, resident killer whales, and wolves. She had generated a list of every change she needed to make and every cause she needed to champion, even though none of them felt truly like hers. And she had met Tess. The situations surrounding their meetings seemed mundane. A talk on the beach, lunch at the diner, a tour of the marine center. But knowing Tess felt momentous somehow, as if she had the key Britt needed to unlock the future.

She shook her head, using her hands to brush raindrops out of her hair. What she felt for Tess was more like lust than a spiritual connection, and she shouldn't let herself make the relationship into something it wasn't and would never be. She carefully balanced her little seal on the dashboard and drove back to the lodge.

CHAPTER FOURTEEN

B ritt parked her car beneath the overhang, close to the entrance
to the lodge, and hurried around to the passenger side. She had
felt a bit foolish driving the short distance to the diner instead of
walking to pick up the trays of food for her cocktail party until she
had stepped outside of the restaurant with a platter of sandwiches
in her hands. Then the light drizzle she had slogged through all day
turned into a serious downpour. Karla and the cook used a blue
plastic tarp to make a sort of tunnel for her as she ferried the dishes
out to her car. They seemed to accept the pelting rain as a normal
November occurrence, but Britt suspected the torrential weather
might be a precursor to an ark-worthy flood or the apocalypse. She
had inched her way back to the lodge with her wipers on full blast,
barely able to see the road directly in front of her.

Alec and Jim came out to help her, and as soon as they had the
food inside, the rain diminished again until it was barely sprinkling.
No sign of the apocalypse, so the party was still on.

Britt used the towel Chris handed her to squeeze some of the
water out of her soaked hair while she looked around the lodge's
reception area.

"It's beautiful in here, Chris," she said. The room was already
stunning, with its mural and immense fireplace, but Chris had added
some extra touches for her party. Fairy lights were draped across
the mantel and the reception desk, and carved animal statues from
Chris's store were standing guard by the tables for food and wine.

Glass ornaments hung from the ceiling, catching the flickering firelight and bouncing it around the room.

"Thank you," he said, opening a bottle of wine with a loud pop. "You're the first guest who has rented this space for a gathering. I think I might branch out into the party planning business."

"You're a true renaissance man, Chris." Britt grinned as she pulled water-beaded foil off the trays, revealing hot wings, club sandwich wedges, and triangles of the ever-present grilled cheese. Nothing fancy, but getting food from the diner beat trying to assemble dainty hors d'oeuvres in her cabin's miniscule kitchen. The casual food fit the atmosphere she was trying to create more than pâté and caviar would, anyway.

The people who were coming tonight represented quite different causes, but they shared a love for the Peninsula and its inhabitants. They were part of a community, and Britt was happy to be part of it for a short while. This party probably wouldn't affect who won the grant, but it would be a chance for these disparate groups to network and for Britt to get to know the applicants in a less formal way.

And a chance to spend more time with Tess. Not that Britt would go through the effort of organizing a party just to have the opportunity to talk to Tess, of course. She wasn't in high school or living in a rom-com, after all.

"I think I need a glass of wine," she said to Chris.

"Me, too."

Britt felt a smile stretch across her face—as involuntary as a leg's response to a reflex hammer—at the sound of Tess's voice coming from directly behind her. She turned around, trying to gain enough control of her facial muscles to appear cool and in control. Tess was standing close, and Britt felt a sudden flush of heat shiver through her, from her neck to her belly. She wanted to blame the wine, but she hadn't had any yet. The fireplace. She was hot because of the fireplace.

"Hello, Tess," she said, hoping a formal tone would mask her lack of composure. "I'm glad you could make it tonight. I was worried the heavy rain might make it difficult to travel on the roads."

Tess grinned. "I wouldn't dare let the weather keep me away

from you," she said, her voice pitched low and intimate. "You might have given my grant to someone else."

Chris gave a bark of laughter at Tess's joke, breaking Britt out of her spell. She rolled her eyes at Tess's presumption. "Chris, this is Tess. She's just one of the grant applicants," Britt said, with exaggerated emphasis the phrase *just one.*

"Uh-huh," Chris said, handing her a glass of wine and giving her a knowing wink. He gave a glass to Tess. "Here you go, Tess."

"Thank you," she said, taking a sip and looking around the room. "Are you the owner? The artwork in this place is gorgeous."

Britt let their discussion about the basket-weaving process fade into the background while she drank some of her wine and regained her composure. Tess had caught her by surprise, but now she was back to normal. Professional. Not blushing. She waved across the room at Melissa and Jake, who had gravitated to the Scrabble table and seemed to be setting up to play doubles with Alec and Jim.

"Well, I guess they're ignoring my advice to mingle," Tess said. "Although I can't complain because at least I managed to talk them out of wearing matching Starfleet uniforms."

Britt shrugged. "I'm a fan, remember? They might have earned the Center extra points."

"Damn," Tess said. "I should have listened to them. Who else is coming tonight?"

"One is an artist named Vince. He organizes beach and river cleanups and creates sculptures with the trash, then uses the money he makes from selling the pieces to fund more cleanup projects."

Tess smiled. "A self-sustaining business. That suits the recycled art theme, doesn't it?"

"Exactly," Britt said, feeling more at ease as she started talking about the other top applicants. If she had an unlimited supply of money, she would have been perfectly happy spending the rest of her life getting to know amazing and talented people like the ones she had met through this grant and giving them money.

"His application sounded kind of sketchy at first. I pictured him wandering along the beach all day, and then piling up a bunch of trash and calling it art." Britt shook her head, remembering how her perception of Vince changed dramatically once she saw the photos of his sculptures included in his grant packet. She had definitely learned a lesson about not making snap judgments. "He's an incredibly talented artist, and his work crews have had a major impact on the waterways along the coast and in the park."

"Which improves the habitat for salmon and other fish, which in turn helps to ensure the survival of species that rely on them for food."

"I know, I know," Britt said, rolling her eyes and imitating Tess's irate diner voice. "*It's all connected.*"

Tess smiled and clinked her glass against Britt's. "Who else?"

"You and I talked about the Makah Wolf Sanctuary when I visited the marine center," Britt said, remembering her talk with Tess on the shore and their trip out to sea. The misty sea air settling on her skin and taste of salt when she'd licked her lips. Tess's arm draped along the boat rail behind her, not touching, but close enough to cause some sort of chemical reaction in Britt's body…

She cleared her throat and took another drink of wine. What had she been talking about? Wolves. "I haven't had a chance to tour the sanctuary yet, but I had an interview with the head caretaker, Felicity. She'll be here tonight, along with some of her volunteers. Oh, and there's Rose, from the native plant society. They're involved in all sorts of activities, like protection, restoration, and education. I drove to Port Angeles last week and heard her speak at Peninsula College about native grasses." Britt shook her head and looked at Tess. "I've spent most of my life in cities, and I always thought of grass as the green stuff suburban people have in their yards. I'd never realized how many functions wild grasses serve, and how important they are to the environment."

"Erosion control, protective spaces for nesting birds and small animals, food sources," Tess said, her voice smooth and low again, so that the decidedly unromantic phrases sounded like pillow talk.

Britt caught herself when her gaze dropped to Tess's mouth the second time, as if reading her lips would help Britt better catch her quietly spoken words. She laughed and took a step back. "Does that little seduction trick really work?"

"I have no idea what you're talking about," Tess said, hiding her grin behind her wineglass.

"Don't act innocent," Britt said, playfully elbowing Tess in the side. "You know exactly what you were doing."

Tess shrugged. "I was talking about native grasses. You, on the other hand, were staring at my mouth."

Britt struggled with the temptation to deny it, but she really had been staring. So much for professional and in control. "I'm going to go say hello to Rose now. Do you want to come and meet her?"

Tess shook her head. She had monopolized Britt enough for the evening. She had been sure to arrive early, hoping she would beat the other candidates and could indulge her desire to have Britt all to herself, for a few moments at least. Now she needed to back off and let Britt be the host. "You go. I'll have a chance to talk to her later this evening."

She watched Britt walk away, deciding this view of her might be her favorite, with those rain-wet jeans hugging her slender hips. Britt needed to get into some dry clothes, and Tess would be glad to help her. She'd slowly peel the damp denim off Britt's cold, soft thighs, and then rub them until she was warm again…

Tess looked around for a distraction—anything to get her mind off Britt and jeans and the removal of those jeans. She noticed a young guy with long reddish-blond hair enter the room and hesitate just inside the door, as if he wasn't sure he was in the right place. He was wearing a navy shirt with a large green recycling symbol on it, and Tess figured he was Britt's artist. Nothing like a discussion about beach trash art to take one's mind off sex. Tess headed over to say hello.

She moved around the room for the next hour, talking to Vince and Rose and drawing Jake and Melissa into conversations with other guests. She was always hyperaware of where Britt was standing, of her bright and beautiful smile, and the obvious pleasure she found in being around this group of people and learning from their stories. Tess loved the company, too. She had only been thinking of seeing Britt again when she looked forward to this evening, and she hadn't realized how much she missed her interactions with colleagues at

Evergreen since she'd been away. This evening gave her a similar sense of camaraderie and collaboration that she felt at the college, even though they were all vying for the same grant.

Tess didn't envy Britt the decision she was going to have to make. Everyone in the room not only deserved the money but would do great things with it. Naturally, she believed her killer whales were the most deserving—her personal feelings aside, they were the ones in the most imminent danger if drastic efforts weren't made to protect them—but she'd respect any choice Britt made.

She had kept her distance from Britt while they circulated through the room, but as soon as she saw her standing alone by the food table and unenthusiastically munching on a grilled cheese sandwich, Tess went to talk to her again. She tried to make it seem casual, as if she just happened to wander over, but her approach was more beeline than meander.

"Having a good time?" Tess asked, putting a piece of club sandwich onto a plate, as if she had really been coming over here to get some food and not to talk to Britt.

"I am. I was worried it would seem like I was setting up the applicants for an evening of competition, like a cage fighting match. Shove everyone in the lodge, make it rain too hard for anyone to want to leave, and give the grant to the last charity standing."

"I'm in," Tess said. "My killer whales would totally win."

"The evening is going so well—let's try not to start a brawl," Britt said. She sounded stern, but her nose crinkled in the way Tess had come to learn was a sign of Britt trying not to laugh out loud. She considered giving up her job and family obligations and devoting herself to the lifelong mission of putting that exact expression on Britt's often thoughtful and serious face.

"Seriously," she said. "A few plants and some garbage? Smashed. A wolf? Merely a morsel for an afternoon snack."

Britt's scrunched nose gave way to a genuine laugh. "Well, I'm glad to hear your voice is back to normal, even though it means everyone in the room can hear you threatening their beloved projects."

Tess cleared her throat and patted her chest. "I was a little hoarse when I got here, but I'm better now. Must be all this dry weather."

Britt smiled and tossed the crust from her grilled cheese into a trash can. "Ugh. I'm sick of these sandwiches. I'd be better off gnawing on a block of tofu. Do you think if I bring some veggie burgers to the diner, they'll cook them for me?"

"I'm sure they will, but they'll probably add American cheese and bacon before they serve it to you." Tess hesitated, trying to phrase her next sentences without sounding as if she'd ever doubted Britt's resolve. "I'm impressed by you, Britt, and I don't mean just for sticking to the vegetarian plan. You resolved to make huge changes in your life, and you're following through even though it's probably been difficult at times."

"In other words, you thought I'd give up and run back to Seattle, my old job, and the nearest steakhouse."

Tess opened her mouth to deny it, but Britt was right. Tess had seen her share of people get all gung-ho about some new cause or project, only to abandon it once the actual work started. Britt was proving she had truly internalized the changes she was making. Still, her continued presence in La Push made Tess curious about the girlfriend...not that she cared one way or another...and she certainly wasn't about to mine for information...

"So, what does your girlfriend think about your new life?" What was the harm in asking? She wasn't going to *do* anything about it.

"You're fishing," Britt said.

"Maybe."

Britt hesitated, apparently debating what to tell Tess, then she shrugged. "We're not seeing each other anymore."

Interesting. Not that Tess cared one way or the other.

"Oh, that's too bad," she said, making an effort to sound genuine. According to Britt's expression, she failed miserably, which was probably due in part to the smile she felt tugging at the corners of her mouth. "What happened to—"

"Did I hear someone call my wolves afternoon snacks?" Felicity interrupted them. She picked up a hot wing and took a bite, reminding Tess of the old cliché about dogs and their owners starting to look alike. Felicity had a delicacy to her that matched her name, with her slight build, softly curling hair, and gracefully carved features, but there was something predatory about her expression. Devoting one's life to a demanding and challenging cause tended to bring out the warrior in people, and Felicity seemed to be no exception.

"They hunt in packs, you know. If we're going to do this, it has to be a pack, not a single wolf."

Tess would still bet on her orcas in a fight against a wolf, unless Felicity was planning to play the role of alpha in the fight. Then she might put her money on the wolves. She noticed Britt's eyes moving back and forth between them, like she was watching a tennis match and thought the ball might actually be a grenade.

"We're just kidding around, Britt," she assured her. "I think."

"You might be, but I don't joke about my wolves." Felicity smiled, though, and her even white teeth and curved lips seemed innocent enough. She threw her bare wing bone into the garbage can.

Tess laughed. "I believe your wolves are very lucky to have you on their side," she said.

"Ditto, with your killer whales." She turned her lupine attention to Britt. "I'm looking forward to our tour of the sanctuary tomorrow. It'll probably be a wet day, so I hope the rain won't bother you."

Britt smiled. "If we waited for a clear day, I probably wouldn't get my tour until next summer."

"Can I come?" Tess interrupted, surprising the two of them and herself with her question. She had always wanted to visit the wolf sanctuary. She decided not to delve into the motivation behind her question, because she might find uncomfortable issues like wanting to be around Britt every second she could, and petty ones like jealousy lurking there. "As a colleague, I mean, not as a spy for the opposition. Never mind. I can visit the sanctuary another time."

Tess sighed. Britt was watching her with a confused expression, probably thinking she was trying to sabotage the other candidates. Felicity was looking at her with far too much perception in those wide gray eyes. Tess had started out the evening as the suave and smooth flirt she usually was, but too much time around Britt paralyzed her brain cells, keeping her axons from firing like they should.

"I don't mind at all, if Britt is okay with it," Felicity said, glancing between Tess and Britt. "Unless you're going to heckle me on the tour and make me look bad. We have ways of disposing of unwanted carcasses at the sanctuary, you know."

"I'm sure the tourists who visit enjoy hearing that part of your presentation." Tess looked at Britt, who lifted her hands in a gesture of surrender.

"You can come if you want," Britt said. "I can't see any way it would affect my decision about the grant, but we need to tell Rose and Vince. They can join us if they'd like."

Great. A group outing to a wolf sanctuary, where Tess might or might not be on the dinner menu. She muttered something about getting another glass of wine, even though her first one was still almost full, and turned away. Was it worth it? Acting foolish by insinuating herself into the tour and quite possibly—if she was playing the odds—embarrassing herself by saying something awkward or clumsy to Britt at some point during the day? Just to be around her for an afternoon?

Tess picked up another glass of wine she had no intention of drinking since she was her group's driver and wandered across the room to where Melissa and Jake were standing behind Chris's tall baskets. It was definitely worth it, she decided. She'd play the fool all over again if it meant she had even an extra five minutes in Britt's company.

Chapter Fifteen

When Tess arrived at the Makah Wolf Sanctuary, she parked next to Britt's Lexus and climbed out of her car. She had wanted to suggest she and Britt drive together—it only made sense to carpool, since she was certain one of Britt's resolutions must have something to do with not wasting natural resources—but she decided riding in the same car might snap the already stretched level of appropriateness given their potential grantor-grantee relationship.

The sanctuary seemed to be primarily a large parklike area, with oak trees and picnic tables scattered around it. A house with a sign indicating it was being used as the sanctuary offices stood on one side of the parking lot, and another building marked as the visitor center was across the lot, next to a high chain-link fence. Tess was about to wander toward the visitor center when Britt and Felicity emerged from the office building.

She waved and waited for them under the shelter of one of the trees. The rain seemed to have worn itself out last night before Britt's party, and had fizzled to a gentle sprinkle.

"How much property do you have here?" she asked, once greetings were finished and they were walking toward the fenced area. Neither Vince or Rose had been able to join them, so it would only be the three of them on the tour.

"About fifty acres," Felicity said. "The section where our resident wolves live is about six acres in size, and half of it is accessible on our tours. We have larger and much more private pens where we keep our breeding Mexican gray wolves that might be released into the wild at some point. Most of the property is vacant land, but last night I had a chance to talk to Rose about having her society repopulate some of the empty spaces with native species, and possibly opening some trails up for tours."

Tess grinned. Britt's grant was working some magic already, by bringing four previously unrelated groups together and making connections among them. Like her and Vince. She was going to put him in touch with Evergreen's art department, because she knew the faculty would adore his artistic mission. He had promised to do an orca sculpture for the marine center in exchange.

"The extra property gives you plenty of room if you want to expand, too," Britt said.

Felicity hesitated. "In some ways, yes. We want to add another private pen and purchase a breeding pair of endangered red wolves, which you know is why we applied for this grant. Still, we need to keep a large buffer zone around our animals. It helps us protect them, plus it makes the neighbors more comfortable. People can be easily frightened at the thought of wolves living next door, even though we're extremely careful with fencing."

Tess nodded. "With the orcas, it sometimes feels like we have to put more effort into fighting to change the public's negative perception of them than into physically protecting them."

"Same with the wolves," Felicity agreed.

They reached the slat-filled fence and waited while Felicity unlocked the gate. Tess watched as Britt's face, framed by her rain-frosted hair, shifted into an expression Tess had come to know as well as her about-to-laugh one. She was connecting dots in her mind, gathering information and collating it neatly.

"So efforts like your book, Tess, and your study of killer whale communication help people see orcas as intelligent family-oriented creatures, and not frightening sea killers. You know, Felicity, I wondered at first why you bothered to give tours instead of focusing on your breeding programs and letting the resident wolves just live quiet lives. I thought it was just a way to make money for the sanctuary, but it's as much an educational effort, isn't it?"

"Yes. Absolutely, yes," Felicity said with an emphatic nod. "Children grow up hearing stories about big bad wolves chomping on girls wearing red capes and innocent little piggies. We do our best to counteract those stories and give kids and adults a new, more positive mythology of wolves."

Britt nodded, lost in thought. "And it goes beyond negative stereotypes. Rose's grasses, the clean beaches Vince leaves behind...most people take them for granted, or aren't aware of their importance, so they can remain unprotected and unnoticed."

"Like the kelp," Tess said, at the exact same time as Britt. They even turned toward each other like mirror images.

Britt laughed and recounted a brief version of the conversation she and Tess had at the Center about sea otters and kelp. Tess stood still, dropping out of the discussion for a few seconds. She felt her heart beating as if she had been running hard, pulsing through her and into the tips of her fingers. So Britt recalled Tess's words—it was in her nature to learn and absorb and remember. So she and Tess had spoken the word *kelp* at the same time, thinking in sync. No big deal. No need for pleasure and fear to start a war inside her chest.

Tess stepped into the sanctuary and all those insane phrases like *soul mates* and *love connection* were thankfully wiped from her conscious mind, replaced by the thrill of being close to the furry and regal wolves. A gravel path wound through the sanctuary, close to fenced pens Felicity said were about a third of an acre each. Wolves ranging in color from pure white to black, and everything in between, watched them with intelligent yellow-gold eyes.

"Are they eating pumpkins?" Britt asked, laughing with quiet delight and speaking in a hushed tone as if she'd entered a church.

"They are," Felicity said with a grin. "We like to give them different things to taste and smell and play with. They're smart animals and need stimulation."

She stopped by the first enclosure and leaned on the railing separating them from the fence and a steel-gray female wolf by only several feet. "Most of the animals on the tour are rescued wolf-dogs and true wolves, and all were bred in captivity and wouldn't survive even if we could release them in the wild. They're clearly accustomed to people and wouldn't stay away from farms and homes."

Felicity led them along the path, introducing each wolf by name and telling its story. They were almost halfway through—and Tess was nearly bursting to rush home and get Justin because she knew how much he would love this place—when one of the wolves behind them started to howl.

"Here we go," Felicity whispered as the low, mournful sound was followed by another, slightly higher in pitch. Soon all the wolves had joined in with unique voices, surrounding the small group of humans with a haunting, beautiful music.

Tess felt Britt's fingers brush against hers, and then they were holding hands. Tess smiled at her and felt another sensation of being in sync—she was certain the look of wonder and joy on Britt's face was mirrored on her own. Later she might analyze the feeling of Britt's slender, cool fingers wrapped around hers and extrapolate to having those fingers touch other parts of her, as well, but right now she accepted the contact for what it was. A need to share a powerful experience with another person.

Tess shook her head as the howling faded away, Britt let go of her hand, and Felicity gave her a smug smile. After that wolfish display, she could probably kiss the grant good-bye.

Hell, she couldn't blame Britt if she made her decision right now. Tess was even ready to empty her savings account and stuff every last cent into the donation box hanging by the exit gate.

❖

Britt and Felicity walked over to the brush-covered acres where the new red wolf enclosure would go, if the sanctuary could get funding. Tess had tactfully separated from them at the gift shop, claiming she wanted to buy gifts for her nephew, but also ensuring that Britt had plenty of time to chat privately with Felicity and find out about her plans.

She was relieved to have a little space after the day's series of intimate brushes against Tess. Physical ones, when Britt had held her hand or bumped against her hip while they were walking along the sanctuary path. Emotional ones, like when their thoughts meshed, and they seemed to understand each other without effort.

Fortunately, Felicity was a walking wolf encyclopedia and enthusiastic about answering every question Britt had in great detail. They filled every second of the walk from the gift shop to the field and back with information, and Britt was grateful for the flow of words because they let her quickly categorize and tidy away her interactions with Tess. The howling had been magnificent, and Britt would have held anyone's hand during the experience. Well, maybe not anyone's. She hadn't grabbed for Felicity.

Saying the same sentence at the exact same time was hardly anything unusual. In fact, there was the entire game of Jinx based around the phenomenon.

By the time she said good-bye to Felicity and returned to the gift shop, she felt sure she'd be able to face Tess with a minimum of blushing and stammering. Tess was standing by a case full of wolf books, trying to stack one on top of her already precarious bundle of stuff.

"Wow. Are you buying the whole store? They won't need the grant after making a profit on you."

"Very funny. I'm just getting a few things for Justin."

Britt pulled a sweatshirt off the top of the pile and held it up to herself. It would easily fit her. "How old did you say he was?"

"Five," Tess said, with a crooked, sheepish smile. "A big five."

Britt raised her eyebrows.

"Okay, I got us matching shirts. Then I thought my sister might want one, too."

"He seems to have an advanced reading level for his age, too." Britt took the adult nonfiction books from Tess and carried them for her.

"Did you see any more wolves out in the back of the property?" Tess asked, obviously changing the subject.

"No. I was hoping for a glimpse of the gray wolves, but I only had a chance to see them on surveillance footage today. I learned a lot, though, and I'm starting to understand the complexity of reintroducing creatures to the wild, and how much better it would be if we didn't hunt, kill, and chase them out in the first place. At the Center, you talked about how it was possible to bring sea otters back to the coast, but it would be nearly impossible to successfully add new killer whales to the pods in Puget Sound. Felicity said there used to be a large population of wolves on the Peninsula, but they're unlikely to come back naturally because of the I-5 corridor. I think she called it a lack of landscape permeability? And if they can't come back on their own, and people are afraid of them, then they'll never be here again."

Britt paused and took a deep breath. She had missed Tess more than she had thought while on the short walk. She wanted to get Tess up to speed on what she and Felicity had discussed as quickly as possible, so they could continue the conversation. Tess was looking at her with a strange, unreadable expression.

"It's a shame, isn't it?" Britt added, filling the silence. "How few people will ever hear them howl?"

Tess grinned. "I agree with you, Britt. I'd even hug you if I wasn't carrying half the gift shop right now."

"A hug would be very unprofessional," Britt said, but she was smiling, too. "I guess it's a good thing you're a compulsive shopper."

Tess reached over with the toe of her shoe and nudged Britt's calf. "You know, Britt, you might not have discovered the specific work you want to do yet, but I can already see the great qualities you'll bring to any job or cause."

Britt wanted to ask what they were, but she felt she'd be asking for compliments. She really wanted to know, though, since she had no idea what qualities Tess saw that she didn't.

As if hearing Britt's unspoken question, Tess clarified, "You hear wolves singing or stories about what's happening to the killer whales, and you respond emotionally to them. But you don't stop with the feeling, like a lot of people do. You ask the next questions. What can I do to make this problem better? What would happen if we tried this next? You're logical and practical."

Britt sighed. She had liked where Tess was going until the last statement. It just brought her back to the beginning. "Logical and practical, like a chemist," she said.

Tess laughed and bumped against her, nearly flinging them both into a display of jigsaw puzzles with the momentum her purchases gave her. "Hey, grab one of those for me, won't you? And don't knock those qualities because they're the ones that get things done, minds changed, and laws passed. You can change careers if you want, but don't try to change who you are in the process."

Britt smiled and selected a puzzle off the shelf. Tess's words might not have clarified her decision-making process, but they gave her some food for thought. Right now, though, she was going to follow Tess's example and shop.

CHAPTER SIXTEEN

The atmosphere in the pub in Forks was subdued for a Friday evening. Two men were playing pool in the far corner and a group of four young-looking kids—Tess would have done a thorough check on their IDs if she had been their server—were plowing through their second pitcher of beer and playing a trivia game that was showing on the only television monitor not playing an ESPN sports commentary show. Three other tables besides Tess's were occupied by couples having dinner. The place and the people in it seemed determined to maintain the stereotype of a homey and quiet small-town tavern, but they hadn't accounted for Tess's friends.

Lenae came through the door first, quietly drawing everyone's attention to her for the usual two reasons. First and foremost, she was tall and elegant, and the simple lines of her bob haircut and well-cut clothes only served to accentuate her beauty. A close second was her guide dog Baxter, a handsome golden retriever. Everyone loved Baxter. He scanned the room, and Tess saw the moment when he recognized her and turned slightly in her direction. Lenae matched his movements with perfect synchrony and smiled in Tess's direction. They seemed calm on the surface, but Tess noticed an unusual tension on Lenae's face and in Baxter's posture.

The likely reason for the tension burst through the door moments later. A tiny black Lab skittered across the foyer with Cara in tow. She waved at Tess, and then stooped down to pick up the menu board that had clattered to the floor after being caught by her puppy's leash. She untangled the dog from a gumball machine and followed Lenae to Tess's table, bumping into everyone who was seated between Tess and the door and calling apologies over her shoulder.

"Sorry. Excuse us. Oops, I'll have another beer sent to replace that one. Hey, Tess, it's good to see you."

"You just made quite an entrance," Tess said, standing up to hug her friends. "The good people of Forks will be talking about this for years to come."

Lenae sat down and removed Baxter's harness to let him know he was off duty. He came over to politely greet Tess before wedging himself under Lenae's chair.

"You have a beer in front of you, don't you?" Lenae asked, making it sound more like an assumed statement and not a question. "Hand it over."

Tess slid her mug toward Lenae and ordered another plus a white wine for Cara from their server. "Tough car ride?"

"You have no idea. Baxter was trying to roll down the window and jump out."

"She's exaggerating," said Cara. "Cupcake did just fine, except for eating most of the back-seat floor mat and then throwing it up again. On a completely unrelated note, do you know anyplace in town where I can get a new turn signal switch?"

"Cupcake? Seriously?" At the mention of her name, the little black pup jumped on Tess's leg, begging for attention. She had huge black paws and wore a green vest with what was supposed to be *Guide Dog Puppy in Training* written across the side, but actually looked like *Gui g Pupp Tra g* because of numerous rips in the fabric. "What's a *Guig Pupp Trag*?"

"Very funny. We had a small issue with her getting caught on the brake pedal. When we were stopped for gas, and not while we were driving, thank God. Cupcake, come back here."

Tess turned to Lenae while Cara chased the puppy around the pool table. "Wow. This one makes Pickwick seem lethargic." Cara had met Lenae when she did a television episode about her guide dog training program, and Cara had gotten talked into puppy walking Pickwick, a shoe-eating wild-child puppy. He had eventually become a loving and talented guide dog for his new owner, and Cara and Lenae had found love with each other. All in all, worth the loss of a few sneakers.

"I know. But it's the first time she's wanted to puppy walk again since handing him over to his permanent owner, and I made the mistake of letting her choose which one she wanted. I should have at least narrowed it down to a few more manageable ones. Or to any puppy except Cupcake."

Tess laughed. "Well, it's just for a year, right?"

Lenae sighed and propped her chin on her hand. "I've been doing this long enough to be able to judge whether a puppy will make it as a guide dog. I seriously doubt Cupcake will make the cut, and then you know what will happen."

Tess did. "Cara will want to keep her. But Pickwick was obnoxious, too, and he grew out of it."

"Pickwick was assertive and independent and smart. Those are qualities that can make a puppy challenging to handle but will make the adult dog an ideal guide and partner. Cupcake is…I'm not sure how to put this kindly…not exactly *smart*."

Baxter made a sound somewhere between a groan and a sigh under the table as Cupcake returned and pounced on his head.

"I'm back, so stop saying bad things about my puppy." Cara let Baxter take charge of puppy-sitting duties while she took a sip of her wine. She sighed happily. "We've missed you, Tess. Tell us about the exile. Has it been as bad as you expected?"

Tess thought about how to answer. She hadn't realized it before, but her time in Forks so far was defined by her interactions with Britt. When she thought of her first day back in her hometown, it was significant because it was the day she met Britt. Even the Center and her killer whales were connected to Britt now, because of the grant, but also because they were things Tess had shared with her. The dread she had felt before coming back to Forks had made the reality somewhat anticlimactic, and Tess knew a large reason for that was because she couldn't hate this place anymore, now that Britt permeated every corner of it in Tess's mind.

"I'd still rather be in Olympia, or in any number of places

besides here, but it really hasn't been as terrible as I thought it would be," she said, focusing on the family aspect for now because Cara and Lenae both knew her history with them and had been concerned about what life here would be like for her. "My mom and I don't have anything in common except a desire to keep some sense of peace, so we talk about the weather and get along just fine. My dad mostly plays video games and Legos with my nephew. We argue about things like medication and exercises, but we don't bring up any personal topics. Ouch!"

Tess pried Cupcake's jaws open until she released her ankle.

"She likes you," Cara declared with a smile. "Go on. You were talking about your family."

"Let me just stanch the bleeding first." Tess sat in an uncomfortable cross-legged position on the wooden chair to keep her ankles out of reach. "I've actually had some civilized conversations with Kelly, but mainly I've had fun getting to know Justin. Last time I saw him, he was still a toddler. He's talking now, and he's a great kid. I hadn't realized how important it was for me to be part of his life, but now I don't want to lose my relationship with him."

"Has your sister considered getting him a service dog, especially with the new baby coming?" Lenae asked. "They can be very helpful to both autistic children and parents. The baby will require a lot of attention, and the dog can fill in the gaps as a companion. If she wants to learn more about it, have her call me."

Tess pictured Justin playing with a dog like Baxter. He would love the animal, and some of the pressure on Kelly would be relieved. "I like the idea, and I'll bring it up to her. She always wanted a dog when we were kids. Just don't try to pawn Cupcake off on her. Right now, we can be in the same room without wanting to punch each other, and I don't want to mess that up."

"Table Rule. No more disparaging remarks about my sweet Cupcake."

Lenae laughed. "Just one story before you enforce the rule. I have to tell Tess about the first time you and Cupcake rode the bus."

"No. You promised you wouldn't. And it served that woman right for wearing grass-colored shoes."

Tess sat back in her chair with a happy sigh as she watched Cara and Lenae's playful interactions. She had missed the comfort and closeness of their friendship since she'd been away from Olympia, and she had been thrilled when Cara called and said they were coming to spend a weekend with her.

Her first reaction had been a desire to call Brittany and have her join them. She knew the three of them would get along well, and she was willing to bet Britt often felt as isolated as she sometimes did, so far from the familiar friends and places of home. Britt had admitted as much to her at the cocktail party, and Tess wished their interactions weren't so restricted. The damned grant got in the way, though, and Tess couldn't cross the line even if she had no romantic intentions toward Britt.

Well, she *had* them, but she wasn't going to act on them. She had pushed propriety enough by getting herself invited on the wolf sanctuary tour, and she had only done so because the other people in contention for the grant knew she was going. She would have welcomed any one of them to tour the marine center, as well.

Cara and Lenae stopped scuffling over Cupcake stories, and Cara leaned toward Tess, twirling her wineglass on the tabletop.

"I'm glad to hear you're getting along with your family, Tess. At least reasonably so. It makes it easier for me to tell you why I'm here."

Tess raised her eyebrows in surprise. "You had an ulterior motive? I thought you were just here to see me."

"We were already planning to come visit in December," Lenae said. "We just moved up the date several weeks."

Cara nodded. "President Carden asked me to come talk to you. She got the grant proposal you sent her."

Tess tamped down the urge to fuss with her beer mug like Cara was with her wineglass, trying to remember when she had ever seen her friend look so serious. Tess naturally had let Evergreen's president know about the work she hoped to do at the marine center. "There shouldn't be a conflict of interest, but why wouldn't she just call me if there was a problem?"

"It's not a problem. It's good news."

"Then why are you about to snap the stem off your glass?"

Cara laughed, and Lenae reached over to hold her hand. "It's complicated, I guess. Carden wants you to do the research you proposed, and she pitched the project to *Fading Song*'s publisher. They've offered a contract for another book by you. Evergreen's board is very interested in getting more involved in the efforts to protect the resident pods, and a book written for the general public is exactly the kind of high-profile project they want to support."

A chance to write about her killer whales and share their story with the public again? Tess had no idea why this would be making Cara nervous. Or why President Carden had asked Cara to relay the news in person instead of just calling Tess. "I'm not seeing a downside here," she said distractedly, already forming an outline for the book in her head.

Cara reached down and wrapped Cupcake's leash around her calf to keep the puppy from roaming the pub. "You'd have to withdraw your grant request, for starters. The college wants ownership of this research and your book, and they don't want any chance of the donor causing problems in the future. It's easier if they pay you and provide a subsidy to the Center."

Tess barely registered the fact that she and the Center would benefit financially from the change in funding source. The book mattered a great deal to her, and so did the money for the struggling lab. Her overriding thought, however, was centered on Britt. They could be friends, and the simple fact of that statement made Tess's stomach flip with anticipation.

"Done. Now tell me the bad news."

"You'd have to stay here for the full academic year. And probably next summer, too," Cara added in a rush of words.

Tess paused with her beer mug halfway to her mouth. She set it down again, directly in the center of her coaster. Stay in Forks for almost a *year*? Now her stomach was flipping for entirely different reasons. Britt surely wouldn't be here that long. She would have nothing to make Forks bearable, except her whales.

Tess remained silent, and Cara elaborated, "Starting next

semester, we'd be sending small groups of students to stay for two weeks at a time, and we're working on a summer joint program with the communications and biology departments. We want to do a student-made film about the killer whale situation, and I'll be here in the summer to lead the project. You'd be able to teach, and you'd have an extended period of time to collect whale songs from the offshores."

Tess shook her head. She had to say yes, without a doubt. The benefits outweighed her petty desire to stay far away from her family. And Cara would be here for at least part of the time.

"I'll do it. You know I will. It's just…yuk."

Baxter sat up and rested his head on her knee. The dog was always able to sense when someone around him was feeling distressed. Cupcake just continued to gnaw on the leg of Cara's chair.

Tess rubbed Baxter's soft ears and steeled herself to accept the situation. She was being offered a wonderful chance, and she wouldn't waste any part of it feeling sorry for herself.

"Do you have more delightful news, or is that it?"

Cara grinned and picked up her menu. "I'm done with official business. Now we can focus on enjoying the hell out of this weekend. What should we do tomorrow?"

"Preferably something strenuously physical to wear out the demon pup. Then we might actually get some sleep at night," Lenae said. "How about a hike in the rainforest? It'll be cold, but I've never been. I want to know if the air feels different there."

"It does," Tess said. She hadn't been on a good hike since she had come to Forks, but she was eager to feel the exploding sense of peace she always had experienced in the rainforest where the air was dense and damp. "You'll enjoy the textures of the different kinds of moss and lichen, and scents are amplified in the humidity. I can't be away from my dad for a full day, but I know some nice shorter trails. Do you mind if I invite a friend to come along?"

Tess didn't think her voice had betrayed her interest in Britt, but both Cara and Lenae snapped to attention.

"A friend? Or a girlfriend?" Cara asked.

"She's not a girlfriend," Lenae answered for Tess. "We never get to double-date with Tess."

"Just a friend," Tess insisted. "Her name is Britt. On my first day here, I went to the ocean in La Push and met her on the beach."

"And you hit on her," Cara said.

"You don't know…okay, I did, but she turned me down. She said she could tell I didn't want a serious relationship because I used a bunch of synonyms for the word *temporary* in just a few minutes of talking."

Lenae laughed and clapped her hands. "I like her already."

"Well, I'm glad someone thinks it's funny. I felt like an idiot. I was stressed about going to my parents' house and angry because I wasn't in Olympia, and…well, let's just say I didn't exude my regular level of finesse."

"Oh, please," Cara said. "I remember the first time I brought Lenae to meet you. You weren't exactly the model of sophistication with her. *Ooh, I'm so sexy. Come inside my lab and feel my killer whale teeth.*"

Tess was certain she hadn't said anything like what Cara claimed, but she did recall Cara threatening to fill her rubber boots with cement and drop her in the Sound if she made any moves on Lenae. "My voice does not sound like that," she protested.

"Pretty close," Lenae said with a grin. "But I thought you were sweet. So back to Britt. What happened next?"

"We went our separate ways, until I saw her again at a store in Forks."

"And you hit on her," Cara said wryly.

"No," Tess said, trying to inject a believable amount of disdain into her voice. Cara and Lenae just laughed harder. "Okay, I offered to be friends. She turned me down again. She's visiting from Seattle, trying to get some perspective on her job, and I assumed she'd be going back right away. Then I went to the marine center and talked to them about working with the offshore whales, and they suggested I apply for the grant. Turned out Brittany was the donor."

"How romantic," Cara said. "Well, besides the two rejections."

"How nonromantic," Tess corrected her. "We couldn't have any kind of a relationship, romantic or not, if I was applying for her grant."

"But now you're not in contention for it anymore," Lenae said.

"Exactly. So we can be friends. *Just* friends," she said when Cara opened her mouth, probably to call the situation romantic again, or to make another comment about Britt's rejections. "We got to know each other a little better during this whole grant process, and she's an interesting person. She used to work for a chemical plant, but she got tired of defending the damage they were doing to the environment. She wants to make changes, but she's trying to find a direction."

Tess left out most of the details of Britt's past, as well as the part about Tess's blowout at the diner. She'd let Britt share what she chose if she came with them tomorrow. She wasn't sure she agreed with Cara's assessment of their encounters as romantic. She wouldn't turn Brittany down if she offered more than friendship—in fact, she'd probably have most of her clothes off before Britt finished offering—but she also wasn't going to turn down the chance to be her friend. She was in uncharted waters with Brittany. Their relationship hadn't followed any of the paths of Tess's usual interactions, and she wasn't sure what would happen next. When she flirted with like-minded women, she *always* knew what would happen next. She was surprised by how much she wanted to take this next step, even if she couldn't see where she would land.

Cupcake came over to her chair and put her front paws on the seat, looking for some ankles to chew. Britt was going to love the dogs, but Tess knew Lenae could be very persuasive when she was on the hunt for volunteers. She'd smell Britt's desire to do good deeds a mile away, and then Britt would be living in a tiny house with an entire litter of Cupcakes to puppy walk. "Just a warning, Lenae. She's going through some tough shit right now, and she's sort of all over the place with causes she wants to support. Please don't do your volunteer voodoo on her."

"I would never take advantage of someone who is vulnerable," Lenae insisted, then she shrugged. "Although, if she has room in her expanding heart for one teeny black Lab, I might be tempted."

"You are not giving my puppy away," Cara said.

Lenae scratched Baxter under his chin. "Sorry, boy. I'll keep trying."

Chapter Seventeen

B ritt was already wearing a T-shirt and ribbed Henley, but she added a heavy flannel shirt and raincoat for insurance. For the first time in a solid week it wasn't pouring rain, and the heavy mist seemed like a welcome respite from the constant deluge. She sat on the ugly plaid couch and pulled on her boots.

Her routine of walks on the beach and lunches at the diner was supposed to be a temporary crutch, a scaffolding to support her days and give her the mental space she needed to think about her future. But it was rapidly turning into something permanent, and Britt was going to have to put an end to it soon.

She was sick of thinking about her future. Going round and round in circles inside her head. Her work at Randall had comprised tidy projects. Puzzles to solve and problems to tackle, each one wrapped up and completed once she figured out the correct formula or combination. The grant had given her a project to research, study, and finalize, but it would be finished on Monday. Britt would no longer have a real reason to stay in La Push, to be near Tess.

She'd decided to give the money to Tess for her killer whale research. She had agonized over the decision, determined to make sure she wasn't letting her interest in Tess as a person influence her rationality. Last night, though, as she sat bundled on her back porch, listening to the waves thump and splash below her, she had realized she was approaching the grant in the wrong way. She had initially set it up because she wanted to support someone who was passionately working to make a significant change in the world—the same type of work she longed to do herself. Tess was the obvious choice.

A knock on her door made her freeze. Since she'd been here, no one had knocked on her door. The housekeepers knew her schedule and performed their cursory cleaning of the cabin when she was out, and no one had visited her since Cammie. She hadn't noticed it before, but something as commonplace as having a person arrive on her doorstep had become strange and unexpected.

Another knock broke her out of her paralysis. She was supposed to answer now. She was heading across the room when she heard Tess's voice clearly through the thin walls.

"I know you're in there, Britt. The weird guys in the lodge said you don't leave for your walk for another three minutes."

Britt opened the door, unable to stop the wide grin from stretching across her face at the sight of Tess. Her dark hair was dotted with drops of mist, but her smile was all sunshine.

"Hey, Tess. Come in." Britt was slowly remembering the protocol for being a normal person. Answer knocks, invite people inside. When had she officially become a hermit?

Tess looked around, picking up objects as she walked. The book Britt was reading, the seal figurine. She stopped by the kitchen sink and admired the view.

"What a great location. I've always wanted to live right by the water. My apartment in Olympia looks out over the harbor, which is wonderful, but it's not the same as having the ocean this close, with the beat of waves and smell of seaweed."

She turned away from the window and leaned back against the kitchen counter. "I've come about the grant. I need to withdraw my proposal."

Britt was still adjusting to seeing Tess in her cabin. So close to the bed that it would only take a small push against her chest to move her over to it. Another gentle shove to make her sit down on the quilt so Britt could lean down and…

Whoa. Britt's fantasies dissipated abruptly once Tess's words registered in her mind. She didn't want the money? Was she going away? Britt dropped onto the bed, feeling as if the one stable part of her life had been knocked out from under her. "What? I was planning to tell you Monday, but I decided to give the money to the marine center. Why don't you want it anymore? What about your killer whales?"

Tess laughed and held up her hands. "I'm not abandoning them, don't worry. I really appreciate knowing we would have gotten the grant, but I just heard from Evergreen. They want to sponsor the research and have me write another book. The college doesn't want to share the limelight, so I can't accept money from another source." She frowned and took a step toward Britt. "I hope you're not upset or offended."

Britt managed to stand again on shaky legs and moved a few inches away from Tess. The strength of her reaction made her realize how much she had come to rely on having Tess in her life. "Are you kidding? This is good news."

"Especially for the wolf sanctuary, I'm guessing."

Britt nodded. She had been torn between the two applicants, but now both of them would be getting some much-needed financial help.

"I thought so." Tess paused. "You know, Britt, even though your money isn't going to the Center, none of this would have happened if I hadn't applied for your grant. You might not have a clear direction for yourself yet, but you're already making a difference."

"Thank you, Tess. And I'm really happy for you. I read *Fading Song*. Your writing style is lyrical and powerful, and I don't know how anyone could read it and not be inspired to do their part to protect the orcas. It's important for you to write another book." Britt *was* happy for Tess, but she felt wrapped in a fog of melancholy at the same time. The grant process was over. Even worse, her tenuous connection to Tess and her world was about to be severed.

"Great. So now we can be friends, right? And friends do things together, like hike through the rainforest?"

Or like having sex. Britt kept this other suggestion to herself, for now. With Cammie and the grant out of the picture, there was no reason to say no to Tess anymore, but Tess apparently had other activities in mind. "Sure, like going on hikes."

Tess pushed away from the counter and clapped her hands once, as if something had been settled between them. "Cool. Let's get going. Cara and Lenae are waiting for us in the car."

"What? Who…?"

"Cara is another professor at Evergreen. She came yesterday to give me the news about the book. Lenae is her partner. You'll love them, but I should maybe warn you about Cupcake…No, best not to mention her, but I'm glad you're wearing boots that cover your ankles."

"I'll need to stop by the lodge and cancel my Scrabble grudge match with Alec." Britt locked the cabin door and shoved the key into the pocket of her slicker.

"Alec must be the one who was muttering something about wiping the floor with you today," Tess said as they walked toward the main lodge.

"In his dreams. He'd better spend today reading the dictionary because he needs to learn some new words if he's going to beat me."

"So is this your new career plan? Are you going to become one of those old men who plays board games in the park?"

Britt laughed even though Tess was giving voice to her own concern that she would petrify in this place, following Alec and Jim from Scrabble at the lodge to dominoes at the store for the rest of her life.

She had reason to be worried, given her anxious reaction to the simple act of meeting new people. Once they finally got out of the lodge, Britt saw Tess's two friends wandering around the edge of the lot with their dogs. Well, one was wandering, and the other looked like she was a water-skier being towed behind a black puppy. Britt jolted to a halt.

"Are you okay?" Tess asked, retracing her steps to come back to Britt's side.

"Sure. I just haven't spent time with people my own age like this for weeks. My ex-girlfriend came to see me soon after I got here—well, like I said, she was my girlfriend when she arrived and my ex by the time she left—but other than her, I've been either alone or hanging out on the edge of local life. I guess I'm a little nervous," she admitted. Or a lot nervous. She had always been focused on school and science, and socializing had been a much lower priority, but now it was nonexistent in her life.

"It'll be fine," Tess said, taking her arm and urging her forward. "And if you decide you're not having a good time and want to come back to the cabin, well, we'll be in the middle of the wilderness, so you'll be out of luck."

"Comforting words," Britt said, playfully jostling Tess's shoulder.

"You'll enjoy the day. I even brought lunch for us. You do like American cheese sandwiches, don't you?"

Britt stopped again, and her face must have reflected her horror because Tess laughed. "I'm kidding. I brought good food. Uh-oh, prepare yourself."

The black Lab puppy was careening toward them, dragging a blond woman at the end of her leash. Tess's friend looked like she was only a sash and a swimsuit away from being a beauty pageant winner. Yeah, not intimidating at all.

The woman stumbled to a halt and stood with her hands on her knees, panting to catch her breath, while the puppy jumped on Britt and nearly knocked her down. She laughed and squatted down, smothered in licks and kisses.

"Britt, I'd like you to meet my friend Cara. And this tornado is Cupcake."

"Hey...nice to...meet you...sorry..." Cara waved in the direction of the frenzied pup.

"Nice to meet you, too."

"And this is Lenae, and Baxter."

Britt disentangled herself from the puppy and stood up again. Lenae was gorgeous, too, but not in the magazine-cover way of Cara. More reserved and understated. Her smile was warm, though, as she held out her hand for Britt to shake. "Hi, it's good to meet you."

At least Cupcake's antics kept all the formalities from feeling too stiff and awkward. Britt was silent through the process of piling into Tess's car—she got to sit in the front passenger seat, while Cara,

Lenae, and the dogs squished into the back—and the get-to-know you portion of the trip. Britt learned Cara produced a local television show and taught in the college's communications department. Lenae owned a guide dog training center. And Tess, of course, had her killer whales, book deals, and professorship.

Britt would normally have been confident in her own career. She had graduated at the top of every class from elementary to graduate school, and she had her pick of places to work once she was finished. She had always been driven and tightly focused. Now her interests were spreading, but shallow-thin, and she missed the security she had found in having a depth of knowledge in one field. She was designed to be a one-trick pony, not a jack-of-all-trades. She just needed to find a new trick.

After they had been driving for about fifteen minutes, everyone fell silent for a moment and she realized she hadn't spoken much since they had left La Push. She searched for something to add to the conversation, but settled instead on asking questions.

"Are we going into the Olympic State Park?"

"Yes. The rainforest zones are found in a series of valleys within the forest. We're going to the Hoh Valley, and the others are Bogachiel, Queets, and Quinault. Did you know that two-thirds of the world's temperate rainforest acres are in the Northwest?"

"No, I really don't know much about this type of ecosystem."

"It's a fascinating place to visit because you can see the different zones right next to each other. The valleys have steep sidewalls, and up there you'll find the Douglas firs and Pacific silver firs of the forest. In the valleys you'll find Sitka spruces and hemlocks."

Britt's comment about the ecosystem had the desired effect, and Tess spent the rest of the drive describing different types of trees and their individual moisture requirements. Britt allowed herself a few moments of peace, letting Tess manage the conversation, but soon she would need to step forward and speak for herself. She couldn't spend the rest of her life hiding in other people's shadows just because she was changing jobs.

Tess stopped when she got to a deserted parking strip and shut off the engine.

"We walk from here."

"What a relief," Cara said, getting out of the car and stretching. "Thanks for the lecture, Teach."

Tess frowned at Britt. "Did I sound like I was delivering a lecture?"

"Of course not. Well, sort of. But it was interesting, and I learned a lot about trees. I even remember most of it." Britt joked about Tess's long-winded description of the rainforest, but she secretly had enjoyed every second of her talk. Not because she cared much about Sitka spruces—even though she now knew more about them than she ever cared to know—but because she liked watching Tess's enthusiasm come to the surface. Her gestures and facial expressions were more pronounced, as if she could barely contain her excitement about fungi and old-growth fir trees.

Cara laughed as she snapped a long leash onto Cupcake's collar. "I zoned out for the whole drive. Say, Tess, you didn't really need the blanket you had in the back seat, did you?"

"I thought I did, but I assume my answer should be no. What did Cupcake do to it?"

"Nothing a little run through the washing machine won't fix."

Cara and Cupcake started down the trail, and Tess hurried after them, asking for more of an explanation about the blanket. Britt held back and walked with Lenae and Baxter, who made a much calmer and more collected exit from the car.

"Do you know how long this hike is?" Britt asked as the path wound through thick stands of trees, some too wide for her to encircle with her arms. She really needed to make a few statements and not just ask questions all day.

"Tess said the edge of the rainforest zone is about two miles along this path. We'll probably walk five total to get to the river where we'll have lunch and back again."

Britt had expected her and Baxter to set a leisurely pace, but they walked quickly, zipping around roots and embedded stones. She soon found a rhythm with their strides, though, and couldn't help but remember her hike at Cape Flattery when she had been ill-equipped, both mentally and in attire, to go traipsing through the woods. Weeks of beach walks had gotten her more functionally fit than gyms ever had, and she enjoyed the feeling of moving easily across the ground, even when the smooth entrance to the trail gave way to rougher going.

"Tess hasn't told us much about you," Lenae said after a few minutes of companionable silence. "She said you used to work at a chemical plant but became disillusioned with some of the practices you saw there. You're looking for a different direction to take now?"

She phrased the last sentence as a question, opening an opportunity for Britt to continue the story.

Britt smiled, appreciating the way Tess had protected Britt's private life, giving her the option of being as vague or forthcoming as she chose to be. She chose honesty. "Yes, but the search isn't going well. I've been researching other options, but all of them feel like I'd be putting on someone else's clothes. I can appreciate the work people like Tess are doing, but I haven't found anything to connect with like I did when I first discovered chemistry."

"What about using your schooling at another plant? Surely there are some that respect the environment more or are actively looking for ways to improve it."

"That was one of my first ideas," Britt said. The answer had seemed to be the easiest one. Why start a career from scratch when she could just redirect her previous knowledge and experience onto a new path? "I found some options, but nothing seemed right. Eventually, I'm just going to have to get a job instead of searching for a lightning-bolt arrival of an avocation. That's probably the direction I'll take if I can't decide on a better option."

"Don't settle too quickly. It's only been, what, a month or two?"

Britt nodded. "Yes," she said. "But I'm not sure what will vanish soonest, my bank account or my patience."

Lenae laughed. "Did Tess tell you I used to work in broadcasting? Not in front of the camera like Cara, but behind the scenes as a writer." She shuddered. "The field was terribly cutthroat and stressful, but I was very good at my job. I was terrified when I gave it up and started training my dogs."

"But you seem very good at this job, too."

Lenae shrugged. "I like to think I am, but in some ways, it doesn't come as naturally to me as writing did. I have to work harder at it, but the change in lifestyle saved me. Plus, I met my beloved Cara, who is plunging down the path toward us right now."

Britt caught the sound of snapping branches and hurrying footsteps seconds after Lenae did and just before Cupcake and Cara careened around a corner and into view.

Cara leaned against a tree while Cupcake jumped all over Baxter. He tolerated it with a stoic expression and a complete lack of involvement in the game.

"Whew. Came to see what was holding you two up. Hey, Britt, can you hold Cupcake for a sec?"

"Of course," Britt said. She took the leash and tried to unravel it from Baxter and his harness. She was rethinking her whole *adopt a black dog* idea, unless she could be sure the dog in question was going to be a calmer one.

"Thanks," Cara said. She started walking along the path again, pausing at the bend and waiting for Britt to catch up. Lenae mumbled something about finding Tess and hurried ahead of them with Baxter.

Britt aimed the puppy in the right direction, and Cara fell into step with her.

"I thought you wanted me to hold her while you tied your shoe or something," Britt said, climbing through a thick mass of ferns after Cupcake.

Cara laughed. "Sorry, but people have stopped saying yes if I ask them to lead her for a while. Tess didn't even fall for the *just a sec* comment."

Britt smiled. Did she always grin like this at just the thought of Tess or the mention of her name? She decided to take advantage of this chance to hear more about who Tess was outside of Forks. She had learned that Tess's casual-player image of herself was only a small part of who she was. "Have you known each other long?"

"We've been friends for five years now. No, six this September. Evergreen doesn't really have traditional classes like other colleges. They offer seminar-type courses focused on a single theme, and professors from a variety of departments teach them. Since Tess studies marine mammal communication, our disciplines naturally intersect. We became friends after teaching together."

Britt thought back to herself as a college student. "I can see the appeal of an interdisciplinary educational model now, but I would have hated it when I was in college. All I wanted to do was study chemistry, and I would have been annoyed if part of my class time was spent relating it to Greek mythology or psychology or whatever."

She switched the leash to her left hand and looked at her palm. "I think I'm getting a blister. I hope the person who eventually gets Cupcake as a guide dog has a thick pair of gloves."

Cara laughed. "Hold on to her long enough and the blisters become calluses. It doesn't hurt as much then. So you have more of an appreciation for big-picture learning now?"

Britt thought for a moment. "Maybe it's more of a recognition. I didn't look up from my test tubes long enough to see where different subjects intersected, but one day I did. I was testifying for my company and looking at the results of what we'd done, and I suddenly saw connections to the world beyond our plant where I hadn't before."

Cara stopped on the path and looked at her with an inscrutable expression.

"What?" Britt asked. "Are you about to yell at me for not coming out of the womb with an environmental conscience? Because Tess already did."

Cara laughed. "Tess," she said with a rueful shake of her head. "I love her, but she doesn't always filter well. No, I wasn't going to yell at you. Quite the opposite, in fact, because I was thinking how impressed I was by what you said."

"Impressed," Britt repeated with disbelief.

"Yes. You said *our plant* and *what we'd done.* A lot of people would separate themselves after having a revelation like yours, but you're taking ownership for where you were and where you're going now. I know Tess feels the same way about you, since I could hear the pride in her voice when she told us about you and the changes you're making. And if she yelled, it was probably because she was thinking about her killer whales at the time. She gets very emotional about the danger they're in, and she doesn't always know how to express it well."

Britt took a moment to find her voice. Cara had somehow identified the values Britt was trying to express in her new life. She wasn't sure if Tess really saw the same integrity in her as Cara seemed to, but she appreciated hearing it just the same. "You're very perceptive," she said.

Cara shrugged. "I have an appearance-conscious family and I work in television. In order to survive, I needed to learn how to look beyond the surface. That's one of the things I like most about Tess. She's one of the most genuine people I've ever met. She's exactly the same on the surface as she is deep down."

Cara glanced sideways at her when they started walking again, reaching over to take the leash from Britt's hands now that Cupcake was getting tired and more manageable. "She said you figured her out from the beginning, too."

Britt smiled at the memory of Tess asking her out the first time. She wasn't about to tell Cara how many times she had wished she could go back and say yes instead of no. "Is this where you warn me that Tess is a player? Or where you try to push us together like couples do with their single friends?"

Cara laughed. "You don't hold back, either, do you? Neither one. I wouldn't call her a player since she doesn't chase every woman she sees or have hundreds of one-night stands. She's more of a homebody than she lets on, and she spends a lot of time with friends. And she's actually very picky about the women she chooses to date. She just is very clear about what she wants from a relationship."

"No strings?" Britt asked. She had thought she wanted something more serious, something completely opposite of what Tess offered, but she wasn't sure anymore. Maybe the new Britt could handle something casual. She sighed, knowing she was still the same stability-loving Britt, even though she hadn't found a solid surface on which to build her life yet. The truth was, she wanted

Tess, and she was trying to rationalize her way into Tess's bed. But even though she was after a real relationship in the long term, she didn't think a short-term fling would necessarily be a bad idea as long as she went into it with her eyes wide open.

"No strings," Cara agreed. She hesitated. "You have to imagine what it was like for her to grow up here, in her traditional family. She's brilliant, fascinated by the world around her, compassionate. She was like a fast-moving river living in a glacial home. She refuses to be stifled like that ever again. Maybe someday she'll join another river permanently, and maybe she won't. Lenae and I would never try to get her to change. We just want her to be happy, and—No, Cupcake, stop!"

She tugged Cupcake out of the shrub where she was rolling in something decomposing and unrecognizable.

"At least her fur is dark enough to hide the muck," Cara said, gingerly stepping out of the undergrowth and back onto the path. "Don't tell Tess until we're back in Forks, or she won't let us in her car."

Britt pulled the collar of her flannel shirt over her nose and spoke with a muffled voice. "I won't say a word, although the smell is going to give you away. If you need someone to hold her while you tie your shoe, you're on your own."

CHAPTER EIGHTEEN

Tess had been worried about the way the trip to the rainforest started. She should have given Britt more than thirty seconds of notice, especially when she was inviting her to join a trio of people who had been friends for a long time. Britt had been friendly, but quiet at first, and Tess had nervously jumped on the topic of rainforest trees to take the pressure of conversation off her. She had intended to stick close to Britt on the trail, but Britt had seemed to slip into easy conversations with Lenae and then Cara, and Tess had given them space to get to know each other on a one-to-one level, rather than as a crowd of four. By the time they crossed into the rainforest and got to the river, Britt seemed like she had always been part of their group.

Tess leaned back against a fallen tree and relaxed. They had stayed in the shelter and relative dryness of the tree line while they ate lunch, but the river was close enough for them to hear the sound of its current and see the eddies and ripples on its surface. Behind them, along the path, a carpet of bracken ferns colored in muted autumn shades of yellow and brown filled the spaces between large coniferous trees and more delicate and yellowed vine maples. The spruces closest to them were a deep shade of green, almost black, but Tess could see more distant trees through their branches, and these were softened to a sea-foam green by a veil of misty fog.

"I can't tell if it's raining or not. It's just wet," Britt said, popping the last bite of her hummus, cucumber, and feta pita into her mouth with a happy-sounding sigh.

Tess grinned and pushed her hood farther back on her head. "I know. You get rain, fog from the ocean, and vapor condensing from the leaves and ground in the rainforest. Sometimes as much moisture is going up as is coming down."

"Maybe all this water will wash off whatever Cupcake was rolling in," Lenae said.

"Oh, yeah. I was hoping no one would notice," Cara said. "I'll rinse her off in the water fountain once we get back to the parking lot."

"There should be plenty of traffic on 101 since it's Saturday," Tess said, wrapping up their trash and stowing it in her backpack. "I'm sure the two of you won't have any problem hitching a ride."

"Cupcake is the second dog you've puppy walked, isn't she?" Britt asked.

"Yes. My first one was Pickwick." She sighed and looked toward the river. "Ah, Pickwick."

Tess and Lenae said, *Ah, Pickwick*, in exaggeratedly dreamy ways at the same time as Cara, and Britt laughed along. Cara threw fir cones at all three of them.

"It must be hard to give them to a new owner after getting attached," Britt said, with a sympathetic tone behind her laughter.

"I was sad, sure, but it was rewarding at the same time," Cara said. "You know it's going to happen and you can prepare for it, sort of like doctors caring about their patients while remaining somewhat detached."

Tess burst out laughing. "Please. You cried for *weeks*."

"I had to pry her fingers off the leash during his presentation ceremony," Lenae told Britt.

Cara crossed her arms over her chest. "Just for that, I'm not rinsing her off in the water fountain. The two of you will just have to suffer through the smell. Sorry, Britt."

Britt poked Tess in the leg with a stick. "So, you said hitchhiking is pretty easy around here? I might have to try it."

Tess got up and reached out her hand to help Britt to her feet. "Nonsense. You have shotgun. We'll just strap Cara and Cupcake to the top of the car."

Tess held Britt's hand a moment longer than necessary, but she finally let go. She took her time getting her small amount of gear together, until Lenae and Cara headed back to the car and she and Britt could have a little time together.

"Your friends are awesome," Britt said. "And lunch was great, too. Thank you for bringing me along today."

"I'd hate to have you miss seeing the rainforest while you're here." Tess veered toward her and bumped her shoulder before moving away again. "And I wanted to spend more time with you."

"Oh, how sweet." Britt smiled and reached over, pushing Tess a few steps off the path and into a fern.

Tess laughed and brushed a stray frond off her jeans.

"Have you told your parents you'll be staying in Forks longer?"

Tess groaned. She hadn't gotten around to telling them yet, but she knew exactly how her predictable family would react. She would bet every cent she had that her mom would cry and clutch Tess to her in a five-minute hug. Her dad would say something noncommittal like *huh* or *okay*, never once taking his eyes off the TV screen. And Kelly would say something snarky and the two of them would snipe at each other, because that's what they always did. It was only going to annoy her when everyone did exactly what she expected them to.

They would be happy, though. A month ago, Tess wouldn't have believed it, but now she did. She wasn't sure how to react to her family now that she realized that her need for distance from them was one-sided.

"Not yet. As soon as my dad is healed enough for me to go, I'll probably rent a place closer to the Center. And farther from them."

Britt rested her hand on Tess's arm. "I'm sorry," she said.

Tess leaned into her touch. Even though she had only voiced part of her thoughts, Britt seemed to have noticed the emotions underneath the simple words. "We're surviving. What about you? Any horror stories from childhood?"

"Nothing worthy of a Lifetime movie. My parents got divorced when I was young, and my dad raised me. He's the quintessential absentminded professor, and I used to joke that I raised him and not the other way around."

Britt and Tess had to walk single file around some roots, and Britt let go of her arm as they navigated the short maze. Tess missed the contact between them but couldn't think of an excuse to renew it once they were walking side by side again.

"He's a theoretical mathematician, and I got my ability to focus and my love of science from him. My mom was a dancer and now is a choreographer. I didn't get anything from her."

Tess smiled. Britt's description of her parents and her assessment of herself was illuminating. She seemed to believe she was one-dimensional, but as her attention to the world around her expanded beyond the flat plane of single-minded focus, she would hopefully begin to see just how much substance she had to offer as a person. "You have more artist in you than you think, Britt. It shows in the way you connect concepts together and in the way you're beginning to value the natural world."

"Thank you. I guess I never saw it like that."

Britt was quiet for a moment, and Tess waited before she asked another question. "Do you still keep in touch with them?"

"I talk to Mom once a month or so, but I haven't called her since I came to La Push. I guess I didn't think she'd understand what I was going through, but maybe she will. Dad certainly doesn't. He tries to be supportive, but he can't comprehend the idea of giving up his math. It makes it difficult for him to sympathize with what I'm feeling, and he's kind of confused by the whole process." Britt gave a flat laugh, devoid of humor. "So am I, though, so I can't fault him for it."

"You'll figure it out," Tess said. "In the meantime, try to enjoy the process."

"That's the kind of thing people say when the process is miserable. It's like saying something will build character." Britt smiled, though, and the back of her hand brushed against Tess's when she skirted around a fallen tree partially blocking their path. Tess wasn't sure if it was intentional or accidental. "Speaking of building character, are you getting along with your dad all right?"

Tess was concentrating on the way she could still feel vibrations where Britt's skin had touched hers, even though they had moved apart again. Even a conversation about her dad wasn't enough to ruin the way she felt. She shrugged. "I am. We'll never be close, but at least we're not screaming at each other like we used to do."

Britt was quiet, watching Tess with a sideways glance.

"Go ahead and ask what's on your mind," Tess said. She usually disliked prolonged chats about her family, preferring to answer any unwelcome questions with monosyllables, but she didn't mind allowing Britt to see more of her than most people did.

"You caught me," Britt said with a smile. "I was just wondering whether you fought so much with your dad because the two of you are alike or different."

"I've been thinking about the same thing," Tess said, surprised to hear Britt voice the question she would never have asked when she was younger. "If you had asked me that when I was fifteen, I would have said we argue because we're absolute opposites. And I would probably have added some obscenities and thrown a few plates against a wall for good measure," she admitted. "I was a bit volatile when I was young."

"No," Britt exclaimed with an exaggerated expression of shock. "You're so mellow now, it's hard to believe."

"Ha ha. Trust me, though. I was the ultimate angsty teenager. You would have hated me if we'd met back then."

Britt tried to deny it, but Tess could see she thought the assessment was probably right. "Were you disruptive in class? I never liked it when undisciplined kids interrupted lessons."

"I would have annoyed the crap out of you, then. But once I realized my best option for getting out of the house was to study hard and get myself to college, you would have liked me again."

"You're very sure of yourself."

"Hey, I'm irresistible. Why pretend otherwise?" Tess laughed, although she sometimes felt that everything she had been certain was truth in Olympia was being challenged here on the Peninsula. By Britt, by her family. "Back to your question. Since I've been back in the Forks house, I've started to understand that when you wade through all the differences between me and my dad—in values, tastes, ways of looking at the world, *everything*—we're much more similar than I ever would have accepted in the past. I think one of the reasons I've been able to be back in that house without too much drama is because I understand how difficult it would be to need him like he needs me now."

"Personal growth. It's character building."

Tess grinned. "Yes, I'm really enjoying the process."

"So what were some of your arguments about?"

"The list could provide conversational fodder for the rest of the hike," Tess said. She was surprised, though, at the lack of bitterness behind her words. Usually she felt an acrid taste in her mouth when she talked about her family, but somehow the gentle scent of Britt's citrusy shampoo, heightened in the humid air around them, made her feel clean instead. "The main issue was logging. It's how he made a paycheck, and he always accused me of being ungrateful when I went on my tirades about how awful it was for the environment."

"I can understand how he would feel, I guess. He's paying the bills and raising you while you're criticizing the work he does." Britt grabbed Tess's hand and gave it a quick squeeze before letting go. "Not that I don't agree with you or am challenging your right to have said what you did."

"No, you're right. I was a pompous ass at times, but I stand by the arguments I made against heavy deforestation. We really didn't stand a chance of bonding with such a major issue driving us apart. Now we ignore the topic completely, but at least we're civil with each other."

"I suppose that's all you can expect sometimes. I'm sure it's easier on your mom this way."

Tess exhaled with a puff of breath. Her mom's frailty had scared her enough that she would have left the house for Edith's sake if she and her dad hadn't found their way to a truce. "Much easier. When I first got here, she seemed on edge all the time, like she was happy to have me back in the house, but expecting me and Dad to explode at any moment. She's been much more at ease lately."

"It was horrible to see all those clear-cut areas we passed on the way here," Britt said, returning to the topic of logging. "I'm glad some of them are replanted, though."

Tess tried to make a sound of noncommittal agreement, but it came out sounding like she was being strangled.

Britt stopped and put her hands on her hips. "Go ahead," she said. "You know you want to."

"Want to what?" Tess asked, laughing in spite of Britt's stern expression.

"Deliver a lecture on the evils of reforestation. Go ahead. Educate me."

Tess frowned. "I never want to treat you like I think you're uneducated. I know you got your doctorate from Northwestern and that you know more about chemistry than I ever will. And probably most other subjects."

Britt rolled her eyes. "I know, Tess. I don't feel as if you're talking down to me, and I would call you on it if you did." She paused, and her impish smile returned. "Did you google me?"

"Maybe. Changing the subject now." Tess felt her cheeks flush, but she hoped her raincoat's hood would hide it. She had used the excuse of the grant to search online for anything she could find about Brittany James.

"Look at this," she said, determined to keep Britt from teasing her more about her internet search. She brushed carefully past a huge fern and stopped next to a massive fallen tree. "When thousands of trees are planted in a clear-cut area at the same time, destined to be chopped down when they're only about forty years old, you won't find anything this magnificent among them."

"Um, I'm looking at a big, dead tree trunk. What are you seeing?"

"Physically, it's a tree carcass, you're right. But it's also a highway for animals and insects. It releases nutrients into the ground and replenishes the soil for other plants. It might be a home for woodpeckers and carpenter ants. And it's a nurse log." Tess gently moved clumps of moss until she found a dainty green shoot. Britt pressed close to her side, nearly derailing Tess's train of thought. She clung to her description of the log as a lifeline to keep herself from drowning in imagined kisses she and Britt would probably never share. "See this tiny sprout? It's a germinated spruce that will feed off the log and possibly reach the ground if it survives long enough for the log under it to decay."

She could have droned on for another hour, describing the marvels of the dead log, but she faltered to a stop. Britt stood next to her, shaking her head slowly.

"I love this moment," Britt said, her voice hushed. "Like when you showed me the killer whale photos and at first they looked the same, but then the individual whales stood out. And here, I only saw a fallen tree, but now I see all the life it supports."

Tess put her fingertips under Britt's chin and turned her head so they were looking at each other. "Or when you sat in the courtroom looking at the types of photos you had been shown numerous times before, and suddenly you really saw what they represented."

She brushed her thumbs under Britt's eyes, not sure if the moisture she felt was from the rain or tears. "What happened to you back in Seattle, and what you're going through now—they're beautiful things, Britt. They're going to make you very strong and influential, whatever direction you decide to take."

Should she kiss her? Yes…no…yes, *just try*. Tess was caught in her indecision when she heard Cara's voice calling for them from a mere few feet away.

"They're over here, Lenae. Making out by a dead tree. Very romantic."

Britt laughed and stepped back. "Well, that kills the mood."

"Remind me to leave them at home next time," Tess said as they emerged from the forest. She was about to hurry to catch up with Cara, Lenae, and the dogs when Britt grabbed her arm and held her back.

"I was thinking…maybe we could go on a date sometime? If you want to," she said, speaking rapidly and not meeting Tess's gaze.

"I want to," Tess said. Britt smiled at her and turned, jogging toward Cara.

"Very much," Tess added in a quiet voice no one was around to hear.

Chapter Nineteen

B ritt paced back and forth in her cabin, impatiently waiting until it was time to pick up Tess for their date. Seven steps, from wall to wall. Not much chance to burn off nervous energy. The winds were too strong for a walk on the beach, unless she wanted to arrive in Forks looking like a castaway who had just washed up on shore. She had tried distracting herself by hanging out in the lobby, but Alec had teased her relentlessly until she couldn't take it anymore. She had used Jim's tiles to spell *F-J-O-R-D* with a triple letter score for the *J* and stormed back to her cabin.

She stopped pacing and stood in front of her closet. She couldn't even do the clichéd first date move of changing her outfit several times while she decided what to wear. She still hadn't brought her old clothes out of storage, and she had a limited number of recently purchased options from which to choose, so no chance of helping time pass in that area.

Britt flopped onto the sofa with a sigh. She was anxious to see Tess again, even though it had only been three days since their hike in the rainforest. Everything had seemed to change between them, although the only evidence of the transformation was contained in the few words she had used to ask Tess on a date. During the past few days, in between her visits to the wolf sanctuary and the heated Scrabble matches between her and Alec, she had slipped back into the comforting habit of making lists. *Where to go on our date* was depressingly sparse, as was *What to wear*. She had thought about writing some conversation starters—a trick she had often used before office parties when she'd gotten out of college and started working in the real world—but this was Tess. They had never had trouble talking to each other, and if there was a lull in the conversation, Britt could easily come up with a question that would launch a Tess Talk. *Paper or plastic? What are your thoughts on recycling?*

The most interesting and revelatory list was the one Britt had made as she struggled to analyze her change in heart. Her attraction to Tess had been constant from the first meeting, as had Tess's admission of a lack of interest in pursuing a long-term relationship, so why had she suddenly felt right about asking her out?

One significant addition to her list was the realization that she would be the first to leave the Peninsula. She had assumed Tess—who was the one determined to keep things casual—would go when she was ready, and Britt would be left behind. But Britt had sat on the damp ground near the river and listened to Tess and Cara make plans for seminars they would teach together in the spring and summer. Tess, although she had been planning to go home to Olympia as soon as her dad was better, was now going to stay in the area. Britt still wasn't sure where she'd go next, but she certainly wasn't planning to stay in La Push beyond the new year. If she hadn't made a life decision by then, she would travel to another spot, maybe in an unfamiliar city this time, and continue her Quest for a Meaningful Life. She would go and leave Tess behind, and this realization made her feel as if they were on equal footing, both transients in this place, with one foot already on the path leading them away from each other.

The other reasons were less easy to verbalize, but still important. Seeing Tess with her friends, watching her soak up the atmosphere of the wolf sanctuary, and spending time talking with her in a social, unprofessional setting had given Britt a more dimensional view of her, and not just a flat and unreliable physical interest in Tess's gorgeous body and eyes. Britt had come to appreciate the qualities that made her a person, from her intelligence to her bullheadedness. Her perception of their potential relationship shifted along with her growing desire for Tess—for *all* of Tess. Even if their relationship wasn't destined to be a long-lasting one, it no longer had any hint of superficiality to it.

Britt checked the time on her phone and got up to leave. She'd get to the Forks diner where she was meeting Tess and have a cup of coffee while she waited for her to finish taking care of her father. She drove along the road from La Push to Forks, by now familiar with every inch of the winding highway. She hadn't been fazed when Tess asked to meet her in town instead of having Britt come to her parents' house. She was having a difficult time relating to her mom and dad as it was, and Britt understood why she wouldn't want to add another person to the mix. It wasn't like she was going to become a permanent fixture at family gatherings.

Britt pulled into the parking lot, surprised to see Tess already there and waiting for her. Early. Britt smiled, warmed by knowing Tess was looking forward to being with her, too.

Tess had been sitting in her car, but she got out and jumped into the passenger seat of Britt's car. Even the short time outside had drenched her, and Britt cranked up her car's powerful heater. "It's raining harder here than it was by the ocean."

"It's Forks. What do you expect?" Tess asked, shaking her head and spraying Britt with water.

"Stop that," Britt said, laughing and holding up her hands to shield herself. She put the car in gear and backed out of the parking place. "So Forks is the cause of all evils in the world?"

"Yes. At least the evils of constant downpours and eternal boredom." Tess nestled into her seat and sighed. "Your gas-guzzling, foreign-made car is exceptionally comfortable."

"Remember this next time, when I pick you up on a Vespa. I should get a good trade-in deal." She accelerated once they were outside the city limits, heading south. She considered taking Tess's hand, then thought better of it. Then changed her mind again. She sighed, annoyed with the indecisiveness that seemed to follow her everywhere. At least she had suggested this date without hovering in the realm of doubt.

Tess shifted a little closer and dragged her index finger down the back of Britt's hand where it rested on the steering wheel. "You still haven't told me where we're going."

Britt had to forcefully make herself focus on the road ahead and not on the warmth in her belly when Tess touched her. She reached over and took Tess's hand.

"A new restaurant in Kalaloch. Jim and Alec recommended it."

Tess interlaced her fingers with Britt's and laughed. "You're taking dating advice from the Scrabble playing guys?"

"And dominoes. They play dominoes, too, so they know what they're talking about."

"You can't argue with those credentials."

Britt grinned. "Alec also said you should be warned to keep an eye on your wallet around me. He's decided I'm morally bankrupt since I helped Jim with a Scrabble word the first time we met."

"A good word?"

"A triple word score with a *V*."

"Wow. That's an arrestable offense in Clallam County. We take our Scrabble playing very seriously."

Britt laughed, relaxing into comfortable banter with Tess as they made the forty-minute drive to Kalaloch. She felt an unaccustomed lightness inside, and it took her almost ten miles to put a name to it. Contentment. She had felt moments of happiness while she had been in La Push, and she had spent time laughing and marveling at the beauty of the place. But underlying everything had been a constant hum of low-level anxiety. What if she had made the wrong choice in coming here? What if she made another wrong choice going forward? For the first time since her frantic escape from Seattle, she felt content in the present and momentarily free from concern about the past and future.

Britt hadn't been to Kalaloch or Ruby Beach yet, but after driving along the coastline to their restaurant, she was determined to come back sometime when the weather was clear. Or at least rainy without quite as much wind as they had today. She parked by the restaurant—unimaginatively named the Kalaloch Restaurant—and reluctantly let go of Tess's hand as they ran for the door.

"It must have taken them weeks to come up with this name," Tess whispered as they followed the hostess to their table.

"I can imagine all the brainstorming sessions, with heated debates over names like the Kalaloch Eatery or the Restaurant de Kalaloch."

"Chez Kalaloch," Tess suggested when they were seated.

Britt laughed and picked up her menu. The tagline at the top promised local, seasonal offerings. Not a grilled cheese sandwich in sight.

"This looks amazing," Tess said. "My compliments to the old dudes."

"They're quite savvy, those two," Britt said. She took a sip of her water and exhaled softly at the view. The entire oceanfront wall was curved and filled with large windows. The sandy beach stretched off to the south, unbroken except for random, massive basalt formations that Britt thought might be accessible at low tide. On the north side of the panoramic view was the mouth of a large creek. The deep twists and turns of the waterway were lined with tangled piles of weathered driftwood trunks, their circles of roots worn to a powdery gray finish. The clouds were still dark and angry looking, but they had bunched together in clumps, exposing ribbons of pale blue sky around them. The setting sun was hidden behind one of the cloud masses, and thick rays formed a halo around it.

Britt was startled out of her admiration of the view by their server's voice, asking if they wanted to start with a drink.

"Wine?" Tess asked.

Britt nodded. "Only if it's red. Can you suggest something local?" she asked the server.

He pointed at one of the offerings on her wine menu. "The Olympic Cellars Syrah is one of my favorites. It pairs well with just about everything on the menu."

"The winery is owned by three women," Tess said. "I went to a tasting there once with Cara when she was doing an episode on Olympic Peninsula wineries. It's right on the highway, so you passed it on your way from Seattle."

Britt tried to recall any landmarks she had spotted on the drive, but she couldn't. "I didn't even notice it," she said. "I only remember seeing the broken yellow lines of the highway dividers. I just kept following them." Broken.

They chatted about nothing in particular until after they had given their orders. Then Tess sat back in her chair and toyed with her wineglass.

"Do you mind if I ask what happened with your ex?"

Britt shook her head. "Not at all. I guess the easy answer is, she wasn't willing to put up with all this." Britt punctuated the *all this* by making vague circles in the air with her hands. Quitting her job, running away from home, and holing up in the desolate town of La Push, all condensed into a tiny gesture. "She didn't seem to mind me wanting to do something different with my life, but she didn't understand why I had to come here to think. But I had to, otherwise I would have lost my conviction and would have gone back to work after stewing at home for a few days."

Maybe she would have run away again after her next court case, or maybe she would have sublimated all her newfound feelings and would have spent the rest of her life knowing something precious had died inside her, like the tiny bird in the photo. She had only known that she had to be far away from the temptation. Cammie hadn't understood.

"When we talked on the beach the first day we met, I thought you sounded hesitant when you said you had a girlfriend. Like you had a question mark in your mind about her."

"I heard the same thing in my own voice," Britt admitted. "Cammie and I had been dating awhile, and we got along fine. No big fights or conflicts. We enjoyed similar things, had friends in common, all that. But even before I called her from Neah Bay, I had a suspicion she wouldn't be part of my future any more than my old job would be. I think a couple needs more depth of commitment and love to be able to get through a major change together. And from the start, I knew I would choose the journey I was taking over her, if I was forced to pick one."

Britt took a drink of her wine, hearing the truth of her words even though she hadn't realized it at the time. She had felt completely lost when she got to La Push, and making decisions had felt like slogging through quicksand. But even though she had considered going back to her old life, some small part of her had been determined to march forward.

"You know how it is when you're separated from people you love, but you know they're always close to you? Cammie never was here with me. She came to visit the one time, and I hoped having her actually come to La Push would help me establish more of a connection so I'd be able to hold her in my mind, but she just skimmed the surface, said good-bye, and was gone again."

"Do you miss her?"

"No," Britt answered without hesitation, although her quickness made her feel guilty. "I mean…well, I really do mean no. Once she left, she vanished from my mind. I feel awful for saying it, but I guess it only proves we didn't have a solid relationship from the start."

Tess didn't answer, but Britt could see her trying to hide a smile by taking a drink of wine.

"Stop looking so smug," she said. She paused while their food was set in front of them. "It's my turn to ask a question."

"I'm an open book," Tess said, spreading her arms wide. "You might not like what's written on the pages, but you won't find any fiction there."

Britt laughed. "For someone who claims to be comfortable with the whole casual dating bit, you take on a very defensive tone whenever it's brought up. Now tell me about the stories on those pages of yours. Not the details, please, but just the general theme."

Tess cut off a piece of batter-dipped fish and dunked it in tartar sauce. She chewed and swallowed before answering—making a blissful sound of contentment as she ate that made Britt's insides wiggle like a jellyfish.

"This is delicious," Tess said. "So, my dating life is pretty simple. I enjoy the company of intelligent, attractive women, but I'm not interested in tying myself down in a relationship. The routines, the expectations, the inevitable boredom you feel after spending a lot of time with one person. None of it sounds appealing. I make sure I'm clear about it from the start." She gave Britt her usual sheepish, lopsided grin. "I usually try to be more tactful about it than I was with you when we met. It was a tough day."

"Yes, it was," Britt said. She heard the words Tess was saying, but she was starting to see some of the currents deep under them. She changed the subject, for a moment.

"Who the hell eats fish and chips with a knife and fork?" she asked, trying to conceal the effect Tess's obvious ecstasy over her food was causing to Britt's insides.

Tess looked around them and leaned across the table. "It's a nice restaurant. Do you want me to shovel the food in my mouth using my hands like a barbarian?"

Britt laughed. "Yes. It's fish and chips."

Tess shook her head and stabbed a french fry with her fork. "Why are you using silverware? Wouldn't you rather cram wads of food into your mouth with your hands?"

Britt kicked Tess playfully under the table, starting a minor skirmish that lasted until the woman across the aisle gave them a glare. She ate some of her salad, crunching through hazelnuts and greens with pleasure, enjoying the respite from soft grilled cheeses. Warm, sweet pieces of roasted acorn squash added another interesting texture.

"I liked Cara," she said. "You've been friends for six years?"

"Yeah, she's great." Tess happily accepted the supposed change in subject. "She met Lenae about two years ago, and the three of us have been friends since then."

"Do you spend a lot of time with the two of them?"

"We have dinner together most Sunday nights, and they always rope me into going to their theme nights. Book clubs, bridge games, that sort of thing. They come up with something new every month or so, and of course I have to go, no matter what it is."

Tess was grinning as she used a fry to scoop out the last of her tartar sauce. "The last one before I came here was Pictionary night. She and Lenae were a team, and they drew the clues on each other's arms with fingers. They destroyed the rest of us. I was very careful not to ask how they got so good at doing that." She arranged her fork and knife neatly on the edge of her plate. "I see Cara at school and at the lab, too. We team teach, so we spend a lot of time together preparing for classes."

"Oh, my," Britt said. "You must be about ready to look for new friends, then."

Tess snapped her attention from watching the sunset to staring at Britt. "What do you mean?"

Britt drank the last of her wine and gestured with the empty glass. "All those routines and expectations. Not to mention the inevitable boredom. You must be getting tired of all those strings."

Tess looked stunned for a moment, and then she laughed, waggling her finger at Britt. "You're a cunning one, Brittany James. I'm going to have to get together with Alec later and compare notes. He's the only other person who is aware of your deviousness. But having a friend is not the same as having a partner."

Britt was going to ask how it was different, but she could see she had proved her point. She gracefully let the matter drop and they talked about inconsequential things as they paid the check and drove back to Forks. Somehow, though, inconsequential things took on new meaning after they had shared more serious thoughts.

Britt parked next to Tess's car and they sat in silence for a minute, with the raindrops beating a steady rhythm on the car. She reached over with barely any internal debate and held Tess's hand.

Tess turned toward her, cupping her cheek in her right hand—Tess's left still tightly holding Britt's—and slowly trailed her fingers across Britt's temple, and down along her jawline. Tess watched her fingers as they moved lower, and Britt wasn't sure if Tess's touch or her gaze was causing the most commotion in the nerve endings just below the surface of her skin.

Tess grazed the edge of Britt's top, fiddling with the fabric, dipping slightly under the edge of the shirt and back to the outer surface of it. Britt rested her left hand on Tess's thigh and leaned toward her. At the first touch of Tess's lips against hers, Britt involuntarily closed her hand, gripping the inner thigh of Tess's jeans and making her gasp against Britt's mouth.

One moment the kiss was barely there—two sets of lips hovering close, occasionally coming into contact with brief bumps and strokes—and the next moment, Tess's mouth was fully against hers, and Britt felt an ache growing inside. Mingled pleasure from the friction of tongues and teeth tempered by the steady, pulsing desire for *more*. And always, always, the anchoring sensation of Tess's hand still tightly holding her own.

They broke apart, resting their foreheads together and both panting slightly, even though the kiss had been gentle.

"Come with me to Thanksgiving dinner at my parents' house," Tess said, her voice barely above a whisper.

Britt gave a burst of laughter, then covered her mouth quickly. "Sorry. I think that would have been the sentence I least expected to hear from you." Before she really got to know Tess, she might have expected to hear a trite and generic pickup line obviously used on every woman Tess met, or another awkward proposition. After spending time with her, she thought she'd hear something heartfelt and intimate. Apparently, there were more layers to Tess Hansen than Britt had uncovered, because she was a continual surprise.

Tess swiped a hand through her hair, making the curls go every which way. "It wasn't the first thing I expected to say, either."

Britt smiled, still reeling from the kiss, but slowly coming down to earth. She smoothed out Tess's hair, lingering in the softness. "Don't worry, I won't hold you to it."

"No, I wanted to ask you, just not right after…" She gestured back and forth between them.

Thanksgiving at the Hansen house? Unexpected, yes, but something in Tess's expression convinced her to go. She probably needed support, plus a stranger in the room to encourage everyone to keep peace on the holiday. Britt realized with a jolt that the words Tess had spoken were probably the most intimate ones she could have said, even more than anything sexual or romantic. Her family life was painful and deeply personal, and she had just invited Britt inside. She couldn't do anything other than accept the invitation, recognizing it for all it meant.

"All right. I'll go."

❖

Tess sat in her car long after she reached her parents' driveway. She didn't have a set of rules about dating, but if she had written one in August it would have included *Don't introduce her into your circle of friends* and *Absolutely do not invite her to Thanksgiving dinner with your family. In fact, why are* you *having Thanksgiving dinner with your family?*

She finally got out of the car and walked toward the dark house. Even if she had written a set of rules, she would have tossed them out once she met Britt. She was starting to feel as if she was in uncharted waters, ready to throw away her usual map and draw a completely new one. Unfortunately, the one time she wasn't afraid to let even the smallest possibility of a future enter a relationship, neither one of them was sure what lay ahead. She was stuck here for an indeterminate number of months, and Britt's next steps were completely unknown.

Tess checked on her dad and found him sound asleep, so she continued up the steps to her old room. She lay down on the bed, still wearing her rain-dampened clothes, and stared at the ceiling as she replayed every nanosecond of their kiss. It hadn't been a long one—asking Britt to Thanksgiving with her parents had been kind of a mood killer—but its intensity more than made up for duration. Tess's kisses in the past had varied from okay to spectacular, but they had always felt like pockets of time when she was temporarily sharing physical closeness with someone. When she kissed Britt, it was as if everything was right there with them—Britt's sense of humor, her expressions of delight when she learned something new, her kindness. Tess hadn't been just kissing a woman, she had been kissing *Britt*. All of her.

And for the first time in her life, Tess wanted even more.

CHAPTER TWENTY

Tess was in the kitchen holding a pan of gravy when Britt got to the house. Kelly called out that she would answer the door while Tess frantically searched for some empty counter space where she could deposit the scalding hot dish.

She finally managed to extricate herself from the kitchen and nearly tripped over Justin, who was aiming for his mother. Both Kelly and Tess's mom had met Britt at the door, and she looked a little overwhelmed by the mob greeting until she looked up and noticed Tess standing a little apart from the rest of her family. Then she smiled, with the same smile she had worn when she picked out individual whales from the photographs for the first time, or when she had really seen the new life springing from the fallen tree.

Tess was falling in love with her.

She wanted to run upstairs and hide in her room so no one—especially Britt—would recognize the emotion in her expression until she figured out what to do with her feelings, either how to make them stop or how to stand back and let them grow.

For the moment, she just needed to try to hide them. She walked over to Britt and gave her a quick and friendly kiss on the cheek. Britt blushed—maybe the kiss had been a little more lingering and a little less friend-like than Tess had intended—and handed her a ceramic dish.

"I brought candied yams," she said. "It's one of the few things my dad can cook, so we had them every Thanksgiving. For most of my childhood, I had macaroni and cheese almost every night except for a full week of candied yams in November."

Britt winced at Tess with a *Save me, I'm rambling!* expression, and Tess was about to suggest they go to her room or out for a walk.

"They smell wonderful, dear," her mom said, putting an end to her plan for some time alone with Britt. "Now, why don't I introduce you to Tess's dad while she puts those yams in the oven to keep warm."

"Um, okay, Edith."

Tess stood in the living room and stared after them, unsure what to do. Born-again activist Britt and her logger father. Yeah, nothing could go wrong with that combination.

"The oven is this way," Kelly said, jabbing her in the arm and pointing toward the kitchen. Her expression softened, and she shoved Tess a little more gently in the right direction. "Your girlfriend will be fine, and you said you'd mash the potatoes."

Tess reluctantly followed her. Her mom came back to the kitchen a few moments later, and between her and Kelly, Tess couldn't get away. She mashed potatoes, drained green beans, and tossed a salad before she was able to rush down the hall to Britt's rescue. Or her dad's. She wasn't sure which.

As she approached the door, she heard the usual background noise of her dad's favorite video game, and then Britt's voice raised above the laser fire.

"Seriously, you have no idea what you're talking about. You're wrong, and I'll prove it."

Tess launched into the room and saw Britt perched on the bed next to her father, holding his game controller.

"See? You needed to pick up the antigravity boots back in level eighteen, but you can't use them until your dragon hatches in level twenty-one. You need to crush the discarded shell fragments and use them for traction."

Britt glanced away from the television and saw her standing in the doorway. "Oh, hey, Tess. Your dad is such a noob."

She playfully—and very gently—pushed him in the arm. He took advantage of her distraction and grabbed the controller.

"Britt showed me an entire planet I could have visited three levels ago. Do you realize how much platinum I could find there?"

Britt stood up and came over to Tess's side. "You keep practicing, Roland. Let me know when you get to level twenty-nine, and I'll show you how to make a fireproof shield out of the bucket you picked up in level six." She put her hands on her hips and gave him a stern look. "You did take the bucket out of the well in level six, didn't you?"

"No, damn it."

Tess paused once they were in the hallway, on a tiny island of privacy sandwiched between the sound of television and her mom's and Kelly's voices. She stepped closer to Britt, until she could feel the warmth of her, but not quite near enough to touch.

"He likes you," she said in disbelief.

"Gee, you sound so surprised. I'm flattered," Britt said, laughing and placing her hand on Tess's jaw. "You've got some sort of pulsing thing going on here. Just relax."

She rubbed the tension out of Tess's clenched jaw and slowly moved until she was massaging the sensitive area where her neck and shoulder met. Tess's tension was draining away under Britt's touch, replaced by a slow wave of arousal.

She rested her hands on Britt's hips and pulled her closer until their bodies were in contact from thighs to breasts. "I'm not surprised because of you, but because of me. I never imagined I would bring a..." Tess hesitated. Kelly had used the word *girlfriend*, and Tess hadn't minded. She didn't know how Britt would react, though. "A woman here that he would approve of."

"Sometimes the point is just to get along peacefully for an evening, not to come to an agreement about the meaning of life." Britt laid her palms flat against Tess's chest, just below her collarbones. "Maybe let him teach you how to play his video game sometime. The two of you will probably never bond on a deep philosophical level, but you can still connect in little ways."

Tess wasn't sure about turning water buckets into shields, but she got the point. Her alternative was to go back to Olympia when she was done with her research and lose contact with her family again. That had been her intention from the start, but she wasn't convinced it was still what she wanted. She sighed and wrapped her arms around Britt's waist, hugging her close.

"It's funny," she said, her breath ruffling Britt's hair as she spoke. "When we first met, you seemed like the lost soul, and I was positive I had life all figured out. I'm starting to wonder if I was the lost one."

Britt laughed, and Tess felt the gentle vibrations move through her. "I'm probably a bad influence on you, with all my indecision and doubt."

Tess held Britt's shoulders and moved her a few inches away so she could look her in the eyes. "Exactly the opposite. No matter what you decide to do next, you'll always be the type of person who is constantly asking questions, wanting to dig deeper and learn more. You helped me realize that I needed to ask some questions myself."

Kelly cleared her throat to get their attention, and Britt jumped backward and out of Tess's arms.

"We're ready to eat, Tess. Can you get Dad to the table?" Kelly made a shooing motion at her—apparently meaning for Tess to get moving—and disappeared into the kitchen again.

"I'll help get the food out," Britt said, ducking around Tess.

Tess caught her arm before she got too far away. "Everything but the gravy is vegetarian," she said. "Well, and the turkey."

Britt smiled her thanks before walking away. Tess went back into her dad's room.

"How do I get away from these trolls?" he asked without turning away from the screen. "They have magic bicycles and I can't run fast enough."

"I have no idea," Tess said.

He looked over at her. "Oh, I thought you were Britt. I'll ask her about the trolls at dinner."

He paused the game and started to shift his legs off the bed. Tess went to his side and put her arm around him, ready to lift, but he didn't move right away.

"I think she's nice," he said, looking in the direction of his closet and not directly at her.

"I think so, too."

He gave her an awkward pat on the shoulder and let her help him off the bed.

❖

It was the oddest Thanksgiving Tess had ever spent with her family. Not just because of the lack of arguments. They had usually managed to get through the holiday without too much fighting, mainly because everyone stayed apart until it was time to eat. Her dad would watch football, her mom would cook, and Kelly and Tess would alternate who was in her room and who was helping their mother in the kitchen, swapping places every half hour or so. This Thanksgiving was different because they stayed together, orbiting around Britt.

Tess stayed on the outskirts, hovering close in case Britt needed her but watching in fascination as Britt charmed her entire family without even trying. She laughed with Kelly and her mom, answered her dad's endless and annoying questions about the stupid video game, and even got Justin to describe every type of dinosaur to her.

Tess wouldn't have minded if they had liked Britt a little less, though. Just enough less so they had a little time together without everyone clamoring for her attention. After their hug in the hallway, Tess only managed to sneak a quick kiss when she showed Britt her old bedroom—until Justin burst in with yet another dinosaur to show her—and to sit close enough to touch on the couch while Kelly played the guitar at the end of the night.

She walked Britt out to her car when the evening was over, and they stood facing each other on the small patch of sheltered driveway while the rain dripped heavily off the edge of the garage roof.

Britt hooked her finger around the top button of Tess's shirt and popped it open. She lowered her head and brushed a featherlight kiss over the skin she had exposed, and Tess bit her lip to keep from moaning out loud.

"Are you tired?" Britt asked. "Or do you think you could find the energy to come back to my cabin later?"

"I'm exhausted," Tess said, sliding her hand through Britt's hair. "I think I'd rather get some sleep."

Britt laughed and backed into the rain. "Hurry," she said.

Tess watched long enough for Britt to get in her car and drive out of sight before she ran back into the house.

CHAPTER TWENTY-ONE

Britt opened the kitchen window in her cabin. Its western exposure meant she could have the sounds of the ocean come through unmuffled by glass without worrying about being flooded by rain. The wind blew in misty droplets that dotted the countertop and chilled the air in the cabin, but she just added another layer of clothes.

She had found that the rhythmic waves helped her think, but at the moment she was trying to use the steady beat of the surf to distract her from thinking too much. Tonight she just wanted to feel. She wanted to burn the sensation of being with Tess onto her skin and into her mind so she would be able to remember every moment with her once Britt moved on.

She had already told Chris she was going to leave. He had seemed sad to have her go—probably because she was one of the few guests at the lodge and the only customer he ever seemed to have in his store. Jim had given her a hug good-bye, and Alec had told Chris to be sure to check the signature on her credit card to make sure she hadn't stolen it. Sentimental old fool.

Britt sighed and dropped onto the couch. She was going to miss her tiny cabin, with its ugly plaid sofa and magnificent view. And she'd miss playing Scrabble with the guys and hearing Chris suggest increasingly bizarre ways for her to retrieve her soul. She'd miss the beach and Karla, but not the grilled cheese sandwiches.

And she'd miss Tess most of all. Britt hadn't fully made the decision to give in to her desire and be with Tess until she made the choice to leave this place. She was the one who had initially refused to consider a date with Tess because she didn't want a casual fling, but now there was nothing casual about it. She was going to be heartsick when she left, but she would hurt worse if she stayed, either stifling her attraction to Tess or being with her and having Tess walk away afterward.

An even scarier thought was having Tess offer her more than her usual short-term relationship. What would happen to Britt then? She'd have her future mapped out for her, delineated by someone else's dreams. She hadn't gone through the ordeal of leaving her job and home just to be plugged into another person's life.

Fortunately, Tess would make no such offer.

Britt bounced back up and looked through the window next to the front door, watching for Tess's car even though she knew it was too soon to see her. Tess had to help clean up after their meal, and then get her dad settled. Then she'd come here. Britt picked up her book to pass the time, but she couldn't focus on more than a sentence or two before thinking of Tess again.

Eventually, she started to shiver even with her heaviest shirts on, and she reluctantly closed the kitchen window just as she heard a knock at the door. She smiled as she opened it and saw Tess standing on her porch with her hair soaking wet from either the rain or a recent shower.

"Come in quick, before you freeze," she said, stepping aside.

Tess kissed her on the mouth as she walked past and into the cabin. She stood in the small room and rubbed her arms. "It's just as cold in here as it is outside."

"I had the window open. It should warm up soon. In the meantime, we should get your wet layers off." Britt walked over to Tess and unzipped her jacket, sliding it off her shoulders and tossing it onto a kitchen chair.

"My jeans are wet, too," Tess said with a wicked grin. She left her soggy shoes by the door and sat on the couch.

"I should hope so." Britt grabbed the quilt off the bed and

settled down next to Tess. She covered them both with the quilt and curled close to her.

Tess wrapped her arms around Britt and kissed her temple. "Thank you for coming tonight. My dad told me to bring you back for another visit soon, but I think he has an ulterior video-game-related motive. When I left the house, he was shouting something about trolls stealing his antigravity boots."

"He should know not to wear them in front of trolls. Jeez." Britt sighed. Tess's dad apparently didn't have much common sense.

"You have a standing invitation for Christmas dinner, by the way." Tess poked her finger through a hole in the cuff of Britt's flannel shirt. "Remember when we first met? Your clothes were so new they still had tags on them. Now you look like a local."

"I snagged it when I was climbing the big rock at the end of the beach," Britt said absently, with most of her attention fixated on Tess's first sentence.

"Tess, I won't be here for Christmas."

Tess looked at her, and her hand grew still where it rested on Britt's wrist. "Are you going to spend the holidays with your dad? Or are you going back to Seattle?"

"Neither. I'm not sure where I'm going, but it's not just for Christmas. It's for good. I guess I'm feeling restless and ready to find someplace new. I haven't found any answers here, so I'll look elsewhere."

Tess placed her hand over Britt's chest. "The answers are in here, Britt. Not in a place outside you. Give yourself more time to think."

"I am," Britt said. "But somewhere else. I'm getting too settled here, but I don't have real purpose to my days. If I get too attached, or too comfortable in my rut, I'll lose the incentive to find my way."

She covered Tess's hand with her own and pressed it close to her heart. Tess dropped her forehead onto their joined hands and used her other arm to pull Britt tightly against her. Britt draped her legs over Tess's thighs.

"Stay, please," Tess said. "We can get a place together near the marine center, and you can be part of the research team if you want. You'll love seeing the orcas out at sea and hearing their voices. You pick up new ideas so quickly—I'll bet you'll have plenty of insights to share. Just give us more time."

"Time until what? The inevitable boredom arrives?" Britt knew her voice sounded bitter, but she had no reason to be angry at Tess. She was angry with herself for being tempted by the offers both to live with Tess in a temporary home and to experience the excitement of learning more about the killer whales. She took a deep breath and tried to soften the harshness of her words. "We both know this won't last. You've been clear about that from the beginning. I'm not going to wait around until you decide you're ready to move to someone new, or until you go back to Olympia where you have plenty more options than you have around here. I can handle this, but only if I know the expiration date ahead of time."

"And what is the date you've picked?"

Britt closed her eyes. "Tomorrow."

Tess grew very still and quiet.

"You wanted something temporary," Britt said, breaking the silence between them. She knew her tone was unnecessarily defensive, but she was fighting to protect something vital to her. Her choices, her future. Still, she couldn't have pulled away from Tess's embrace if she'd tried. She had no idea how she'd find the strength to leave tomorrow.

"Yes. I did."

"And that's what I'm giving you. But I'm also giving myself the chance to walk away with some dignity."

Britt felt the tension in Tess as she struggled with her private thoughts, and she also felt the moment when Tess gave in. A sigh rippled through her and she enfolded Britt in her arms, gathering her close and kissing her softly on the neck.

"Okay, then. We should make the most of tonight." Tess punctuated her sentence with a kiss that turned into a gentle bite.

Britt shuddered, shocked by the way Tess had managed to replace Britt's anxiety with arousal in an instant. She tilted her head, and Tess buried her hands in Britt's hair, her kisses growing more insistent. She licked Britt's neck, nipped at her chin, and then captured her mouth.

This was nothing like the delicate kiss they'd shared in the car after their date. She had been aroused by Tess's touch then, but now desire rocked through Britt with every stroke of Tess's tongue. She shifted, straddling Tess's thighs and pressing against her, praying Tess wouldn't ask her to stay again, because right now, Britt would promise her anything. Everything.

She slid her hands under Tess's shirt and fitted them around the curve of her shoulders. Too many clothes. No time to take them off. Britt felt Tess's hands on her hips, pulling and releasing until the rhythm of breaths, bodies, and tongues were synchronized. Britt gasped, feeling the pressure of tears behind her eyes. After months of feeling wrong, *this* finally felt right.

Tess's hand was on her belly, stroking her skin under her shirt, dipping below the edge of her jeans. Fumbling to undo the buttons and reach past denim and cotton. Then Tess was touching her, joining her fingers to the rhythm set by their kiss.

Britt pushed against Tess's hand, desperate for faster, harder, more. She was determined to drive Tess to the edge, and triumphant when she felt Tess moan against her mouth. Her body attuned to Tess, sensing what she needed, changing her movements, until Tess cried out as she came. Britt's own orgasm took her by surprise, following Tess's as naturally as cause and effect.

She rested her head against Tess's shoulder as she caught her breath and slowly released the grip she'd had on the back of the couch. She was surprised she hadn't torn out handfuls of stuffing.

Tess stirred beneath her and removed her hand from down the front of Britt's jeans. She kissed Britt's cheek and nestled her close. "Yes, this would get boring very quickly."

"Inevitably," Britt said with a weak laugh. Maybe in a million years, she thought, but she kept her opinion to herself.

She heard a whisper inside, asking how could she walk away from Tess? And an even louder shout, demanding how could she not? Leaving tomorrow was going to shatter her, but it would be much worse if she waited. Already she had a hard time chasing away thoughts of forever, even though she had been well aware of the deal she had made with Tess.

The muscles in her legs began to grow stiff, and she climbed off Tess's lap and sat beside her, but the warmth she had felt while they were melded together quickly began to dissipate in the cold room. The quilt had fallen on the floor at some point, and Britt picked it up and spread it over them again.

She had to stop thinking about leaving Tess, or she'd never stop shivering.

❖

Tess felt Britt tremble and she sat up, tucking the quilt snugly around Britt. She went over to the heater and turned it up a few degrees before taking off her rain-dampened jeans and tossing them on the chair with her jacket. She sat down on the bed, and Britt came over to join her. They rummaged under the quilt, shedding various articles of clothing, and soon were wrapped around each other again with no clothing barriers between them. The skin-to-skin contact warmed Tess more than any heater or flannel shirt could.

She should have felt even more aroused on the bed than she had when they were fully dressed on the couch, since she now had Britt's inner thigh draped across her legs, and her hand was drawing slow circles around Tess's navel, but Tess had too many thoughts racing through her mind. They had been kept at bay by sex, but now threatened to overwhelm her. Even the involuntary act of breathing became manual, and Tess kept needing to remind herself to inhale again after every exhale.

She had finally found someone who made her want to plan for a future, and that person had decided to have sex with her and leave town the next day. She was sure Cara and Lenae—as well as some of her past dates—would relish the irony of her situation. Tess didn't. The crazy part was, Britt thought she was giving Tess exactly what she wanted, when in fact it was the complete opposite. Tess had protested. Somewhat. But she hadn't mentioned the word *love* or made a dramatic effort to get Britt to stay.

As soon as she had heard herself tell Britt she could help with Tess's research, she had realized what a mistake she was making. Not because she didn't believe Britt would be an insightful member of the team—naturally she would be—but because she had been steering Britt toward Tess's passion, not hers. She was no better than Cammie or Britt's ex-boss, or even her own parents, if she tried to overshadow Britt's search for her place in the world. Tess had to back away and let her go, hoping that maybe, someday, Britt might come back. She had never allowed thoughts of next week to permeate her dating life, and here she was thinking in terms of months, possibly years down the road, with no guarantees included.

At this moment, though, Britt was in her arms. Tess smoothed her hand down the length of Britt's back, following the curve of her hips. She pressed Britt onto her back and kissed her on the mouth, slowly exploring with her tongue. She had one night—only a few more hours, really—to map Britt's body in her mind. She moved to her temples, then to the curve of her ear, using her lips and tongue as cartographer's tools. Britt shifted under her, as if unable to keep still, as if needing to be closer to Tess.

Tess focused her attention on Britt's shoulders. The top of them, where they sloped elegantly down to her arms, and the front, where they ended in a smooth curving hollow above her breasts. Tess decided she could stay there for hours, balanced between collarbone and the swell of her breasts, but there were other regions to explore, and she dragged her lips and tongue over Britt's breasts. All of her senses coalesced here, mingling with the sound of Britt's gasp, the friction of a tightened nipple against the skin of Tess's lips, the sight of Britt's beautiful body that had always been hidden from Tess by layers of clothes.

She had to keep moving, to reach every part of Britt before her time was up and Britt was gone. Her stomach, tense with desire. A detour to her calves and thighs, defined and gorgeous after hours spent walking on the beach. And finally, to the very center of her, where the scents of sex and citrus and ocean drew Tess like a homing signal.

Britt is going away. Tess shut her eyes, slamming a door

between this bed and those words, burying herself in Britt until every hint of sad anticipation was gone, leaving only Tess and Britt and the movements connecting them. But when Britt climaxed, calling Tess's name, and Tess's own body cried out in response, the door crashed down and the sorrow came stampeding back into her head.

She rested her cheek on Britt's stomach, feeling the rise and fall of her breath as it gradually slowed to a normal rate and the small shudders that vibrated through her.

When Britt reached for her, Tess shifted up the bed, resting her head on the pillow. Britt smiled at her, but Tess was surprised to see that her cheeks were wet with tears. She traced their paths with her index finger.

"I'm going to miss you," Britt said, twining her fingers through Tess's hair.

"Me, too," Tess said, when she really meant *Please, stay.*

CHAPTER TWENTY-TWO

B ritt sat on the patio of a restaurant in Olympia, near the harbor. The view was lovely, with tall-masted boats rocking against the pier and gulls and cormorants swooping low over the water. Britt barely noticed them, though, since her main focus was on the apartment buildings clustered by the dock across from her. Which would most likely be Tess's home? The one with stained wood and small decks looked more natural, more her style, but the building with gray siding looked like it had the best water views.

Britt had been playing this game ever since she had arrived in the state's capital city three days ago. Every time she sat by a café window or drove along the streets, she would wonder if she was near where Tess lived when she was in Olympia, where she shopped, where she ate.

She had taken her time getting here. She had stopped in the tourist town of Ocean Shores, and then had spent several days in Aberdeen while she decided which direction to take. She had the choice of continuing along Highway 101, down to Long Beach and across the state line to the Oregon coast, or changing to Highway 12 and going to Olympia.

She had decided to leave the ocean behind for a while because it only reminded her of Tess. Of course, going to the city where she lived and worked wasn't exactly the best way to get Tess out of her mind, but Britt hadn't been able to resist. She had managed to keep herself from turning the car around and heading back to Forks during her drive here, and that had taxed her willpower to its limit.

Besides, she needed to meet with her lawyer, Cathy, and finish the paperwork for the grant.

Yes, she could have signed the papers digitally instead of coming here in person. Britt sighed and took a bite of her black bean burger. She had cried for the first three hours after leaving La Push and had sniffled for a half hour more. She missed Tess, and if it made her feel a teensy bit better to come here, where Tess's shadow seemed to hide in every doorway, then Britt was going to give herself that small comfort.

Britt dipped a sweet potato fry in a small metal cup of house-made aioli. At least the food around here had brought back the joy of eating for her. This city was a vegetarian's heaven, making dining a pleasure instead of a plasticky-cheese chore. Wandering through the downtown area was fun, too. There were entire shops dedicated to items like candy, books, and shoes, rather than just a single shelf of each in the La Push general store. She imagined being here with Tess, window-shopping and laughing together. Meeting Cara and Lenae for dinner at one of the local pubs.

Aargh. Tess, Tess, Tess. She needed to come up with another topic to think about. She had definitely made the right decision to leave. She had questioned her initial choice to run away from Seattle, too, and she had finally come to terms with how important it had been for her to do so. And she hadn't run away from Tess.

Well, yes, she had. But for some good reasons mixed in with the more embarrassing, fear-based ones. She didn't want to be hurt, so she hurt Tess first by walking away. She didn't want to invest in the relationship only to find out Tess was just playing around. Although she honestly had a hard time believing Tess's feelings for her weren't real, and potentially—a big *potentially*—lasting.

But the serious reason she had left was her need to find her own path, before she lost herself in Tess's world.

Britt threw down her napkin in disgust. She was sick of thinking about what to do with her life. Sick of making lists and chasing after her One True Passion. Sick of being somewhat interested in hundreds of topics, but unable to locate one that spoke to her.

She was meeting with Cathy later this afternoon and would have no reason to stay in Olympia once her business here was finished. Her hotel was beautiful, but far too expensive for a prolonged stay, and a long-term rental was out of the question. She'd move on, maybe to a small coastal town or inland to the less expensive eastern sides of Washington or Oregon.

But today she was going to indulge herself, just a little. She paid for her meal and left the restaurant, driving a few miles down the highway to Evergreen's campus.

The proximity of the city seemed to fade into the background as she drove along the tree-lined road leading to the college. The setting was wild and natural, perfectly suited to Tess. Britt parked in one of the lots and skirted the edge as she walked toward the main part of the campus. She was a little worried about running into Cara, but she figured she'd be safe if she kept close to cover. There was no way Cara could sneak up on Britt if she had Cupcake with her, so she should have plenty of time to duck behind a tree if she heard them coming.

She stopped at a large information board and studied the map of the college, memorizing the path to the marine biology department's lab. She wandered around the central area of the campus for an hour first, though, admiring the blend of modern architecture and Native American inspired buildings. She stumbled upon the communications building and hastily backtracked in case Cara was hanging around outside, and then she visited the library where she was sure Tess spent a good amount of time, and the bookstore where signed copies of *Fading Song* were on display. The Evergreen staff had gone all out, decorating the bookshelf with killer whale cutouts and interrelated books on topics like the declining salmon population and underwater photography, but they still couldn't top the marine center's Tess shrine, in Britt's opinion.

Eventually, she found the path leading to the lab. The trail made her think about their hike through the rainforest. The day was clear and cold instead of dripping wet, but the two settings were still similar. Ferns covered much of the space between trees, and every fallen log Britt saw made her think of the moment when she had asked Tess on their date.

She apparently took a wrong turn somewhere—while she was obsessing about Tess, no doubt—because she found herself on the top of a cliff, with no obvious way to get down the side of it. She must have misread the map, so she finally slipped and slid her way down a steep hill and came to the college's section of beach. She sat on a weathered driftwood trunk near the base of the cliff and watched students and professors filter in and out of the building. Just as she had suspected, the place practically screamed Tess. If Britt had been told to design a space where Tess would work, she would have produced something exactly like the building and boat slips in front of her.

Okay, so maybe it hadn't been a good idea to come here. Britt was cemented to her seat, lost in memories of Tess. Britt pictured her standing by the bay with a playful sea otter cavorting behind her. Or gently moving some moss aside on the dead tree to show Britt the baby seedling growing beneath it. Or in Britt's cabin as she reverently touched every part of her—inside and out—making Britt cry because it seemed as if Tess saw her as something much more than a casual lover, but Britt had already made plans to leave.

Britt stood up. Time to get to her meeting. She followed a group of students as they left the lab and discovered a zigzag staircase that deposited her in one of the student parking lots. She cut through the woods and found her car.

The drive back to downtown Olympia only took a few minutes, but the transition from near wilderness to urban area made her feel as if she had traveled much farther. She parked on a side street not far from the Capitol Building and walked to the courthouse where she would be meeting Cathy. She checked the directory for the right courtroom and found a bench outside where she could sit and wait. The uncomfortable wooden bench was shiny with rich brown lacquer, and she worried that if she relaxed too much she would slide right off and onto the floor.

Britt watched the activity around her and felt a sense of the familiar for the first time since she had left Seattle. Everything had been new from the moment of her escape forward, but this courthouse, even though she had never testified here, was a connection to her old life. She felt a quiver of excitement inside, as if she was about to go on the stand.

This was part of her past, and unless she took to a life of crime—or if Alec falsely accused her of stealing his Scrabble tiles and got her arrested—she'd rarely be seeing the inside of a courthouse in the future. She had expected to feel some anxiety coming here today because her last day in court had precipitated her decision to leave her job, but she felt fine.

During one of her list-making episodes, she had written down every aspect of her old job that had excited her. She had thought she could take those bits and pieces and use them to build a new, ideal career, but she had gotten so uncomfortable with the process she had needed to stop. She was easily able to identify what she loved about chemistry, like logical problem solving. Her issues arose when she was forced to admit how much she had enjoyed going to court. She had torn up the list, ashamed to admit she had liked it. Her testimony there had come at a great cost—to the environment, yes, but also to her conscience.

Still, she couldn't deny that she had loved the process of preparing for trials, although not the reasons behind them. She had to study each case, anticipate questions, and think fast while on the stand. She usually learned new things because the cases often involved other chemists' projects and not her own, and she had to understand all aspects of their work.

Britt had never considered herself to be an artistic person like her mom until Tess claimed she was. Since that day in the rainforest, Britt had actively looked inside herself for the traits Tess had seen in her, and she was surprised when she saw them, too. Testifying in court utilized those more artistic skills of persuasion and cultivating empathy as well as her science and logic-oriented abilities. And she had been damned good in the courtroom.

Until her last case, of course.

She vividly remembered how she had felt on the inside, and she was certain some of her anguish had been visible—and therefore influential. She had stuttered over some of the words, and she hadn't been able to stop staring at those photos. Britt laughed to herself. She might as well have been working for the other side.

I might as well have been working for the other side.

Britt stood up but didn't know where to go, so she sat down again. Could this be her answer? She frantically checked her pockets, but she didn't have pen and paper handy. She wanted to make a list or a mind map or something to help her sort through the thoughts speeding through her mind and determine whether this idea would be feasible.

She gave herself thirty seconds to fantasize about the possibility before she would have to examine the idea in more practical terms. She pictured a little office building—nothing fancy or expensive, but kind of homey—filled with the staff members she had hired because they were idealistic and determined to do good. And her personal office, with a sign on her door identifying her job title as environmental lawyer. Or animal activist lawyer. And her desk, with a stack of file folders, each containing information about a case she had chosen because the issues involved mattered to her. And here was Tess, meeting her for lunch where they would discuss everything Britt was learning about her cases and all the different killer whale songs Tess had heard that day…

Her daydreaming time was up, and she had to come back to reality. Good thing, too, because her mind had taken a bit of a detour at the end there. Even though the images in the fantasy might be idealistic, she could compromise as long as some parts came true.

Even though she couldn't write them down, she started forming action steps. She'd have to go back to school—she loved school—and…well, she wasn't sure exactly what else she'd need to do. Research, first of all. Write lots and lots of lists…

"Brittany?"

Britt was startled out of her reverie. She looked up and saw a woman standing next to her with short blond hair and wire-rimmed glasses. "Yes," she said, getting to her feet. "Hello, Cathy. It's nice to see you again."

"You, too. I have all your paperwork with me, and there's an office we can use right over here."

She led them down the hall and into a small, bare rectangle of a room with several desks inside, each with high partitions for privacy, so they looked like little cubicles. Cathy sat at the one in the far corner and pulled a stack of paperwork out of her briefcase.

"We just need a few signatures, and we'll be all set to transfer the money to the sanctuary." She paused and smiled at Britt. "I've never been there, but my youngest daughter adores wolves. We're planning a weekend trip to visit it this spring."

"She'll love it," Britt said. The grant was already doing its job and bringing more attention to the sanctuary. Just one family so far, but it was a start.

Britt had already read through a copy of the papers, so she skimmed each section quickly and signed.

"If you decide you have more money to give away, let me know," Cathy said once they were finished.

Britt laughed. "I wish. I'm going to need a grant of my own soon unless I find a job."

"I know it was a big decision to donate money you've rightfully earned, even though you had ethical reasons for doing so. Do you feel better now that the money will be used to do something good?"

Although she had already spent some of the bonus money in the past, the process of giving away what was left was one of those symbolic gestures that marked an end. And a new beginning. "I feel lighter, but I still want to do more," Britt said. She hesitated, and then decided to try on her new idea and see if it fit.

"I've been thinking about going to law school." For all of ten minutes. "I'm interested in advocating for either animals or the environment on a legislative level, where I could feel I was making a real difference in the world. But I'd have to go to law school. And get accepted first, of course. And take the LSAT. Oh God, and a bar exam? I really haven't thought this through, but I hadn't even considered it until I was sitting in the hall out there just now. Maybe I shouldn't even—"

Cathy held up her hands, palms out, and stopped Britt's flow of words. "Don't talk yourself out of this so quickly, without even giving it a chance," she said, laughing. "I think you have the potential to make an excellent lawyer, Brittany. Well, as long as you don't argue against your own case in the courtroom like you were doing just now." She opened her briefcase on the desk and rummaged through it before pulling out a stack of business cards, selecting two and handing them to Britt. "I have some friends who would probably be willing to talk to you about what those jobs would entail. Cameron lives up near Monroe and works with a large animal sanctuary, so her focus is on anticruelty laws. Harry works mainly with community groups that are trying to protect wildlife habitats and wetlands in their neighborhoods."

Britt took the cards, amazed by how two slender, flimsy bits of paper could make her plan seem more tangible. These were real people doing work she might love.

"Call me if you have any questions, especially if you're considering going to the University of Washington like I did. I can give you advice about the admissions process and the different fields of study."

"Thank you," Britt said. She said good-bye and walked outside. She was getting hungry for dinner, so she walked downtown and hunted for a place to eat. For the first time in months, her days were different from each other. Her La Push schedule was no longer in effect, and she felt a sense of freedom. Part of her missed the regularity of her ocean days, though.

She stood outside a café and read the dinner menu. Then she continued on her way, pulling the business cards out of her pocket and looking at them again. This plan might work. Did it leave any room for Tess in her new life—provided, of course, Tess wanted to be in it? Seattle wasn't far from Olympia, if Britt went to school there. And after she graduated…

Britt kept getting ahead of herself. Far, far ahead. She needed to concentrate on learning as much as she could about a law career, just as she had researched killer whales and wolves for the grant. If it seemed right for her, then maybe she would contact Tess. At least let her know that she had finally found what she was looking for.

She found a microbrewery with a great-looking menu and went inside, taking a vacant seat at the bar where she ordered an amber ale and a vegetable curry. She wished Tess was here with her, even just as a friend. Britt felt a sharp pang of loneliness that had nothing to do with eating alone, which she never minded, and everything to do with being out of contact with Tess.

For now, though, Britt had to go solo, and even though she had chosen to come to Olympia because Tess lived here, she suddenly felt she had come to the right place at the right time for herself, too. She had thought La Push was the perfect place where she could make decisions, but now she saw it in a new way. There, human beings and all the trappings of their social lives were secondary to nature. The starkness of the coast and the unimpeded openness of sky, ocean, and forest had shot her with a much-needed antidote to her past, leaving her with a cleaner palette of ocean grays, spruce greens, and primal reds, whites, and blacks. If she had come straight to Olympia from Seattle, the bright colors would have blended, and she would have traded one city for another, possibly making small, barely discernible changes in her lifestyle rather than the drastic shift she really needed.

She shook her head. Enough drama and philosophy for today. She missed Tess. If she was here, they'd take a break from these serious thoughts and shift to joking and laughter. But Tess wasn't here, so Britt would have to have fun in her own weird way, by making more lists. She got out the new pen and notepad she had bought on her way here from the courthouse and wrote a heading at the top of a fresh page: *Law School: Pros and Cons.* Tess straddled both columns, with a question mark by her name. Britt thought for a moment, and then wrote her first pro.

Would learn the skills needed to sue Alec for slander.

CHAPTER TWENTY-THREE

Tess got to the marine center before Jake and Melissa arrived, and she hauled several boxes of supplies into the hallway. She had been working nonstop for two weeks, ever since Britt left, and she still wasn't able to keep from thinking about her. If she let herself pause, though, she was overwhelmed with sadness. This must be how the women she had dated in the past felt when their affairs were over and Tess was gone.

She laughed, glad she at least had a smidgen of humor left inside. Her lovers had always seemed as unmoved by the inevitable ends of their relationships as she had been, and Tess had liked it that way. She'd *planned* it that way, being careful never to get involved with someone who might want more. She had recognized her growing disinterest in the whole game for a while now, but she hadn't considered the reasons why she often would rather spend an evening with friends or working late in her lab or reading and writing in the peace of her own home. She'd blame research for an article, or plans with Cara and Lenae, for her slackening social life, while ignoring the melancholy she sometimes felt when she was alone in her apartment or when she was out with her friends and saw how much pleasure the small intimacies they shared gave them.

And ignoring the loneliness she felt when she was out with a woman who wanted nothing more from her than a few shared hours.

Tess got two folding chairs out of her trunk, slammed the lid shut, and carried them into the Center. She had briefly considered puppy walking for a year but had been careful not to mention it to Lenae because she was relentless when she smelled fresh volunteer blood. Looking back now, she wondered if she had subconsciously been wanting to use the puppy as an excuse to slow her dating even more, giving her a way to get out of the game without having to face the real reason she was getting so little enjoyment out of it. Then Britt had come into her life, and Tess hadn't been able to remain in denial any longer. She wanted the *more* she had always been so careful to avoid. She wanted love, companionship, routine, and expectations. She wanted to share those things with Britt, a woman who would never become boring to her.

But Britt was gone. Maybe Tess would ask Lenae for a puppy to help ease her loneliness, although the Cupcake experience had left her a little wary. She had been working like a demon at the Center, as she organized seminars with other Evergreen faculty members via the internet, and at her parents' house. She had even gotten her mom into the garden again, where they had finished all the winterizing chores of pruning, deadheading, and mulching. She had done most of the work while her mom had given directions— sometimes delivered in a shriek, like when Tess had been about to pull up her mother's favorite rosebush because it looked dead.

Tess pushed and shoved until all the boxes were in the empty storage closet at the far end of the hall. She had cleaned it out last week, removing the mess of old brooms, mops, and questionable, expired cleaning fluids that no one used anyway. Most of the equipment was beyond repair, and she had thrown it out. The few items she had kept were shoved in a corner in the break room. She started unpacking the stuff she had brought and transforming the room into something new.

She heard Melissa and Jake arguing over some television show as they came through the door, and she went out to meet them.

"Hey, you two. I have something for you. We'll be having more traffic here for a few months, and I know you've been a little concerned about it."

A little concerned was her polite way of saying *having routine panic attacks.*

She handed each of them a key and gestured for them to follow her to the storage room.

"Do we have to clean some more?" Melissa asked in an exasperated tone.

"No," Tess said with a laugh. She opened the door and showed them what was inside. "There are only two keys, so no one else can come in here. Whenever you feel the need to get away and have some privacy, you can use this room. You won't need to hide behind the rain slickers or under your desks."

Melissa walked to the center of the room and slowly turned around. It was almost small enough for her to touch both walls at the same time, but Tess had managed to fit two chairs and a folding table inside. She had been rather indiscriminate in her science fiction choices for the decor—partially because she had bought what she could find in Forks, and also because she wasn't well-versed in the genre. *Star Trek* and *Star Wars* posters vied for space on the walls, and she had found two *Battlestar Galactica* puzzles, one from the original series and the other from the more recent shows. A stack of books—anything she could find with an alien or a spaceship on the cover—filled a child-sized bookcase. She had thought of Britt the entire time she was shopping and decorating the space—Britt would have loved the experience, and she would have known exactly what to get. Melissa and Jake seemed pleased enough with the result, though.

"This is great. Thank you, Tess." Melissa gave her a hug, and Jake waved at her from the far corner of the room.

"It's perfect," he said, examining a model of the TV version of the *Delta Flyer* that she had placed on top of the bookshelf. It was Tess's favorite part of the room.

"Just promise me you won't spend all your time back here, and no bringing work with you, or you'll never leave. Work at your desks, even if there are students around, and come back here only when you need a break." They nodded in agreement, but she had a feeling she was going to have to repeat those instructions hundreds of times over the next semester. She herded them out and used Melissa's key to lock the door behind her. "Jake, can you find out if any of the offshores have been seen today? Melissa and I can get the boat ready."

Tess jumped from one activity to the next, unable to stand the gaps in between. Kelly and Justin were coming out on the boat today, and she was hopeful that her sister's usual abrasiveness would make her irritated enough to forget about being sad.

She made another trip to her car to get a cooler full of snacks and water. She put the Justin-sized life vest she had bought on top and carried it around the Center and to the dock. Melissa was already on board, checking the microphones and stowing extra sets of headphones in the metal trunk. Tess secured the cooler and went to do an engine check. She paused by the bench where Britt had sat when she had visited the Center, and then continued on with a sigh. Was she doomed to spend the rest of her life thinking *I wish Britt were here*? It was going to get old real fast.

When they were ready to go, she jumped back onto the dock and saw Kelly and Justin standing at the edge of the boulders and watching the sea otter diving and resurfacing in a hunt for food.

"I see you've met Scrabble, our center's mascot," she said, fighting to keep her balance when Justin ran at her and grabbed her around the knees in a hug.

"Careful, Justin, don't knock Aunt Tess into the ocean," Kelly said, and Tess could hear the exhaustion in her voice. "He's been very excited about this boat ride all morning."

Kelly put a hand on her lower back, arching in a stretch, and Tess was surprised to see how much more pronounced her belly was than when Tess had first arrived. She realized she would be here for the birth this time. She'd sit in the hospital waiting room with her parents, and then hold a newborn niece or nephew. Strange. She wasn't sure how she felt about all this family bonding crap, but the thought of seeing the baby was one thoroughly positive aspect of it. As was Justin.

She knelt down and helped him put on the life vest, tightening straps and checking the fit before she turned him loose again.

"I'll watch him while we're on the boat, so you can relax and enjoy the water today." Tess waited until Justin had walked over to the retaining wall and out of earshot before she asked her next question. "Did you have a chance to call Lenae?"

"Yes. She's got a good prospect in mind, so Josh and I will take Justin to visit her when he's home from sea in January. If they get along well, we'll adopt the dog, but I don't want to tell Justin what's going on until we're sure they'll be a good fit."

Kelly perched on the wall a few yards from her son and continued, "I agree with your friend about a dog being a good companion for Justin, and a playmate so he won't feel lonely while the baby needs more of my attention. I'm kind of ashamed to admit it, but I'm excited to have a dog in the house for selfish reasons, too. I've always wanted one."

"I remember," Tess said. She sat on the wall next to her, keeping an eye on Justin to make sure he didn't leap into the water after the otter.

"It was a lonely way to grow up," Kelly said. "I used to feel like we were part of an experiment. Someone took four people who hardly had anything in common and put us in a house together, told us we were a family. I wouldn't have been surprised to learn that all our mirrors were two-way ones, and a group of sociologists was behind them, observing us as we tried to interact and failed. I don't ever want him to feel like that."

Who was this woman? Civil, understanding, sharing her emotions. Kelly must be even more exhausted than Tess had realized, or she had become a pod person with an alien inside that was controlling her voice. Tess decided she had spent far too much time reading the back covers of those sci-fi books.

"He never will, Kelly. I think a service dog will be wonderful for him, but he doesn't need one to make him feel loved or part of a family."

"I'd like to think you're right, and that the dog will be happy to be with us, too."

"Of course it will." She hesitated, wondering whether she should change the subject to one that was more comfortable and less personal, or if she should broach the topic she had on her mind. What the hell. She might as well give it a shot. "You know, I always thought you were fine at home. You didn't fight with Mom and Dad like I did, and you never left."

"You fought them enough for the both of us, so it was hard for me to get a word in edgewise," Kelly said, but she smiled and poked Tess in the arm. "You handled the situation by getting more belligerent, while I handled it by withdrawing. I read a lot of fantasy books and I spent as many nights as I could with my friend Ann. You and I needed stimulation and vibrancy in our childhoods, but our home life was barren. Stable and secure, but barren. I think we could have helped each other through it better if we had stayed close, but we didn't."

Tess thought back to the imaginative games they used to play and the elaborate stories they invented. "Why did we stop playing together?"

"I don't know," Kelly said. "But I'm sure it was your fault."

"Hey. Was not." Tess tossed a pebble at her, and Kelly batted it away. "Well, it probably was. I wasn't easy to be around sometimes."

"No, you weren't. But you're getting better. Sort of."

Tess smiled and watched Justin carefully line up his dinosaurs on the surface of the wall. Kelly was filling her house with music and games, and now with a playful dog. Justin was going to be fine.

She turned back and saw Kelly looking at her with an expression she couldn't read. "What?" she asked.

"I was just thinking about how we both have tried not to become our parents in sort of the same way. You know, the way you sleep around—"

"You cheat on Josh?" Tess asked, shocked.

"No, you idiot," she said with a scowl, but then her expression softened. "But I did pick a man who is away a lot of the time. This lifestyle sets up a certain cycle that made me comfortable, I guess. Long periods when I have my space and don't have to worry about intimacy issues. And when he does come home, it's kind of like a honeymoon all over again, so our relationship stays exciting and not boring."

Ugh. Way too much sharing. "First, gross. And second, I don't sleep around."

"When I called about Dad, you had a woman in your apartment, didn't you? You were whispering on the phone. But not long after, you showed up here with no girlfriend and with no mention of one."

"Oh, yeah. Lydia. She doesn't help my case much."

Kelly smirked. "I knew I was right. But now there's Britt. Your feelings for her must be scaring the shit out of you."

"My feelings for her don't matter anymore. She's gone," Tess said, surprised at the harshness of her tone. Kelly was picking away at the truth, and Tess hated to admit how accurate she was. She sighed. "Yes, I was scared. But not enough to stop falling in love with her."

Kelly patted her on the knee, looking as uncomfortable with the gesture as Tess felt. They needed to go back to mock punches and jabs.

"Give her time. You're a strong person, Tess. Obstinate, successful, sure in your convictions. It would be easy for someone to be overshadowed in a relationship with you. I have a feeling that once she chooses a path to take, she'll be the one overshadowing you. It'll be good for you to be challenged."

"Gee, thanks, sis. So how did you become so wise?" She injected the words with more sarcasm than she actually felt.

"I'm the older sister," Kelly said with a shrug, then she grinned. "Plus, I'm in therapy. It helps. I think I'm ready to have Josh home full-time. To have a more normal marriage instead of a part-time one. One or both of us could find a job around here, or maybe move if we need to."

Tess liked the idea of the two of them being together, especially with a second child on the way. "Do you think Josh would like the idea?"

Kelly laughed. "I know he would. He seems to understand how I feel, and he's waiting for me to be the one to bring it up. Maybe you and I are both ready to stop being defined by our parents."

Maybe, Tess thought. But it would be up to Britt, because Tess couldn't imagine wanting anyone else the same way. Britt made love seem worthwhile. Tess was rescued from the need to tell Kelly this when she looked up and saw Jake running out of the Center, waving his arms frantically to get her attention.

"Orcas," she said. She scooped up Justin, and Kelly grabbed the dinosaurs, and they ran toward the boat.

CHAPTER TWENTY-FOUR

B ritt walked into the marine center, stepping carefully as if she might encounter land mines. She wasn't sure how Tess was going to react to her being here, if she would be angry with her for leaving, or happy to see her again. Maybe Tess would give her the silent treatment since Britt hadn't been in contact with her for almost a month. The worst-case scenario in her mind had her encountering a neutral Tess who had already moved on and was going on a date tonight, maybe with Karla from the La Push diner. She had asked Britt about Tess's *situation*—really, who said things like that?— after they had met there for the grant interview and had said Tess was fiery. Jeez. Britt had never mentioned it to Tess, but she knew how fast gossip traveled in this place.

She was relieved when that particular train of thought was interrupted by Melissa, who was coming out of the break room with a big bowl of popcorn.

"Hi, Britt. Are you looking for Tess? She's out there." Melissa waved in the general direction of the ocean, which wasn't particularly helpful, and then disappeared into a storage room.

Huh. Britt walked through the deserted lab and went out the back door of the marine center. She scanned the shoreline in both directions, but no one was in sight. She went to the boathouse next and tried to peer through the windows, but they were too densely covered with mineral deposits from the sea air for her to see much. The door was unlocked, so she went inside.

"Tess?" she called, but no one answered. She checked in the closet and under the tables, just in case Tess had seen her coming and was hiding, hopefully not with Karla. No luck. The boats were the only other option, so she went aboard the trawler.

She didn't see anyone at first, but on her second pass by the wheelhouse she saw two feet and a very nice jeans-clad ass poking out of a large storage cubby.

"Tess?" she asked. Eventually. She was glad no one was around to notice how long she stood there and stared before speaking.

She heard a thump and a curse, and Tess wiggled out of the compartment. She stood up, rubbing her head, and turned around.

"God, Melissa, you...Oh. Britt."

Britt wasn't sure how to interpret her tone. Did she sound pissed? Dismissive? Exhausted after last night's sex with Karla?

"Hi, Tess." Her own voice sounded lovelorn. No doubt about it.

"You're back."

"Yes."

This was going well. They had whittled down their conversation to single words. At this rate, it would take them all night to share even simple concepts, let alone the complex one Britt had come here to discuss. She took a deep breath and started again.

"I went to Olympia after I left. I had to sign papers for the grant before the money could be transferred, and I went to Evergreen while I was there. Then I went to Seattle, and then I came here, which was strange because I retraced the route I took when I ran away, but this time I wasn't quite as shell-shocked, so I saw more than the broken yellow lines." She paused and took another breath. She hadn't been shell-shocked this time, but she'd been worried about how Tess would feel about seeing her again. "I even stopped at the Olympic Cellars Winery and bought a bottle of wine."

For us to share, she added. She'd save that sentence for later, though.

Tess was watching Britt in her usual unperturbed, calm way. "Evergreen has a beautiful campus."

"Yes, it does."

Tess looked out toward the horizon with a visible sigh and ran her hand through her hair. "How was Seattle?"

"Interesting. I had a lot of questions and I think I found the answers I needed."

"Good, Britt, I'm glad. Now, I have more work to do here, and I'm sure you need to get back to the city, so I'll see you later."

She left Britt standing in the wheelhouse, unsure what to do or say next. It took her several minutes before she realized what emotion Tess had been trying to hide behind a veneer of nonchalance. Not anger or indifference or a Karla-induced lust. It was fear.

She slowly walked through the narrow door and onto the deck, where Tess was uncoiling and recoiling a rope.

"That looks like an important job," Britt said softly, standing close behind Tess.

"It's a high-tech piece of killer whale research equipment. If it isn't coiled just right, it won't work."

Britt saw a hint of a smile on Tess's face and she exhaled slowly. "Can we sit down for a while and talk, Tess? I've made some decisions and I'd like to share them with you."

"I guess so. Okay."

They were heading to the bench where Britt had sat on her first boat ride when Melissa and Jake flung themselves out the back door and jumped on the boat.

"A good sighting," Melissa said, panting. "Not far."

She and Jake started unmooring the boat, and Tess turned to Britt. "Do you want to wait here? We can talk when I get back."

"Are you kidding? You can throw me overboard, but I'm not leaving on my own. I want to see killer whales."

Tess gave her an actual grin this time and went to help the other two. Britt sat on her bench as they motored out to sea. She pulled her thick winter coat tightly around herself as they left the inlet and the breeze turned into a biting wind. Her loose hair whipped across her face.

Tess was back soon, and she sat down a few feet away from Britt. "So tell me about your decisions."

Britt hesitated. She had imagined talking about her new plans while she and Tess were alone in her cabin, curled up together and sipping their wine. She brushed her hair out of her eyes and decided this was an even better setting because it was a reflection of Tess. And, unless she was prepared to swim back to shore, Tess wouldn't be able to run away before Britt was done talking.

"While I was walking around Evergreen's campus, I was looking at the different buildings and trying to decide what department I would choose if I was back in college and starting over. I guess it's what I've been doing all along, looking for one subject or passion to replace the one I was prepared to leave behind."

Tess leaned closer to hear Britt's voice over the sound of the boat's engine and the heavy wind. She wanted to touch Britt. To tuck her gorgeous, wild hair behind her ears. To kiss her and let her know how much she had missed her. To grab her and keep her from leaving ever again. But from the moment she had looked up and seen Britt standing in the wheelhouse, all her old habits had come rushing back. Mask her emotions. Don't seem vulnerable. Don't *care*. She focused on what Britt was saying because she sensed that she needed to feel heard right now, and Tess would do that for her. She'd deal with her own mixed-up emotions after.

"But I realized it's what got me into this mess in the first place," Britt continued. "Getting so single-minded that I couldn't see anything beyond my narrow world. That day in court forced me to look deeper and wider. I knew I needed to change, but I was just trying to find a substitute for chemistry." She paused and pushed her hair off her face again. "Does this make any sense?"

Tess nodded, understanding exactly what Britt meant because she had noticed Britt had always seemed delighted when she saw connections between subjects, but she had been determined to find only one to pursue.

"Well, after campus I went to the courthouse to sign those papers. I was sitting on this god-awful bench and thinking about trials, and all of a sudden I realized I was only seeing one side of the courtroom in my memory. There's another side. The ones defending the environment or animals or the people who are trying to protect them."

"Oh," said Tess, quickly catching up with what Britt was saying, and seeing the potential it held for her. She would be formidable if she channeled her energy and passion into a career like that. Tess couldn't contain her grin, even if she had still been interested in trying.

"It's a great idea, Britt. So how many lists about it have you made so far?"

"Two full notebooks. I've even written one about vegetarian options for my sack lunches on school days." Britt shook her head. "You really think it could work?"

"Absolutely." Tess put her arm across the back of the bench, wanting to get closer to Britt, but not wanting to touch her until she figured out where she stood with her. Britt might be here just to get her opinion, or to use her as a sounding board. A friend. "What did you do in Seattle?"

"I talked to a couple of people in admissions at UW and Seattle University, and I met with two lawyers who are friends with Cathy." She hesitated. "I signed up to take the LSAT," she said in a shy-sounding voice. "If everything goes according to plan, I could be starting classes next fall."

"That's a big deal," Tess said, knowing exactly why Britt's whole demeanor had changed when she said it. Making lists, meeting with people…those were part of the thought process. Scheduling a test was a physical move forward. "Your first action step."

Britt nodded, looking pleased at Tess's statement. "My second was to come here. I had to take at least one on my own first, though."

Tess realized she was holding her breath and she exhaled. "Seattle is close to Olympia," she said.

Britt smiled and sat back on the bench until her back was pressed against Tess's arm. "That's exactly what I was thinking."

Tess shifted until her arm was draped over Britt's shoulders, with her fingers trailing up and down Britt's upper arm.

"Maybe—if you aren't too busy with your studies, that is—we

could constantly go on long-lasting dates that would be permanent parts of an unending relationship."

Tess moved a little closer with each word, until she was only a breath away from Britt's lips.

"Oh, my," Britt said softly. "That's a lot of antonyms for *temporary*."

"The word no longer exists in my vocabulary, at least where you're concerned. I've replaced it with the word *love*."

"I love you, too, Tess." Britt closed the tiny gap between them and kissed Tess. Tess pulled Britt nearer, one hand tangled in her windblown hair and the other around her waist. Britt put her hands on Tess's cheeks, and their chill intensified the sensations Tess was experiencing. Elation, arousal, joy. She lost herself in the feel of Britt's lips and tongue, the hint of citrus mingling with the sea air, the irritating sensation of someone jabbing her on the back.

She turned around and saw Jake standing a few feet away, using the handle of a broom to get her attention.

"What?" she asked, highly annoyed by the interruption. He pointed to port.

"Oh," Britt said on a long, awed breath. They stood up and joined Melissa and Jake at the railing, watching the rhythmic movement of graceful black fins as they cut through the water.

"Sorry, Jake," Tess said quietly. He smiled and shook his head, waving off her apology.

"How many are there?" Britt asked. "I can't tell."

"Five," Tess said. "The one in front is the matriarch, and the two with the taller fins are her sons. Then there's a daughter, with a calf of her own."

Tess was mesmerized by the sight, even though she had seen similar ones countless times. She could only imagine how it was affecting Britt, who was seeing them for the first time in their natural habitat, especially after the type of soul-searching she'd been doing for the past months. Tess watched as the mother broke the surface with a puff of air and water, followed immediately by the baby's tiny spray of breath. Over and over, in a beautiful harmony.

She stood right behind Britt and placed her hands on her

shoulders. "Look how the pod surfaces and breathes, matching their rhythms to each other. They're connected instinctively. It's called synchrony."

Britt turned her head and looked at Tess. Tess leaned forward and kissed her softly on the mouth. When she pulled away, they both exhaled at the same time.

Britt smiled.

"Synchrony," she agreed.

CHAPTER TWENTY-FIVE

B ritt entered the parking lot of the marine center and pulled into one of the few empty slots. She didn't see Tess's car, but sometimes she carpooled from Forks with Cara. Tess wouldn't be expecting her until tomorrow, and Britt hadn't called to let her know she was taking a day off from work to give them a long weekend together.

She went inside, waving at the student who was talking to a group of tourists at the reception desk, and followed the jumbled sound of multiple radios into the office. The difference between the Center on her first visit and now still amazed her. Evergreen had descended on the sleepy little lab and brought it to life. At least a half dozen students were wandering through the space, working on computers and making notes on wall charts. She saw another similarly sized group through the back windows, swarming over the *Delta Flyer* and its equipment. One thing hadn't changed, however. No matter how much new equipment glistened on tidily organized desks, or how many locals and visitors were now given tours of the lab, the focus was always on the killer whales and other marine life. Learning about them and protecting them. Tess made sure of that.

Britt was about to go through the back door to find Tess when Cara came out of the tiny kitchen, with her hands wrapped around a mug of something steamy.

"Hey, Britt. You're here early this weekend." Cara gave her a kiss on the cheek, and Britt caught the distinctive scent of Earl Grey tea wafting from her mug.

Britt grinned. "I wanted to surprise Tess. Isn't she here?"

"You just missed her," Cara said, leaning back against the kitchen's doorjamb. "She came in with the tide at about four this morning, so she left a little early."

Even better. Britt had been working as a receptionist at an environmental law firm in Seattle while she waited to hear about her admission to the university. She loved her job and was soaking up as much knowledge as she could, but her favorite time was when she and Tess were able to spend weekends together, either on the Peninsula or in the city. She certainly wasn't going to complain about finding Tess at home rather than at the lab. "I'll catch her at the house, then," she said, turning toward the front door again.

"Yeah, okay. Well, good luck, and all that."

Britt hesitated, caught by the strange tone in Cara's voice. "Why do I need luck? What's wrong?"

"Oh, nothing," Cara said, not meeting her eyes. "It's just… never mind. You'll find out soon enough."

Britt suddenly realized how quiet the hallway was. And nothing was attacking her ankles. She looked around frantically. "Oh God. Where's Cupcake? You didn't give us Cupcake, did you?"

Cara gave an indignant gasp. "She's in the storage room with Jake. He brought a ham sandwich for lunch. And you'd be lucky to have her."

She marched off in the opposite direction, and Britt hurried out to her car, heading toward Forks and the house she and Tess were renting. Britt loved the old place, even though Tess had nearly hyperventilated when they signed the lease because it was only three blocks from her parents' home. Britt spent a few minutes of her drive wondering what Cara had been trying to warn her about, but soon turned to the more interesting prospect of the weekend ahead. She'd walk on the beach, challenge Jim and Alec to a Scrabble tournament, and help Tess's dad install the new expansion pack she'd picked up in the city. Most of all, she'd be with Tess. Britt sighed happily as she parked in the driveway, finally releasing the tension from a busy workweek and the long drive out to the coast.

"Britt? Is that you?" Tess's voice called from the kitchen when she came through the front door. "I wasn't expecting..."

Tess halted as soon as she came into the living room and saw Britt. "Wow. Either you were chosen to be the university's mascot, or you got accepted to the law school."

Britt glanced down at the clothes she had bought this morning. A purple hoodie with a large gold husky paw on the front, matching purple socks, a baseball cap with UW on it, and a school lanyard. "I got in!"

"Of course you got in." Tess was beaming as she hurried over and grabbed Britt in a tight hug. "I never doubted you would."

Britt handed Tess a bag. "I got you a matching sweatshirt, and a...wait, what's that?"

She pointed at the couch, suddenly understanding Cara's dire warning. She should have taken it more seriously. "Did you buy a guitar?"

"I did," Tess said, going over to the sofa and picking up the instrument. She strummed some random notes. "I realized the reason I wasn't improving was because I only got to practice when I managed to sneak Kelly's away from her."

"Right. That's why," Britt said weakly. It certainly had nothing to do with Tess's blatant disregard for music theory and her inability to remember any chord for more than two minutes.

Tess sat down and patted the cushion next to her. "Do you want to hear a song?"

Britt fidgeted with the empty plastic card holder on her lanyard. She wouldn't mind hearing a song, but she had serious doubts about Tess's ability to play one. She should just be thankful Tess wasn't trying to play the drums or a tuba. And thankful that she had come into the house in the first place with a determined plan to distract Tess from whatever she had been doing.

She slipped the lanyard over her head and tossed it next to Tess. "You can play the guitar, or you can come over here and find out exactly how much school spirit I have," she said, pulling off her cap and letting her hair tumble down to her shoulders. She tossed the hat toward the couch and Tess caught it before it landed. She propped the guitar against the end table and balanced the baseball cap on top.

"I've had enough guitar for the day," she said, getting up and walking over to stand in front of Britt. "I want to play something else now."

"I was hoping you'd choose me," Britt said, raising her arms as Tess tugged off her hoodie, revealing a logoed sports bra.

"Every day, every second, every minute I choose you," Tess said. She cupped Britt's breasts in her hands and rubbed the pads of her thumbs over Britt's nipples. When Britt moaned and rocked against her, Tess bent her head and kissed along the top of her shoulder, snapping the bra strap with her teeth.

Britt wrapped her arms around Tess's neck, loosely enough to give Tess room to reach down and unbutton her jeans. She went still for a moment—even though Tess's inspection of her UW underwear made it nearly impossible to keep from squirming—and savored the peace of this in-between place. After a long but fulfilling week at work and the thrill of receiving her law school acceptance letter, and before Tess finished undressing her, and she returned the favor. After a long journey to reinvent her life and find her place in the world, and before Tess reminded her that no matter where else she went or what else she did, her true home was right here, in Tess's arms.

She hesitated in between until she could no longer resist the urge to move forward. She grabbed Tess's T-shirt and pulled her close with enough force to knock them both off balance and against the front door. Tess laughed, bracing her hands on either side of Britt's head and kissing her with as much strength and passion as Britt had just shown. When she paused, nuzzling against Britt's neck and hair, Britt was breathing in short gasps, all thoughts of slowing down and savoring the moment banished from her mind. Tess grinned at her, pressing close and nudging her knee between Britt's legs.

"Welcome home," she said.

About the Author

Karis Walsh is a native of the Pacific Northwest, where she finds inspiration for the settings of her contemporary romances and romantic intrigues. She was a Golden Crown Literary Award winner with *Tales from Sea Glass Inn*, and her novels have been shortlisted for a Lambda Literary award and a Forward INDIES award. She can usually be found reading with a cat curled on her lap, hiking with a dog at her side, or playing her viola with both animals hiding under the bed. Contact her at kariswalsh@gmail.com.

Books Available From Bold Strokes Books

A Wish Upon a Star by Jeannie Levig. Erica Cooper has learned to depend on only herself, but when her new neighbor, Leslie Raymond, befriends Erica's special needs daughter, the walls protecting Erica's heart threaten to crumble. (978-1-163555-274-4)

Answering the Call by Ali Vali. Detective Sept Savoie returns to the streets of New Orleans, as do the dead bodies from ritualistic killings, and she does everything in her power to bring their killers to justice while trying to keep her partner, Keegan Blanchard, safe. (978-1-163555-050-4)

Friends Without Benefits by Dena Blake. When Dex Putman gets the woman she thought she always wanted, she soon wonders if it's really love after all. (978-1-163555-349-9)

Invalid Evidence by Stevie Mikayne. Private Investigator Jil Kidd is called away to investigate a possible killer whale, just when her partner Jess needs her most. (978-1-163555-307-9)

Pursuit of Happiness by Carsen Taite. When attorney Stevie Palmer's client reveals a scandal that could derail Senator Meredith Mitchell's presidential bid, their chance at love may be collateral damage. (978-1-163555-044-3)

Seascape by Karis Walsh. Marine biologist Tess Hansen returns to Washington's isolated northern coast, where she struggles to adjust to small-town living while courting an endowment from Brittany James for her orca research center. (978-1-163555-079-5)

Second In Command by VK Powell. Jazz Perry's life is disrupted and her career jeopardized when she becomes personally involved with the case of an abandoned child and the child's competent but strict social worker, Emory Blake. (978-1-163555-185-3)

Taking Chances by Erin McKenzie. When Valerie Cruz and Paige Wellington clash over what's in the best interest of the children in Valerie's care, the children may be the ones who teach them it's worth taking chances for love. (978-1-163555-209-6)

Breaking Down Her Walls by Erin Zak. Could a love worth staying for be the key to breaking down Julia Finch's walls? (978-1-63555-369-7)

All of Me by Emily Smith. When chief surgical resident Galen Burgess meets her new intern, Rowan Duncan, she may finally discover that doing what you've always done will only give you what you've always had. (978-1-163555-321-5)

As the Crow Flies by Karen F. Williams. Romance seems to be blooming all around, but problems arise when a restless ghost emerges from the ether to roam the dark corners of this haunting tale. (978-1-163555-285-0)

Both Ways by Ileandra Young. SPEAR agent Danika Karson races to protect the city from a supernatural threat and must rely on the woman she's trained to despise: Rayne, an achingly beautiful vampire. (978-1-163555-298-0)

Calendar Girl by Georgia Beers. Forced to work together, Addison Fairchild and Kate Cooper discover that opposites really do attract. (978-1-163555-333-8)

Cash and the Sorority Girl by Ashley Bartlett. Cash Braddock doesn't want to deal with morality, drugs, or people. Unfortunately, she's going to have to. (978-1-163555-310-9)

Lovebirds by Lisa Moreau. Two women from different worlds collide in a small California mountain town, each with a mission that doesn't include falling in love. (978-1-163555-213-3)

Media Darling by Fiona Riley. Can Hollywood bad girl Emerson and reluctant celebrity gossip reporter Hayley work together to make each other's dreams come true? Or will Emerson's secrets ruin not one career, but two? (978-1-163555-278-2)

Stroke of Fate by Renee Roman. Can Sean Moore live up to her reputation and save Jade Rivers from the stalker determined to end Jade's career and, ultimately, her life? (978-1-163555-162-4)